LITTLE
FLOWER

Also by Ted Oswald

The Libète Limyè Mysteries
Because We Are
There is a Land

LITTLE FLOWER

A NOVEL

TED OSWALD

DISPATCH

Cover design and illustration by MECOB

Additional cover images: © iStockphoto.com / hpkalyani, © iStockphoto.com / kevinruss, © Shutterstock.com / Ljupco Smokovski, © Shutterstock.com / krkt, © Shutterstock.com / O.S.

Dispatch Publishing
www.dispatchpublishing.com

Little Flower/Ted Oswald. -- 1st ed.

ISBN-13: 978-0-9886005-4-6 (Hardcover)
ISBN-10: 0-9886005-4-4 (Hardcover)

ISBN-13: 978-0-9886005-5-3 (Paperback)
ISBN-10: 0-9886005-5-2 (Papaerback)

To my brothers and sisters

Pluck this little flower and take it, delay not! I fear lest it
Droop and drop into the dust.
I may not find a place in thy garland, but honour it with a touch of
Pain from thy hand and pluck it. I fear lest the day end before I am
Aware, and the time of offering go by.
Though its colour be not deep and its smell be faint, use this flower
In thy service and use it while there is time.

– 'Flower', Rabindranath Tagore

To: The Apostolic See,
         Bishop of Rome,
         Supreme Pontiff,
         His Holiness,
         Holy Father,
         Pope Francis
         At the desk where he sits
         Apostolic Palace
         00120 Vatican City

From: His lowly servant
         Sister Immaculata
         Mother Teresa Home for Disabled
            and Abandoned Children
         New Delhi
         India

Re: The Miraculous

There was a time not so long ago that I was very afraid, and I told Sister Shanti as much. Why? she asked, and I explained. But fear is nothing, a passing thing, she said. It doesn't feel like it, I said. Even if I am put to death, I will wake in the land of my Lord, she said. And I wanted to have that same sense of safety, and courage, and to someday join her in that place of eternal wakefulness. And then Sister Shanti went on and faced all I feared. In doing this, she set me free.

   Holy Father, I have a story to tell. I hope you have ears to hear.

   It comes with a demand: the canonization of our dear, departed Sister Shanti.

   While certain celebrities of our age (e.g. Mother Teresa) have the masses demanding their ascension to sainthood, I fear our Shanti has none but me to plead her case.

   Others would see Shanti vanish among the ranks of little-known suffering servants. She would be first to accept that she was not much liked. She was hard. And stubborn. But I submit that she loved well, but her love was misunderstood, and her humility mistaken for pride.

You may ask why I would write you directly. 'Why not follow the canonical law, with its exhaustively enumerated steps, and undertake a process that probably won't be completed before you or I die?' I hear you question. The reason, quite simply, is that I am an impatient person.

You may also ask why my petition arrives as a personal letter rather than a coldly-stated reporting of fact: 'John said this', 'Mary said this', 'The prostitute screwed this many'. But that would be a catalogue of the trivial, and I am a person too easily bored.

No: Sister Shanti's story could not be risked to a lengthy journalistic, fact-finding project. The output, whether a 100-page report, a documentary film, or a glossy magazine feature, would do half of what a well-told story can.

And so, dear Francis, the story of a soul I shall write.

It will be a mystery, simple yet mind-boggling;

> Of untold Joy wrapped in staggering Sadness;
> Of Weak Lions and Crafty Lambs;
> Of Miracles – approximately 141. I mean, 142;
> Of Deaths – approximately 5, few natural;
> Of the Sacred and Profane laying down side by side,
> often several times a night,
> always for a pittance.

And so the accuracy of names of people and places has become a relative thing to protect the innocent. Slight and inconsequential modifications of fact have been made for dramatic effect and parsimony. What is most important is the truth that underlies the story. And this tale I tell, if nothing else, is the truest form of truth.

Understand. This is an invitation to come and see. For words to be made flesh. For you to incarnate a story and touch the souls captured inside.

Entering is not for the faint of heart, but if you choose to do so, I believe you will be transformed by the life of Sister Shanti of Delhi, as have I.

I

Ah. I'm happy to see you're still reading. I take this as your informed consent.

Our travels will be confined to the country of India, the city of Delhi and its environs.

Have you ever been?

On a globe my city appears an infinitesimal pinprick, yet it teems with cosmic significance. This choking, sprawling, urban cesspool is full of the marvellous: nearly 25 million bodies, all imbued with souls. It is obvious that the world values some lives less than others. This is a heresy. Their lives tremble with significance, pulsing with the potential for love, for each reflects the image of our loving Creator.

We begin in the old city, Shahjahanabad, and not so very many years ago. The streets are awash in fresh sunlight and lined with a hundred thousand enterprising captains of industry, ancient architectural wonders, and a multitude of pavement dwellers. On these roads have walked kings, rajas, viceroys, the Mahatma himself, and defecating dogs. And I love it despite itself. Just watch your step.

Pope Francis. Francis!

Don't just stand there gawking at it all. You'll have to keep up with me. I wait for no one, the Holy See included!

Just a turn of another corner and…we arrive. Knock twice at the outer gate. You read the sign: 'Missionaries of Charity Mother Teresa *Shishu Bhavan* Home for Abandoned and Disabled Children'. That's right, it's a Missionaries of Charity outpost, an MC home, a convent of sorts. Don't forget to greet Ebenezer the gateman; a respectful handshake will do. Politely decline to see pictures of his grandchildren. Come along…yes, yes. That oval window there looks in on Sister's office and if you stand on tiptoe just *so* you can peer in as Shanti reads her newspaper.

Pope Francis, you needn't duck out of view. She can't very well see us.

Yes, you are correct. We are *here* but you must understand, we are *not* here.

Think of the hundreds – *thousands* – of people you might pass on the road every day of whom you never take note. The two of us are of those people. Unseen – unless we're meant to be seen.

Where were we?

Right. While the other Sisters tend to wet bedclothes and prepare breakfast, Sister Shanti, the superior of the MC home, sits in her office, reading her newspaper.

It is not as though she shrugs off her responsibilities. Whereas the other Sisters rose at 4:40 a.m. at the first stroke of the bell, she was up at 4, already in prayer, both desperate and needful. Mass followed at 7 a.m., and the visiting father, quite new to his priestly responsibilities, enlivened the proceedings when he, to the gasps of the nine Sisters prostrating themselves before the altar, accidentally spilt the cup and sent the Host – Christ's body! – tumbling to the floor.

Shanti chuckles at the memory. Good Lord, she remarks to the open air.

She unfolds the paper and squints, having to adjust her heavy-framed glasses. She hates them. The lenses have only grown thicker over the years she has passed in the religious life, and she fears a new prescription is in order. She sets to reading with a sigh.

Having recently attained 69 years, Sister is comfortable in her late-life routines. Fixtures include starting with the day's paper, *The Indian Express*, gifted by R. K. Dharanipragada (retired accountant and busy-body neighbour), and her enamel cup full of chai, a dribble of donated non-fat Mother Dairy milk, and a teaspoon of sugar.

One article in and a coo outside draws her attention. A pigeon visits a bird feeder just beyond her small oval window before a crow descends and frightens it off. Sister bristles at the scene, but does nothing about this intruder. Her eye drifts to the edge of the rooftops and she slips into reverie, staring absently just past the crow, just over the wall, and at the distant, outside world.

The bell sounds. She rises. We follow.

Sister Shanti climbs to the second floor, touching the spot on the wall she always does, the one where it is painted 'DO WHAT

HE TELLS YOU'. She passes the singing and dancing cartoon characters in the corridor, checks the ward for TB-stricken children, and ascends to the third level. The morning apostolate duties are underway. The other Sisters, paid assistants from the neighbouring slum, and a pair of Swedish university-graduate volunteers clean, wipe, change, launder, clean, discipline, play, cook, and clean. She paces among the bassinets and cribs and small beds, among the cries and giggling and cooing, as she confers with the overnight matron who nearly nods off mid-sentence. Sister thanks her and tells her to go home. Sisters on all levels of the building bring her problems throughout the morning: 'Rakesh had seizures again this morning'; 'Toilet is again overflowing'; 'Milk has gone off'. She makes calls, inspects, assists. Rakesh is a particular burden on her; doctors have been able to do nothing for the 4-year-old. She tasks Sister Neepa, a recent arrival and the only Sister not finally professed, with watching Rakesh.

The air is heavy at the day's start and brutal by midday when lunch is served. It's as if the sluggish ceiling fans are resigned to failure. The children, those who are well, end their games long enough to sit and be served their plate of rice and dal with boiled egg crumbled on top. Then come the mats and naps. Sister Shanti joins the other Sisters for their meal and half-hour of rest before leading a spiritual reading, a chapter from St Thérèse of Lisieux's autobiography, one of her favourites. Then chai, 'proof of God's goodness', Sister Becky mutters under her breath. Little Arjun, a hellion by any definition, has given Sister Becky much trouble today. Sister Shanti very nearly smiles as she sips.

The afternoon follows the morning. The pair of plumbers Sister has called may or may not be resolving the toilet situation. Their looks portend further problems. Rakesh falls into seizures again, and Sister joins Sister Neepa who is terrified in holding him down and protecting his tongue from his clenching jaw. After the episode Sister begrudgingly sends Ebenezer, the gateman, to buy some milk for the children before they sleep this evening. No time to beg it, as the Sisters are meant to.

The sunlight slants, afternoon turns to evening. There is adoration, and they return to the chapel, that same rectangle of a room where they pass so much of their lives. Sister takes up a place on a stool at the back while the other Sisters kneel. Christ is there, perpetually hanging on his cross. And the words Sister has read a million times painted by his side: I THIRST. She puts her head in her hands to pray:

Out of the depths I cry to You, O Lord; Lord, hear my voice.
Let Your ears be attentive to my voice in supplication.
If You, O Lord, mark iniquities, Lord, who can stand?
But with You is forgiveness, that You may be revered.
I trust in the Lord; my soul trusts in His word.
My soul waits for the Lord more than sentinels wait for the dawn.
More than sentinels wait for the dawn, let Israel wait for the Lord,
For with the Lord is kindness and
with Him is plenteous redemption;
And He will redeem Israel from all their iniquities.

And now begins a curiosity.

While recreation hour is at hand, the younger Sisters wheel in cribs until they form an arc around an old piano. Older children are seated on a blanket in the arc's hollow. Sister supervises this quietly.

When the last child is placed Sister Shanti watches the other Sisters step out and close the door behind them.

To God alone be the glory, Sister says, her eyes closed. She seats herself at the piano and plays.

You can hear its beauty. To say Sister is an accomplished musician is to say Sachin Tendulkar is a reasonable cricketer, Gandhi is an OK Mahatma, or Jesus a ho-hum Christ: understatements, all of them.

Sister is enraptured. The poorly-tuned piano turns into a heavenly instrument. Watch Sister as she plays, giving herself to the music. She never improvises. You might imagine with a prodigious talent she might break from those lines of notes and momentary rests to compose her own melodies. She does not. She never allows herself to move beyond her dotted instructions on the page.

You can see it in how her body moves. There is some pain underlying all of this, buried and undisclosed, voiced only through these notes that leap to life, reverberate, and disappear without trace. Much like a prayer.

Sister never permits others besides these children to hear.

Mother Teresa, the founder of the Missionaries of Charity, of which I am also a member, told us to 'See Jesus in his distressing disguise' of the broken, abandoned, and impoverished. In playing for them, Sister plays for Him, offering the most beauty her fingertips can muster for the ears of children incapable of ever appreciating it intellectually. Nevertheless, their jitters settle and crying ceases.

The recital lasts as it always does, for half an hour. When she stops, the Sisters enter to take the children and tuck them into their beds, bless them, and bid them goodnight. Sister touches each child as they leave, a rare smile on her lips.

Dear Francis: Sister Shanti is a complex woman with a complicated story, one of billions of such stories with new chapters written in daily accretions of hope, misery, joy, despair, love and hate that make us who we are until our final page is reached and we are no more. For an old, troubled nun with a regimented life like Sister's, these chapters feel achingly monotonous, but events are in motion that will ensure Sister Shanti's story will never be the same.

Ah, I've lost track of the time. We must be on the move; we have the first killing to attend.

II

Ram Kumar sits sipping chai and wondering whether today is the day he will die.

He looks at the street, and back to his watch, and again to the street. He struggles to bring the small glass to his lips without another tremor of his hand.

A robust Muslim man, the chaiwallah, proprietor of the tea shop in which young Ram sits, watches him from the corner of his eye. Shifting his weight from where he stands behind his simmering pots, the chaiwallah looks out on the narrow, darkening lane outside. A trio of *Jamnapari* goats eat discarded rice. His grandsons kick a neon-coloured ball back and forth. A sad seller hawks shrivelled radishes. A man on a motorbike threads his way among them all. Nothing seen through this small window into the world through which this Delhiite has watched for 36 years seems strange. What disturbs the chaiwallah is this young Hindu in his shop in the Muslim quarter of Old Delhi as night descends, dressed in a tailored suit and very much resembling trouble.

The young boy who mops the shop floor with a rag stares openly at Ram. The child has a strange lip, a cleft palate rejoined indelicately. Ram tries to avoid looking at him; surely some urchin or the chaiwallah's nephew from a desperate Bihari village, and this wondering is Ram's mistake. His restless leg gets the better of him and shakes the table until his tea takes a leap and meets the floor. The glass shatters, the tea spills.

So very sorry, Sir, Ram mumbles, bounding up from his chair, surveying what his nerves have wrought. He gulps. The chaiwallah grimaces. The small boy, unfazed, moves to pick up the broken glass and wipe milky tea from Ram's shining black shoes.

Another chai? Ram asks. He fumbles through his suit and pants pockets in search of his billfold. Upon finding it he takes out an impressive wad of notes. Ram moves from his table to where the chaiwallah stands and holds out a thousand rupees. Any change? he asks, feebly.

Up close, the chaiwallah now seems formidable. His flowing orange-dyed beard. His furrowed brow. The calloused obeisance mark in the middle of his forehead, staring like a third eye.

You should go, he says.

B-but I insist. I broke the glass. Let me at least replace—

The chaiwallah throws down the rag he holds and crosses his arms.

Ram swallows. He knows what is best. Besides, Ram thinks, the appointed time nears.

He steps down the tea shop's few steps, out of its jarring fluorescent light, its blue-and-white chequered tiles, its walls decked with the symbols of Islam. Ram notices the mopping boy still watching him. He waves to the boy, not precisely sure why, and looks both ways.

Off to Ajmeri Gate. Off to Garstin Bastion Road, G.B. Road for short.

Let's follow, Francis.

Everything seems ghoulish to the young man as he walks under snaking power lines and looming shop overhangs. The light escapes the road faster than Ram can. He shudders every time he steps into the shadows where the small lane makes sharp, elbow turns. He wishes for the comfort of a weapon: a gun, a pipe, even a trusty, pointed Reynolds pen.

The decision to leave Delhi was rushed, set upon him by circumstances outside of his control. He had lately failed to visit the temple in his neighbourhood near Jahangirpuri – not intentionally, he tells himself – and he worried that his failure to make an offering, ring the bell, and appease the goddess Lakshmi had brought about this sudden turn in his fortunes. Forced to abandon his apartment, he now flees with the TAG Heuer watch on his wrist, the cash in his billfold, and the suit on his person. His only real consolation is a pair of railway tickets in his inside suit-pocket.

As he reaches the Mughal-era gate the surrounding streets are marked by ordinary chaos. A steady stream of autorickshaws vie for pole position as they circle the roundabout. Honking horns call out in uneven chorus. Bored vendors sell seasoning packs, packed snacks, and fresh juice, hoping for a few extra rupees to close the day. Ram feels at ease merging into lines of anonymous pedestrians at the street's margins, hearing their unhurried, unworried chatter. He glances up at the well-lit billboard picturing local Congress Party lackeys and barely dodges a cycle-rickshaw. Distracted, he stumbles onto a seated street barber taming a customer's ear hair.

Watch where you're going!

S-sorry, Ram mutters, trying to regain his balance.

He sweats. The heat and pollution mingle, making the air

gelatinous. His tie suffocates like a dog collar, and he paws at it. He had thought of dressing down since his Western-cut suit is not inconspicuous, but his jacket hides the bulging package tucked into his waistband.

Of course! The package. Preoccupied by imagined threats, the tickets, departure times, and the one who would accompany him, the envelope has slipped his mind. Ram reaches back, his fingers running over the delicate paper's edges in hopes it will impart instructions as to his next steps. Time is short, but there is still enough to deliver it. It may be his last chance.

G.B. Road can wait, he decides. With a wave of his hand, he hails a passing cycle-rickshaw and names the address and a price. They set off. So must we.

Pope, flag that rickshaw down! That one with the barefooted driver of shabby dress and ill odour over there! No, the *other* one!

Ram's driver, taciturn, exhausted, doesn't talk with him; Ram appreciates this as Delhi, tinged by orange-hued street lights, passes by at a leisurely pace of 10 kilometres an hour. The ride's pulsing rhythm matches the driver's pedalling and sends Ram off into musing.

Ram is not unacquainted with fearing for his life, nor with avoiding those who would end it. The ability to disappear, often by finding ever darker and more dangerous places to hide, has served him well. That he is out and about instead of in a dingy hole confirms the prognosis that, yes, he must be insane. Love will do that.

They arrive, and so have we. Ram takes in the familiar sign above the gate with its cross and heart set aflame, its serene portrait of Mother, and the words:

MISSIONARIES OF CHARITY
MOTHER TERESA HOME
SHISHU BHAVAN
HOME FOR ABANDONED AND DISABLED CHILDREN

I'll only be a minute, Ram says to the driver. Then we go straight back to Ajmeri Gate.

The driver answers with a nod.

Ram knocks at the gate. The night-watchman answers.

Sister Shanti, please.

Not available.

It's very important.

Not possible. Sister is playing for the children. The others are in recreation.

Please. I need to see her.

She's very clear about these things. Not to be disturbed.

Ram considers handing over the envelope to this man, but he spies a nun walking past. (You know her to be Sister Neepa, Pope.)

Sister! he calls. I have an important message for Sister Shanti!

I told you to leave them be! the night-watchman hisses, but Sister Neepa approaches anyway, carrying a tray of short plastic cups emptied of their milk. Her lips purse.

Ram forces the envelope through the gap in the gate. I would most appreciate you giving it to Sister Shanti at an appropriate moment, he says in English. Tell her this is from Ram. And that I have gone away.

She hands her tray over to the watchman and wipes her hands on her apron. She hesitates before taking the envelope and depositing it in her apron's pocket. She nods and takes back her tray before disappearing inside the children's home.

Dhanyavaad, Sir, thank you very much.

The watchman tuts and slams the gate shut.

Ram stands up straighter, breathes easier. That this task is completed is a tremendous relief. Maybe, just maybe, this would make up for his remiss offerings to Lakshmi, he wonders.

Back to G.B., he mutters, sliding back into the rickshaw's vinyl seat.

And back we go into ours, Francis. Follow, driver! Follow!

As his rickshaw stirs back to life Ram feels the warmth that came with doing good get extinguished: a distinct chill courses through him, swirling down about his toes. He takes it to be a sign: is his planned detour down G.B. Road a mistake? Should he push on to the railway station, flash his ticket, and leave this sorry city behind?

He pays the driver for the short trip with a thousand-rupee note, an exorbitant sum beyond what had been agreed. The surprised man touches it to his lips, then to his forehead. Ram slicks back his greasy hair and smiles, sadly. He can see the railway station from where he stands. Just a brief nip through the underground Metro station and he'd be standing safely in front of its gleaming, colonnaded entrance.

But G.B. exerts a gravitational pull on him, just as it always has. More than the place he first had sex – first *paid* for sex, really – G.B. is where he met Meeta.

It is where she is this very moment.

And leaving her is impossible.

He plunges in, and so do we, Pope.

G.B. Road runs along the railway tracks. Its brothels, known as *kothas* here in Delhi, are open night and day, stacked above reputable street-level shops. Columns support the multi-floor buildings and provide a covered walkway. The girls – caked in make-up, bedecked in cheap jewellery – call from barred windows and balustraded balconies.

Ram starts down the street and is set upon by touts. These are the grimy young men in soiled clothes with floating eyes, still high from sniffing glue. These are the women of a certain age, with their sagging jowls, henna-dyed hair, foreheads dotted with smudged bindis in a poor pretence of piety, who can just as easily whisper gracious enticements as lash out with the foulest of tongues.

Nice girls here, Sir. Just up the stairs.

No, thank you, Ram says, brushing the first woman off.

He continues on his way. A young, shovel-faced man appears from behind a column and tugs at his sleeve.

Hashish? Here for *laundi-bazi*? Nepalese virgins are waiting for you.

I know where I'm going.

They're young. Good price. The best price for you. Just down the road.

I *said* leave me alone.

Ram shoves him a bit and the young pimp bristles. He pulls a knife from his pocket, exposing it just an inch or so, and Ram holds up both hands. There is recognition there, on both their parts.

Sorry, Pinku, Ram says. Another time, maybe.

Pinku lets him leave, but not without a curse.

Ram loosens his tie again. He steps into the street to avoid more touts and looks up towards the faded stars, just visible through the smog and cloud. Guilt descends, so sweepingly he nearly collapses in the middle of the road. He gasps, trying to focus on his good deed just completed, and on Meeta: lovely, beautiful Meeta. It is not the honking cars or angry shouting that make him stir, though.

His eyes latch on to those of a stout, sauntering policeman, known widely as Constable Singh. Singh's gaze falls on Ram and his suit and his apparent means.

Ram gulps.

If the officer chooses to pounce on Ram, Ram could easily lose every rupee in his pockets, and, even worse, embroil himself in a dreaded 'police case'. A passing car's side mirror brushes the constable, and this distracts him just long enough for Ram to slip away and disappear in the bustle.

I apologize if you're winded, Pope. This is quite the pace we're keeping! Worry not. A chance to rest is at hand; Ram has finally reached the stairwell to *kotha* No. 201.

Unfortunately, another obstacle positions herself in young Ram's path: Latika floats near the stairwell's entrance.

Though working girls usually remain upstairs – purportedly for propriety's sake, really to keep them from running off – this woman is on the street. She immediately presses herself up against Ram. Her touch makes his head light.

Ram gulps again.

Back for something special tonight? she whispers in his ear, groping him down low. Or are you just here for your *normal, boring,* usual? she chuckles.

Conflict is writ large on his face. He has used Latika before, not infrequently, and close in time to his visits to Meeta. He isn't pleased with the fact. Not because Latika didn't satisfy his fleshly desires – quite the opposite. This particular moment is not so ideal to contemplate his lies.

L-later, he says.

Latika pouts like a spurned lover and leans towards him. Don't stay away too long. Secrets have a way of escaping. She peers over his shoulder, sees an older man eyeing her from a few columns away. Nice suit, she whispers to Ram, and glides away. Ram shudders and climbs, grateful to escape from the world of harsh streetlights and storefronts that sell copper pipe fittings, electrical cable, water pumps, and tiles by day, into a realm much more aligned with who Ram knows himself to be.

The steps are steep, lit only by ambient light from the six *kothas* that branch off at the passage's three levels. He grips the chain running along the wall, there to support those who rise with wild anticipation and leave spent of money and body.

It takes 21 uneven steps to reach the first level, and 23 to reach the second. The air in the passage is dank, smelling unexpectedly of aniseed. As he lingers outside the cracked door to No. 201 he gulps the air in. He checks his watch. Each movement of the seconds-hand is a new imperative. He knocks, pushes in the door, and is greeted by an old woman, Ginna, listening to her clock radio.

She is a tubby old thing, and sits leaning against her side-table while smoking a bidi cheroot and waving a small hand fan. '*Laila, O Laila*', a classic, fills the room. On the wall, out of her view, is the portrait of a beatific, white, blond Jesus.

A smile slithers onto her face on recognizing him. Smoke pours from her nostrils.

Ah, my *son*! My *Ram*! You've *returned*. She struggles to stand, and, finding it too great an effort, falls back into her seat. Here again for my treasure?

Ram takes a small step forward. Girls start peeking out from behind curtains along the corridor, just off the gallery. Yes, Ginnaji. But tonight is a little out of the ordinary.

Ginna looks Ram up and down, notes his incongruous suit. Oh?

14

I hoped to pay extra. Like before. For a whole night. *Outside.*

Ginna's eyes narrow. She sucks her cigarette and exhales before a smile again visits her lips. Which hotel?

The Rose Garden. Just down the road. Like before. He winces at his repeated phrase.

She leans forward, her thick make-up no longer hiding her face's cross-cutting trenches. She sniffs. He keeps his eyes fixed on hers, even as new beads of sweat slide down his face.

It will take more than the last time, she says. The night's just starting. So how much?

That *is* the question. Ram knows the balance is delicate. Pimps like Ginna are anxious about prize girls running off with boyfriends. If he offers her an amount too high, she might suspect he aims to take her away. If too low, she will keep him from her. His calculations have been iterated all evening. And yet:

I received a bonus at the call centre this week, Ram says. You name the price.

Ginna grabs his hand and pulls Ram even closer. She searches his coal-dark eyes again, whispers in his ear. He hides his grimace from her. As you wish, he says. The small dark hair protruding from a mole on her neck makes him blanch. He finally pulls away, but not before she gives his cheek a maternal pat.

Ah. Ginna extends a finger. One condition. Adiba joins you.

A new wave of worry sweeps over Ram.

Adiba. Adiba! *Adiba!* Ginna screams. A door near the entryway opens slowly, and from behind it steps Adiba.

The man, Ginna's son, is of indeterminate age, though not old. His heavy limbs and flab are poorly hidden by his unbuttoned shirt. Sounds – tinny explosions, *dishooms* and machinegun fire – stream from the film he watches in his room.

Wha? Adiba slurs. He sweats profusely and scratches at his days-old stubble, then his balls.

You must go with Meeta and this one. Get ready.

Adiba licks his lips, appearing indifferent even though this assignment means he will be adrift in Delhi the whole night. He lumbers back into his room. When he reappears his shirt is still unbuttoned.

Adiba is a lout, Ram knows, and stupid. Meeta has told Ram how Adiba sometimes forces himself on the girls, on her, when his mother is out. Losing him on the street will be a challenge.

You may *go* to her, Ginna says with grandiloquence. Grab *condoms*! No pollution of the girls! *This* is a *clean* establishment.

Ram gives a deferential nod and moves towards a sink jutting out from the corridor wall. He takes a few rubbers from a box there and placates the old woman by depositing them in his suit-pocket.

Down the short hallway he goes.

He reaches for the handle of the hallway's single door when a stroke of vertigo disorients him. His heart beats like a tabla. This is love. It has to be. His hand planted on the unpainted wall comes away with a powdery dust. He wipes his hand on his trousers, tightens his tie.

Ram knocks.

Come in! is sung from inside.

Entering the room, he is transported.

One first notices the burst of fluorescent light. Then the walls, papered with a collage of Bollywood models, true brassy *chhamak-challos*, in a catalogue of come-hither poses. The room has the illusion of spaciousness owing to a large, full-length mirror, and the flannel-covered floor is cleared but for cushions and pillows should a customer enjoy reclining for a dance performance before doing the deed. Her cot is in the corner, a thin cushion for a mattress, and with relatively clean sheets. A singer's professions of love spring from a small radio and bounce off the walls.

Amid the impressive spell cast by these surroundings sits Meeta.

She is before the mirror, combing out her luxuriant hair. Her jewellery glints, hooped earrings and a golden stud in her nose. She can see Ram's reflection without turning around. Meeta rises, smiles widely. You've come!

I have. And it's time. The, uh, *the* time.

She nearly drops her comb. It's here?

He nods.

I have to pack!

He rushes to her, kisses her. There's no time, my sweet. Ginna thinks we're going to the Rose Garden for the night. If we take much of anything she'll get suspicious. And besides, Adiba is to follow us.

Her angelic features are tinged with the infernal; she looks more like the petulant child she is than the womanly image she projects. Ram should not be too surprised; after all, she is but 17.

Meeta begins changing. No one on the street wears a close-cut choli like she has on now.

Avert your eyes, Pope, just for a moment.

She's in a respectable salwar-kameez now, covered from shoulder to ankle. She sweeps the cosmetics off the bureau and into her faux-designer purse. She adds an undergarment.

Anything else you want to take? He cups his hand to whisper: *This is the last time you'll be here.*

This is all I need, she says, definitively.

Though it is night, on go her 'Guchi' sunglasses, a most-prized possession. A quick check of the mirror turns into an assortment of poses, an adjustment of her hair, as if 'desperate runaway' has its own look. Ram, his eye torn between the face of his watch and of Meeta's, finally grabs her by the hand.

As they lock eyes, the moment registers: Ram, resembling a film actor in his suit; Meeta, appearing as a starlet; both stepping into a vast unknown. They could be cast as heroes in a Hindi-movie; this is not lost on them.

They step into the hallway. Meeta slides her arm into Ram's and they stride past the watching eyes. Meeta holds her chin high while the other girls curse her.

Ginna grabs hold of Ram as he passes and whispers, *Just* remember: I have people who have people who kill people.

Not to worry, Aunty. Meeta will be returned safe and sound tomorrow morning, 7 a.m., sharp. Like before. His voice trembles on the last syllable. He smiles.

Ginna looks him over with just enough of a probing eye to make his knees buckle. She turns to Meeta. Be *good*, she says, her hand tightening into a vise around Meeta's wrist. *A-di-ba!*

He lumbers out of his room. At last most of his shirt buttons have become acquainted with their holes.

You can nearly see the question doing backflips in Ram's head as the trio descend the stairs: *How…to…escape…him?*

They enter the street awash with men, men, men: confused, lonely, bereft. Onward towards Ajmeri Gate, the subway, the railway station, and freedom – *if* Adiba can be lost.

Oh, what an evening we'll have! My love and I, on our own! What glory! What rapture awaits! Meeta sows her florid hopes to the pimply youth trying to look at ease, the tout with a ghastly tumour fastened to her chin, the pervert pleasuring himself in the shadows.

Ram is mortified. They already draw too much attention. He looks to Adiba who shuffles along unfazed, either pondering one of life's greatest questions, or why his anti-dandruff shampoo is so ineffective.

Maybe speak a little more quietly, my flower? Ram hisses. He checks his watch. Only 15 minutes remain. He looks up and nearly collides with another man.

Sorry, sir——

He first sees the man's dark suit. Then his face and the thin, familiar scar running down its side like a worm. They stand loo king at one another as volumes of history are recalled. Ram's eyes glisten. His body quakes. The ManInSuit's presence is a message sent and received: he is here to kill Ram.

Ram renews his pace and Meeta laughs, like all is a game. Excuse us! she calls, giggling. She kisses Ram on the cheek. Ram does not kiss her back.

Moments ago, Adiba posed a serious problem. This ManIn-Suit represents a crisis. Ram doesn't need to look back to realize he is now part of their caravan.

You worry too much, Meeta says. She has no idea, Ram thinks. Visions like shots in a film play in his mind: a bullet entering the back of his head; Meeta, covered in his blood, letting loose a scream; his corpse falling to the ground in exquisite slow motion as the soundtrack soars——

18

Oh! Meeta exclaims. I've lost my shoe!

Ram pauses, infuriated.

What are you—

Meeta silences him, her finger on her lips. Adiba, my dear. *Dear*, dear, Adiba. She saunters towards the lump of a man and thrusts out her chest. Could you go and get it for me? I can see it right back there.

Adiba licks his lips. She takes his hand, giving it a gentle rub. He half-smiles, turns. Meeta shoots off into the street, one foot bare, and signals to Ram to run. Once inside a parked autorickshaw, she shouts, Metro! Now! *Now!*

The driver, shocked, drops his half-eaten roti and obeys.

Oh, how Ram loves this petite treasure! He peeks out the rickshaw and sees Adiba back where they left him, a shoe in his hand, utterly confused. The ManInSuit is nowhere. Relieved, Ram feels a keening sadness. The ManInSuit represents more than mere fear, and not a word of it can he explain to Meeta, not ever.

She talks a mile a minute, casting a vision of their shared future: beautiful children, fabulous wealth, regular promotions at his work, a grand home; the size and heft of her dreams stagger.

Ram nods absently, his eyes fixed on the oval window at the back, scanning for signs of pursuit until the application of the brakes throws him forward.

They burst forth, down the stairs, and into the tile-lined Metro corridors, running – no, *flying* – to the railway station, hand-in-hand, weaving through families with grumpy children and professionals returning home after long days at work and bedraggled *mazdoors* with their tools, dodging ATMs and orange cones indicating renovations underway, past the cautionary Metro signs and watchful CCTV cameras and the suspended clock, gleaming like a moon, seen in a blur: eight minutes till their train departs.

Meeta loves this freedom. She runs ahead, remaining shoe in one hand, her other hand trailing behind to keep hold of Ram. He reaches, struggling to weave through the crowds with the ease her small form allows. New blisters form on his heels. He can't help peering over his shoulder for pursuers. Terror makes his insides wobbly, and her wagging hand feels like a wisp of what could be, just beyond his grasp, just *barely*.

Up the stairs they go, exiting into the night air and a turbid river of parked yellow-and-green autorickshaws. They move among them, Meeta still running ahead, and arrive: the New Delhi Railway Station. Past the columns they go, absorbed by another crush of coming-and-going commuters. Nearly doubled over in need of breath, Ram scans the ominous departure/arrival board as letters and numbers flutter and *chk-chk-chk-chk* into place. Meeta cannot help but smile.

So…where are we…going? she asks between gasps.

Ram marvels that this girl, who really knows very little of him, is willing to escape with him to any quarter of India without hesitation. He points to the bottom-most listing, even though he knows that the letters are as indecipherable to her as little black squiggles on a page. Bangalore, he says.

Bangalore? She is full of wonder. More dreams spring to life in her eyes.

He finally catches her hand. Come on!

Up a staircase they go. Just before flashing their tickets to a disinterested railway employee and passing a barricade of wire and police signage, Meeta stops abruptly, touching her face.

What is it? he asks, fearing the worst.

I need to visit the toilet. The washroom.

Now? But the train—

I need to.

Meeta, this is ridicul—

I will *not* enter our new life looking like what…what I am.

He looks anew at her face, past the flared nostrils and set jaw, to the gaudy bursts of colour.

You mean a…*whore?* The word is uttered under his breath.

She needles him with her eyes. I need to redo my face.

There's no time!

Then go without me! She crosses her arms.

StunnedShockedTerrified, Ram is all three. Go. *Go!* His voice cracks. He steps to the side of the line, scanning faces in the crowd, looking for ManInSuit. You have a minute! he calls after her as his watch's seconds-hand starts another lap.

She smiles curtly, already feeling around in her purse before stepping inside the nearby washroom.

A minute, even less! he says, unable to hide his worry. Peering down a level at the crowded platform he sees their train has already arrived. Passengers climb aboard, coolies haul luggage, sellers hawk snacks, beggars beg, pickpockets pick. He looks back, and what he sees, who he sees, brings a cry: *Meeta!*

ManInSuit, huffing and puffing and searching, looking as if he doesn't want to do what he wants to do. He reaches inside his coat. Ram cannot wait. He sprints towards the ticket checker, shows his ticket again. *Run*…thoughts are…*Run*…impossible and he…*Run*…pushes on through…*Run*…the throng until…

A thought flashes into his mind: the presence of others will protect him!

He scans faces: the older woman with kohl-darkened eyes, the sinewy coolie with his red cap, a spindly man with a plastered comb-over. But Ram has never entrusted his safety to another soul; doing so now is against his every instinct.

His pursuer has somehow worked his way past the checkpoint and follows, his face set. The reluctance Ram glimpsed on ManInSuit's face only a moment ago has evaporated.

A calm voice blares over a loudspeaker: *Attention. Train Number 5609 inbound from Chandigarh will be arriving shortly on Platform Number 3. Please stand clear.*

He considers jumping onto his train, but knows there will be no escape there. Ram continues to run until nearly out of platform. He tries to summon cries, but they are stifled by his stupid fear. He stumbles back into a column. Amongst all the commotion on the platform, Ram feels he is without options, utterly alone in his hopelessness.

Finally, confronting him squarely, the suited man pulls out a knife as he snarls, advancing on Ram. Ram shouts, the sound swallowed up by the screeching brakes of the arriving train.

When Meeta exits the washroom, her allotted minute long since passed, she looks for Ram. He is nowhere. Could he have left her behind? she wonders. Impossible!

There seems to be a commotion down towards the trains but the ticket agent won't let her pass.

What's going on? she enquires. The agent shrugs.

People clamour to exit the platform and head up, up, up, past the checkpoint.

In the crush, she slips past the distracted agent and forces her way down, down, down.

An older, turbaned fellow stands watching on the edge of a group of other sober men who stare at the prematurely stopped train.

Please, Miss. He holds up a barring hand. This is not for your eyes.

But what has happened?

A man was just killed. I saw it happen.

Killed? But how? She looks past the man again and sees porters and railway staff preoccupied with something caught under the railway engine's wheels.

The killer threw the young man on the tracks, just as it was arriving. Then off he ran.

Off he ran, she murmurs. A man extricates half of a bloodied suit-coat from the tracks.

Her hand leaps to her mouth. The truth finally descends on Meeta, and her body, her whole being, is stricken:

Ram, her love, her saviour, is no more.

III

The world is a troubled place, Francis. There is no doubt.

I was not always able to write, especially not in English. In fact, my family and village would be shocked to see how easily I can unlock the combinations of these words. I don't count this as a matter of pride; it is only God's gift, to be sure.

I was not always Sister Immaculata. I was carried to Kolkata by rail with two other young women, just about my age, but from the state of Ranchi. They had green crosses tattooed on their foreheads. At the railway station we were met and driven to the Mother House. We were soon to begin our novitiate, the first stage of our religious life after short, and, in my case, thankfully uneventful periods of aspirancy elsewhere.

I was terrified. I still felt an imposter. I was among other new Indian Sisters, many lifelong Catholics, mostly tribal sorts of girls from far-flung corners of our country. We were a different generation than our predecessors like Sister Shanti who often came from the educated and middle classes. You know better than anyone that the numbers of new vocations are plummeting. Though the MCs are immensely popular, largely because of Mother's enduring fame, I would say it remains a crisis. We are a generation either losing the ears to hear Christ's gentle call, or we're so backward that he simply doesn't want us. But then I am reassured by the fact that I too have been called, and this is proof that the latter view cannot stand.

I'm not sharing this to elevate myself in your view, Francis. It's just that Meeta and I are similar souls. Her pains and triumphs are the only reasons I'm willing to step back with you and inhabit these times and places.

I imagine you looking off to the side, just past the margins of the page. At your piles of correspondence, demands of advisers and archbishops, your calendar laden with appointments. You feel the need to feed your flock. To retreat for time with the Lord. Is this story *worth* my time? you ask. What are the *stakes* of this mystery?

Put bluntly, it's a battle for Meeta's soul. Though I know I can't control what you will do, I hesitate to jump forward for a simple telling of where she ends up would rob her story of its power.

No.

I simply can't indulge the ticking clock, your grumbling stomach, or harried presidents on the line. I humbly demand your full attention. Set aside the day's concerns, step out of your office, and join me again in Delhi.

For my sake. For Sister's. For your own.

*

Take a seat, Holy Father. There will do. I'll stand.

You're correct. Welcome to the view from inside the small oval window of Sister Shanti's office. It is morning, and Sister, the creature of habit that she is, passes a few moments with her newspaper.

She a saint? I can imagine you asking. Ah, you have seen but glimpses of her. To support my claim of Sister's sainthood, you will have to look closer. Detail by fragmented detail will collect, and only then will they resolve into the image of the beatific.

Observe.

First there are the superficial things. Sister is 154.94 cm. Her skin is brown. Her eyes are brown. Though she wears glasses, the younger Sisters in their tertianship remark her eyes are aflame. She has a terrible posture, except when playing the piano. She always favours her left foot; she slipped in the shower a decade ago and fractured her right ankle. It healed poorly, and the effect on her gait remains. Her dental hygiene is fastidious. She has but two missing teeth, both molars, both on the right side. She was quietly grateful they were not in the front. Her hair, a point of vanity in her youth, is shorn and covered by her banded blue-bordered sari except at night. She has not seen herself with a full head of hair since she was 21, when she completed aspirancy and entered postulancy.

She jots a note in a nearby ledger with her right hand – but look more closely. It is a crossword puzzle. Her disobediences are few, and this is one of them. She has always loved the newspaper's puzzles, though the worldly clues have become more remote as she has become more removed from the world. She files her half-filled attempts in expense report folders, knowing no one ever looks there but her. Her other guilty pleasure is reading American legal thrillers. Her most serious abuse of authority is reading novels lent by stroke-afflicted Om Prakash who lives at the MC home in Civil Lines; he collects the dog-eared books from visitors who come from all over the world.

The entirety of her earthly possessions includes three saris, a grey cardigan, a rosary, a small metal crucifix, an enamel bowl, flatware, and her Bible on the side of her desk. Her holy book is holey. Worms have gnawed the bottom of its pages. Grime and tea stains speckle it. Beyond the Gospels, beyond the Spirit of God becoming manifest in the pages of scripture like bursting lights, she resists opening the book except when required. Contemplation comes easily, but contemplative prayer not so much. Sister mostly keeps to herself these days. Her confessor, Father Bartholomew, is no confidante.

She turns from the newspaper again, stricken by something unseen, and takes up her rosary to utter a spontaneous decade. Her rosary is the same given to her by her most beloved teacher, Sister Angelique, an aged French nun from Shanti's convent school days. When Sister Shanti once thought she had dropped her rosary in public, she disobeyed the bell by which all of our nunly activities are regulated until she found it. This is perhaps a portent of more significant losses, and more significant recoveries.

There is work to do at her desk. There are always calls from those eager to visit the home, to volunteer, to *experience* the religious life lived under Mother Teresa's Rule. Whenever they come, starry-eyed, Sister does not disabuse them of their notions of life lived simply in service and prayer, but also does not fail to emphasize the heaps of dirty diapers. A family from Illinois is stopping by in about an hour, and she crosses this from her calendar. There are the details to be coordinated for the upcoming MC retreat. The odious task of tracking finances that rears its head monthly. And there is her responsibility for the spiritual care and discipline of those Sisters and children and staff under her oversight. Meetings, sessions, gatherings, etc. She pushes all of that to the side for just a few more moments of quiet with her news.

She returns to the front page. It is filled with the abhorrent and inane from all around Delhi and the world; she *tsks* even as she scans the headlines. Another rape, she mutters. Another murder. Another minister indicted on corruption charges.

Just as her eye passes over the mention of a grisly death last night, a knock comes from the doorway and disrupts our prying.

Yes? Sister Shanti finally says, her voice harsher than she intends. Sister Neepa, standing before her, immediately looks downwards. There are deliveries for you, Sister Neepa says. Two. One from the morning post. A second from last night, left for you at the gate.

Last night?

Sister Neepa swallows. Yes.

Why was it not delivered to me then?

You were with the children. During the Great Silence. I know you do not like distraction when you play the piano for them.

And who delivered it?

I did not know him. A man – a young man – a worried young man – was bringing it to the gate. Said it was important.

Sister Shanti returns her eyes to her newspaper and sighs. She extends her hand to the open air. When Sister Neepa fails to deposit the letters immediately, Sister snaps her fingers.

Sister Neepa approaches the hand like it is a trap set to spring. When the letters are within her grasp, Sister Shanti examines them closely. Thank you, Sister Shanti says.

Of course, Mother Superior.

And Sister?

Y-yes?

When someone says correspondence they're delivering late at night is of great importance, bring it to me. The Great Silence was made for man, and not man for the Silence.

The young nun is confused. Yes, Mother, she whispers.

You may go.

Sister Neepa flits off, a frightened bird. The first letter has her typewritten name above the MC home's address. International postage, stamped with – can it be? – St Peter's Basilica. Turning it over, her eyes catch on a single word in the return address: 'Vatican'.

Anxiety claims Sister. She rises, looks out on the long corridor outside the office door, and engages the lock.

Sister Shanti takes half of a long-broken pair of scissors in her trembling, knotty fingers. A quick slip between shallow breaths: the envelope is open.

She pulls out the contents: a single page, typed words on heavy stock paper. She reads the single, simple paragraph it contains once, twice, thrice.

She lets it fall to the desk, lets herself slump in her chair.

Her eyes close, her body deflates. We wait a minute before she moves again.

Finally, she pushes up her glasses, pinches the bridge of her nose, bites her lip, breathes deeply. She turns, seemingly numbed, and looks out of the small oval window, at the birdless bird feeder, the tall wall, the apartments set apart across the road. It is all achingly familiar, yet everything outside feels part of a far-off land she will never, ever visit.

There are attempts at prayer, but the words, sentiments, simple feelings of devotion to her God cannot be summoned. She looks at the letter, then at her aged, empty hands. It is a small grace that the door was not knocked at just now, the telephone not rung.

Once she's composed, she opens the door and invites in the sounds of squeaky footsteps on concrete floors, the children's cries and laughter and incomprehensible attempts at speech.

MCs are meant to be cheerful at all times.

She is an MC.

She is the Mother Superior.

Therefore, she is to be cheerful.

She tucks the sadness away and out of view, and is very careful to hide the just-received letter. She picks up the second delivery, her mind still lingering on the first. There's nothing written on the outside of the envelope, not a scratch. It's quite thick; bulging, in fact.

A snip of the scissors and – shock.

Money: hundreds, no, *thousands* of euros, dollars, a few lakh rupees. She lets it all slide out in a pile on her desk and marvels. She looks for some kind of explanation and finds it.

For the children. Goodbye. Ram.

The first letter is all but forgotten, a non-issue now. Sister Shanti tries to recall Sister Neepa's few shared details. A worried young man? At the gate? Last night? Fear, just a drop, spreads in her like tincture in water. Out comes her frayed address book, flipped to R. The only phone number she has for Ram is crossed through. How long is it since she's seen the boy? She immediately regrets the curse that flies from her lips; Sister Neepa had no idea who Ram is to Sister Shanti.

Rosary again in hand, Sister begins running the beads through her fingers, not praying, merely thinking. Her darting eyes flit to the newspaper, finding purchase on the ragged edge of the paragraph she was reading just when Sister Neepa appeared.

> **DELHI.** A young man was pushed before the arriving Chandigarh express train at New Delhi Station last night. Witnesses noticed a brief scuffle before the killer got the better of the victim and tossed him to the tracks as the incoming train arrived at 7.56 p.m. His assailant absconded though local police assure the public they are on his trail. The victim, Ram Kumar, 19, was only immediately identifiable by the contents of his pockets accounting to the severity of his injuries. Kumar was a young BPO employee from Gurgaon. He is survived by his bereaved fiancée who was present at the scene.

Sister claps her mouth to trap her horror.

IV

Take a handful of crumbs, Pope. Spread them widely. The flocks need feeding, and I need to tell you a story within our story.

In 1998, in her 59th year, Sister Shanti was panicked.

She stood in the shadow of a flyover near Kashmere Gate, the one we stand under this very moment, searching the faces of destitute children. Cars and rickshaws passed overhead. Five other MCs slopped porridge onto flimsy metal plates. Sister, despite herself, could not make herself work.

Why, you ask?

She did not see Ram.

The boy was always quick to assemble. He would run to her with a mischievous smile on his lips and hand her a treasure he had collected. A string bracelet. A smooth piece of coloured glass. A crinkled picture of movie star Dharmendra. She would take them, hide them away, stifling any sign of the great pleasure she found in the gifts. She ought not to show favouritism, but over the months she had come to know the boy, it proved impossible. She would pat him on the head and return him to the line as her heart was set aflame.

That day, they were nearly done serving the children and he was still absent. Sister dropped her ladle. Wiped her hands on her royal blue apron. Walked among the children as they ingested the thick mush. She enquired after Ram. Whether he had been seen. And where. And when. Fears of all the damnable things that could claim a child on Delhi's streets played out in her mind. The children looked into her eyes. They wished to tell her what she wanted to know.

Finally, one could.

Sister told the junior Sisters to gather up the pots and ladles and bowls and return with the driver to the MC home. She would search for Ram. Sister Shanti was asked if she would appreciate help; she declined.

She walked the distance from the flyover to the railway station. Waded through all manner of suffering on her search: a small girl and her smaller brother begging on the steps of a pedestrian overbridge; a bearded man without legs lying inert on a sodden square of cardboard.

A kind policeman let her through without a ticket. She scoured the platforms. Pushed through throngs. Crashed through crowds. She found Ram in a daze on the fourth platform. His eyes were distant. The odour of urine climbed off him. High, from sniffing glue. She lifted him up, wrapped her arms around him.

They departed together.

A simple tale, but one you will hear echoes of again and again.

But for now, throw your last crumbs to the birds, dear Francis. Time marches on and we must visit Meeta.

The girl returned disconsolate to the *kotha* last night. It was only later, after the sun had risen, after Ginna had cursed her, after Adiba had bruised her, that two thoughts occurred: (1) she shouldn't have gone to the washroom; and (2) she should have run away.

Ginna was taken aback when Meeta poked through the door with black streaks of kohl running down her face and bleated out Ram's sad fate. Only an hour or so before he had stood before Ginna looking young, dapper, and, well, alive.

Ginna's first thought: At least he had paid in advance.

Ginna's second thought: A valuable lesson was learned – try to escape and people get hurt. They even die.

After waiting 15 minutes for Meeta to compose herself, Ginna re-entered the girl's room. Get *ready* to take another customer, Ginna said, her well of compassion already dry. Off you go to welcome him, she ordered. Meeta would not. The old woman mistakenly believed raising her voice could force Meeta's sobs into submission. It did the opposite.

Quiet that down! snapped a man from the curtained space across from Meeta's room. He was busy with Anu, one of Ginna's other girls. How am I supposed to fuck with all this noise and bother?

Meeta still refused to stir.

Ginna huffed and spat, the spit landing right on the papered face of actress Sushmita Sen. Ginna left, and Meeta dug her face into her pillow to muffle her cries, knowing Adiba would soon appear.

The hours after stretched and twisted. She passed the night puzzling over the reordering of her imagined future. Conjured visions of Ram falling onto the tracks in slow motion, holding up his hands to stop the barrelling train. The coital sounds from all around – hydraulic suction, whispers, men's grunting – were a cruel chorus. Meeta had not felt suffocated like this since childhood when she was nightly tucked away under her mother's bed as it creaked with another visitor's weight.

This is what God made you for.

She had heard these words all her life, whispered by her mother and grandmother. This trade, and the life it brought, were her only inheritance. But she had hopes of more.

The whole journey from childhood to this night had seemed like her life's first act. The thrilling escape was meant to be the climax, the end, at least until the action-packed sequel arrived in cinemas next summer. The realization that life did not move from Act I to Act II, that Fate would not provide an inciting incident to jar her from this existence, was crushing. She was, as she'd always feared, trapped at her beginning.

And so the night progressed. She nursed her wounds. She cried. She retched and vomited. She slept.

When we arrive, the sun has already begun its afternoon descent and she awakes in a sweat. She pulls her face from her pillow to find a ghostly mask imprinted on it. She fumbles around for a hand-mirror. The black eye isn't so bad; not her worst. It could be concealed in part with kohl, and customers loved those black-rimmed eyes.

As Meeta stirs from her cot, new tears slip onto the floor. They are so sudden she can't even wipe them away. The sound of her rising brings the *kotha*'s three other didis, or 'sisters', to her room.

We heard…

It's so terrible…

Yes, so bad…

Their words are hollow, forced. They stand in the doorway with crossed arms.

To avoid their stares and stop her tears Meeta reaches for a baby wipe and daubs at her face.

You thought you were running away last night, says Anu.

And didn't even say goodbye, Rifat says.

You were busy with other customers, Meeta replies, with a wave of her hand.

No, we weren't, Anu says.

You're so selfish, Deepti says.

Meeta turns. Her temper flares. You'd have done the same!

Anu comes close. We understand the chance you took.

Rifat sits next to her. We do. Honestly.

Only Deepti still scowls from the doorway.

Deepti is the worst. She's been this way since Meeta came on the scene. Some would say Deepti is the prettiest, though she is a wilting flower at 27 or 28; she doesn't know her age. Though she has looks to trap customers, she can't 'give them a good time', as it were. She keeps to herself, unless angered, and is often found staring off into space alone while the other girls chat and chew *gutkha* and dance and preen one another.

Rifat is the only Muslim in the place, fair and a bit chubby. Tricked into this *dhanda*, this business, she comes from a provincial Kashmiri village and always has some illness – today it is jaundice – and this leads her to cook and clean rather than take customers. Unfortunately for her, she remains kind. Of this, the others take endless advantage.

Anu is from Malgudi, in the south. She first began working in Chennai's brothels before being shipped to Delhi after her attempt to flee and return to her family. It was her aunts who handed her back to her apoplectic pimp; they had been threatened with violence because of Anu's unpaid 'debts'. Adjusting to the capital had been difficult; she had only spoken Tamil and took to Hindustani poorly.

Meeta eyes them all in turn, frowning. One of Ginna's proverbs echoes in her inner ear: '*Yahan ki dosti, yahin pe khatam*'. A friendship that starts in this place ends in this place.

But it isn't her fault she's Ginna's number one favourite – she has a gift! Excels at dance! Knows best how to stroke men's egos (and their other parts)! The trade was bred into her, quite literally, when conceived in an act of transactional sex! On the scale of prostitution, ranging from the gutter *romni* to the ho-hum *bedni*, followed by the respectable *tawaif* and the courtesan-like *randi*, Meeta figured she fell safely in *randi* territory, only dipping to *tawaif* on her bad days.

She came to Ginna's brothel from neighbouring Uttar Pradesh, U.P., after an '*Incident*' where '*That Girl*' was dismissed after '*Circumstances Most Inauspicious*', as Ginna recounted. Never much discussed, but from what Meeta gleaned, *That Girl* was very active with her teeth. The vacancy meant a new girl was needed, and, through a series of interlocutors and intermediaries, Meeta was procured from her village in Nat Purwa.

I've digressed, Francis.

I feel like a widow, Meeta says glumly, after a minute's silence. I have been robbed of one of the greatest loves ever known.

It wouldn't have lasted, Deepti says flatly. Men like him come, make a thousand promises, and then abandon you over nothing.

All eyes turn to her.

This…has happened to you? Anu asks.

Deepti scowls again.

You *sisterfucker*, Meeta says, rising. You come in here, say things like this, you *romni* bitch? While his remains are on the railway tracks? Ram wouldn't have left me! Not a chance!

Deepti waves her hand and grumbles about needing to piss on the way out the door.

Meeta, *betee*, Anu says, caressing Meeta's arm. You know Deepti is more right than wrong. Move on. You'll be better for it. Another *harami* will be here in a few days, rupees in one hand, beak in the other, promising to give you the world.

You too? You're all…*terrible!* Meeta cries. Rifat is hurt at being associated with the others. Anu shrugs, follows in Deepti's steps. I'll never get over this loss! Meeta cries. Not with all the rest of my life!

Just quit the act, Deepti calls from the toilet. We're already tiring.

With so many storming emotions, it is a surprise the seed of an idea germinates, takes root, breaks soil.

Take note, Francis:

See Meeta's eyes widen; her mouth gape; her heart hop. This is the moment where one plot line has been cut short, but another, motivated by the twining threads of revenge and justice, is newly spun!

Meeta throws herself into the corridor and shouts: I'll show you all! I'll not let it be. If I've been denied love, then I'll have my hate! I'll find the murderer! I'll spend my life hunting down my love's killer!

Peels of laughter erupt, and muffled complaints can be heard from the floor above.

Rifat, the only one not to laugh, whispers after Meeta's pledge has a moment to air. But…you can't even leave this place. Ginna would never…

You think she'll keep me from my vengeance? Do you?

Rifat shrugs. I do.

Meeta pushes past Rifat, tears down the hall through a curtain of drying bras, scaring a surveying rat back into hiding. Ginna, despite the shouting, dozes as a bleary recording of the Nizahud-din qawwalis drones and drones.

I need to leave, Ginna. I have to catch Ram's killer. And kill him.

Ginna blinks awake. She picks the sleep from her eyes, examines it. She stands. She slaps the girl. Does Adiba need to beat you again? Get back to your room!

Meeta swallows. She reaches for a knife that Ginna left on the table as she chopped a white radish.

A threat.

A-di-*ba!* Ginna calls, quite unaffected. Stupid one here is acting up!

Adiba pokes his head from his room.

The knife trembles in Meeta's hand. Unexpectedly, she lifts it to her own throat.

This gets Ginna's attention. Her golden goose, a knife to its neck, and with stupidity enough to act!

Let's be *reasonable*—

I'm leaving.

Just put the knife down, my *treasured* one—

I need time to find who did this.

Of course you do, but there are *considerations*—

I will kill myself.

But why, my *dear*? You have such a bright—

Give me a week. One week.

Ginna glowers, mulls her options. Five days.

Six.

Starting now.

Tomorrow.

Meeta's eyes flick between Adiba and Ginna. She gives a silent, sideways nod.

Terms, Ginna says. Adiba goes with you *everywhere*.

Meeta sneers. Alright.

Your debt will *increase* every night you don't work.

I expected that.

No running away. Ginna wags her arthritic finger. *Consequences*.

Meeta unconsciously lowers the knife and Ginna eyes it warily. *What* do I have to run from? the girl says. Now that Ram is no more, and I am trapped, life is…

Ginna rolls her eyes. Just get back in your room and get that swollen face of yours decorated. Customers are coming soon. You'll scare them off.

Meeta slams the knife down. All watch her. She dabs at a new (genuine) tear as she retreats to her room.

That same seed is flourishing, sending up a sprout: rising hope makes her head light, offers a hope that despite this day's darkness, one day, things might be better.

Meeta sits and picks up a comb but does nothing with it, just stares at herself in the mirror.

Rifat enters wordlessly. She takes the comb and begins running it through Meeta's hair. Anu comes in with a sigh and takes Meeta's hand. Finally, Deepti enters, brings a chair, and places it facing Meeta. She begins to powder Meeta's face. None speak, their minds heavy with what they suffer and all they will never know.

V

Walk with me now. Across the old city. Back to the river. We have a very specific meeting to keep.

You seem anxious, Pope. I wonder if you're not at ease? Maybe wishing to be finished with all of this? I know I offered warning as to what our story would entail, but I suppose you are unaccustomed to visiting brothels? I joke, of course. The *kothas* may seem the darkest places I'll take you on our travels, but this is not so.

Judging by the sun's position, we're still a few minutes early. I see you scan our surroundings wondering where we are. That massive river is the Yamuna. We stand on its western bank, north of the city in an industrial zone. Just *look* at all these bilious towers pumping without end...

That river, despite appearances, is Delhi's lifeblood. In the past, this water was a cleansing thing. It gave life. Took waste away. The muck before you is the price paid for our way of life. I see you leaning down to take a closer look; you will only be disappointed. It is a vitriolic sludge. I sometimes think it comes into contact with us, with our sins, and bears them. They're so overwhelming, the river cannot handle all the misery we churn out.

I fear for our generation. And the next. And the next.

When I first found myself in the Mother House for aspirancy, it was a surprise to learn how sinful I was. I was relatively new to the Church and its teachings, carried into the religious life more with a conviction to love than anything else. Dogma and doctrine were soon to follow, and I have since embraced them, but in those early days it was so easy. Just...simple love, spiritual milk for an infant believer.

I was amazed they let me remain. I wasn't able to speak English, not really. I couldn't even navigate the Holy Book to which I had pledged my allegiance, with all of its numbers and letters, letters and numbers. Fortunately, the Mother Superior took my deficiencies in her stride. Showed much forbearance. Gave me extra reading instruction. Taught me to use a fork and knife.

36

And, of course, the MC vows:

Poverty: I was ambivalent about embracing this one. I have since come around.

Chastity: *Not* a problem. We are fully devoted to Christ alone. No time for menfolk.

Obedience: Another concern. Not previously a strong suit of mine.

And then our fourth vow, our religious community's reason for being, some might say,

Wholehearted and true service to the poor: Why I came. The main event. The star attraction.

You're probably quite familiar with all aspects of the religious life, so stop me if I'm a bore. I can't really say if the MC period of aspirancy is different from any other religious community's. Work in the mornings. Obey the bell. Pray and study in the afternoons. Obey the bell. It was a regimented existence, but I took to it, like some do to military training. Many aspirants struggled with the vast hours of prayer. I did at first. I soon found them to be the source of tremendous consolation and healing.

Ah. The sun has slotted into place and…yes, rounding that corner just now are Sisters Shanti and Neepa.

They walk along the industrial track otherwise alone. Sister finds the streets almost restful compared to the clang and clatter and chaos and crowding of Delhi's byways and roadways and flyovers. There is no chatter between her and Sister Neepa. Sister Neepa looks up at a flock of crows circling overhead like kites in formation. We nuns are meant to keep 'obedience of the eyes' when outdoors, to not let our gaze wander and pray the rosary as we walk. Sisters don't have pedometers to measure the time and distance between two points: they have the rosary. Thus far, despite two intervening commuter bus rides, Sister Shanti has prayed many, many decades. She runs her fingertips over her rosary again, but as their destination nears her thoughts are a million miles from Our Father and Hailed Mary.

Sister stops abruptly, and Sister Neepa is shaken from her own prayers. What is it? Neepa asks.

Sister Shanti spins around. She withdraws a carefully folded, pencil-drawn map from a plastic bag. She tilts her head. No good at all, Sister mutters. There is not one person to direct them. Despite a breeze, it is so hot, all the factories' guards are hiding in shaded corners.

Not far off she sees a car turn onto the road. She is unfamiliar with most makes and models these days – the need for such knowledge fell away long ago – though this car she knows. It is an Ambassador, an Indian classic. Her family had one once, when she was growing up. It had taken her all over Delhi. To school, to piano lessons, to the temple, back home again. Flashing memories of rides with her parents are pleasant, at least at first.

She tries to wave the car down as it approaches her but its driver refuses to slow down. With hesitation, but not much, she steps into the car's path, prompting a cry from Sister Neepa and forcing the Ambassador to skid to a stop. Sister admires the car's shape and chrome before bothering to look up at the driver who appears very, very angry.

With his torso half out the driver-side window, he hollers, What do you bloody think you're doing, eh?

Sister stares him down as she passes Sister Neepa (her head down, in shame or prayer, Sister Shanti doesn't care) to face the driver directly. He shrinks back into the car like a turtle tucks in its head.

She sizes him up. He has a long beard, well-tended and flecked with grey, and puffy eyes. He wears a khaki bush shirt and turban.

You are standing in my way, he says, sheepishly.

I am. The car's rear windows are tinted and she can't resist peeking through his opened window at the passenger. A woman, older than Shanti but not so distant in age, sits staring into space from the back seat. Her head is a clash of colour: wrapped in a floral print scarf, her eyes are shaded behind buggy purple sunglasses while the lower part of her face is painted to an extent she appears clown-like. She is Indian by her looks, very light-skinned, and dainty.

38

Well, what is it? The air conditioning, it escapes, the driver says.

Indeed it does. The mild cool was refreshing and Sister luxuriated in it.

We're a bit lost, Sister finally says, and without help. We're looking for the Public Crematorium. The electric one. The duffers have not placed any signs on the road, and we've never been this way.

The driver leans forward to observe Sister Neepa, who still peers at the ground. He looks at Sister Shanti again and his expression softens just so.

Drive, Malhotra, *drive*. I'm too tired to trifle.

Malhotra turns to his passenger. Just a moment, memsahib. These two have lost someone as well. We'll be on our way shortly.

Too *tired* to trifle, she says, her voice trailing off.

Malhotra grimaces at her remark. He turns to Sister. You saw where we turned from a moment ago?

Sister nods.

Go down not two hundred metres more. There's your crematorium.

Sister gives a tilt of the head. I thank you, Malhotra sahib.

The woman in back raises her hand to her head as if pained. Just *drive*...

With a shrug, Malhotra rolls up his window.

An interesting pair, Sister remarks as the car accelerates and turns around a bend.

Most, Sister Neepa replies. Shanti looks at Neepa: the young nun is perpetually tense. Sister sighs and moves on.

The crematorium is surprisingly small, set behind a chain-link fence. It is a radical departure from the open-air funerary ghats along the Yamuna where Hindus bring their dead. The electric burning was meant to limit deforestation and reduce air pollution, but all of the environmental and cost benefits in the world couldn't make up for the alien-ness of this dark-looking box. Electric ghats like this are mostly used by the poor and for unclaimed victims whom no one comes forward to claim. The Ram Kumars of the world.

The shock of learning Ram was dead lasted all morning. Immediately labelled in Sister's mind as the Profound Sadness, at the ring of the bell, so conditioned was Sister that her tears dried up, her sorrow ceased, only to be replaced by *weight*: imponderable and unmovable. Composed again, she wandered the rest of the day through an emotional fog so thick that it levelled highs and lows alike.

Sister called a local policeman in their district, a desk officer who had been of help on several past occasions. Within three hours there was a return call and an address given. A check of an old Delhi map in her office displayed the main road but showed the area surrounding it as devoid of settlement or industry. Delhi, ever metastasizing, had been on the move.

The crematorium's main gate is ajar. The chowkidar dozes where he sits. They do not disturb him as they step inside under a prominent sign which declares BURNING OF THE NON-DEAD FORBIDDEN.

Dear God, Sister mutters.

They find themselves in one of the dark chambers used for cremations. It has space for attendees to gather around a rectangular central platform with a slatted, sliding door. A track lies on the floor running up to the slats, with a sort of sled locked into place. Red lights glare from a control panel built into a side wall. There are no mourners, no bhajans being sung, no prayers being offered.

Wait here, Sister Shanti tells Sister Neepa, and sets out looking for an attendant. The squeaking of her sandals echoes, bouncing off the utilitarian walls and floors.

Anyone here? she hollers.

A door opens at the end of the corridor. A slight, middle-aged man appears, his hands sheathed in yellow kitchen gloves and his fingertips facing upwards. He wonders at the old woman decked in white.

You are?

Here to mourn, Sister says, matter-of-factly. I received notice you are – processing – the body of a young man. He died last night.

Here for the, uh – he signals with a chop – train one?

Yes, the 'train' one. Her features curl.

He's underway.

Burning?

Burning.

I hoped to see him.

You wouldn't have wanted. His face – he rams one hand into the other. Interesting mode of death. Normally it is the bullets, head trauma, stab wounds…

Sister clears her throat. At least it was quick, Sister says.

Haan, says the attendant. True. I can take you to him. He is finishing at any moment.

Sister stands inert, as if put on pause.

Finally: Did he have any effects?

The attendant looks at her dumbly.

Any *things*? When he came? In his pockets? On his person?

Glumness sets in, as if he's been left on the sides at a cricket match. The dead from the streets are well picked over when they arrive, he says. Police, or the men who bring the bodies do it. Vultures, all of them. There is a billfold, but not a paisa to be found inside.

May I see it?

That's not allowed.

Please.

No exceptions.

Sister grimaces.

It's, ah, generally wise not to go against Sister Shanti's wishes, Sister Neepa says, finally making her presence known.

He coughs. It's so very difficult. My precious daughter, Prithri, all of 7 years, she is needing new shoes. All I can think about, in fact. Though his tone is flat, his eyebrows are buoyant.

Sister Shanti comes close, and despite her diminutive size, scares him. Do *not* ask for baksheesh. The boy burning in that little box was as a son to me. Either there are rules, and you cannot do it, or, out of respect for me and my loss, you *will* do it.

The attendant swallows. Yes, memsahib. I am seeing. Daughter's shoes can wait. He goes to the back room. Sister Shanti ignores Sister Neepa's surprise and returns to the crematorium chamber, hears the hiss of the flames at work.

Are you alright? Sister Neepa enquires, rejoining her.

A simple reply: No.

When the attendant returns he has removed the gloves.

The billfold is covered with a bit of Sir's remains, but I was able to find these.

He places two items in Sister's outstretched hand. She raises them to her eyes and squints. The first is a business card:

SHAH JEE & SONS ANTIQUES AND METAL RECYCLING
A subsidiary of Shah Jee & Sons Co.
Chawri Bazar

The second is a railway ticket. She reads: passenger, Meeta Chandralekha. Destination, Bangalore. Likely the fiancée mentioned in the article, Sister realizes.

Are they to your satisfaction? the attendant asks Sister.

They are.

Your young man is the final cremation of the day.

We'll only stay a few moments then.

As you wish.

Sister Neepa waits awkwardly as Sister Shanti stands before the concrete box in silence, still wondering at Sister's reference to Ram as her 'son'. Figuratively, of course. But it helps her understand what has taken hold of the usually inscrutable Sister Shanti.

Touching other Sisters outside of what is necessary is prohibited under the MC rule. It is an attempt to avoid 'particular friendships', a euphemism if ever there was one. Sister Neepa worries Sister Shanti will take it poorly if she offers her a consoling hand. Sister Neepa does so anyway.

Sister Shanti responds slowly. She takes her hand in her own. The Profound Sadness is written on her face.

Thank you for accompanying me, Sister Shanti whispers. It means much.

They turn, waiting the remaining minutes for the buzzer to sound and the cremation to end, but depart before the attendant comes to dispose of what remains.

VI

I have told you my name was not always Immaculata. Sister's was not always Shanti.

In 1956, in her 17th year, Sister Shanti was still Heera Chayn.

She passed her days in a convent school in Delhi. She admired the nuns. Most of them, anyway. There was a portly French Sister, Sister Angelique, who lacked patience but was quick-witted. Open and honest and joyful. This spoke volumes to Heera.

Heera excelled in her studies. Maths and English were her favourites; music was a passion. This makes her mother very proud. It makes her father very sad.

Heera loved the daily walk home with her girlfriends. When they could get away with it, the boys from a nearby school troubled Heera, but worry not: Heera troubled the boys. Her affections were inconstant, her romantic infatuations turning over almost daily.

She was an only child. Wished for a brother. There was one, before she was born. Dead, after two days. Her arrival three years later was met with much rejoicing and she was loved deeply from the start. Her parents never attempted another child for the staggering fear of potential loss.

Daddy, her father, was a stern bureaucrat in the Ministry of Railways, made of imperious stuff like in the Indian Administrative Service, and an old-order Anglophile. He wore tweed coats even in beastly heat. Only drank English gin. Had friends from abroad bring him the newest Graham Greene novels. Questionably ranked English composers Tallis and Byrd above Mozart and Beethoven. He had always dreamt of study in the (former) imperial motherland, but on reaching middle age knew that ship had long sailed.

Her mother, Mummy, from a successful Punjabi business family, was an amateur singer and accomplished sitarist. Also stern. Her infatuations with the West tended towards continental Europe, but the Second World War dampened her affections for all things German and French, except their music. It was from her and her alone that Heera's own extraordinary musical aptitude had sprung. Yet she no longer sang or played. Not since her son passed away, her brother died fighting for the crown, her country ripped in two. Her life moved from one bout of depression to the next.

The family migrated from Amritsar to Kolkata (then Calcutta) in 1947 when Partition came. Sectarian strife: the only explanation that needs saying. They arrived with their Ambassador full of possessions and empty of petrol. Their most valuable things had been stolen or abandoned in their swift flight, but ties in the new independent government remained intact. Strings were pulled. Favours called in. A job and an apartment were secured, as was a place at an elite Catholic school for Heera. A Western education was to be had for this one, Daddy said. Indeed, Mummy said, indeed.

On this day, sitting around the dinner table and part-way through a meal of curried lentils, her father asked Heera what she wished to become. He revisited this question on occasion.

She laid down her fork, dabbed at her mouth with a napkin.

Her first answer: a pianist.

Her mother smiled. Her father tutted. Too impractical, he said.

Heera sat. She thought. Her second answer: a jurist.

He smiled. That's good. Very good. Exams are coming up. Go to UK, maybe?

She pondered over the proposition. No, she stated definitively. I will stay here. Closer to home. To you both.

He grumbled something about missed opportunity, but he loves her for this.

They went on to finish their meal, and Heera felt a stab of regret. She was an honest, guileless girl. Smiled freely. Did her homework. Harboured no secrets. As fleeting as this moment was, it stayed with her. Why? one might ask. Because in appeasing her Hindu parents she failed to mention that she wonders if she is meant to become a Catholic nun.

Go back to Old Delhi, to G.B. Road, to the darkened stairwell with the chain running along the wall, to *kotha* No. 201, and knock.

Step in.

Meeta has worked the entire night. It is agony between her legs. Wisps of what could have been swirl about: *a space to call her own* freedom to amble *holding her head up high in the streets* a loving husband *lack of want* the line between inside and outside her body unbroken unless she allowed.

Two regulars complain when Meeta will not accommodate their 'requests'. These men, like so many, arrive with heads full of Internet pornography, demanding re-enactments. Adiba has to throw them out, refunds in hand; Ginna fears her star attraction may be fading. She has seen such ruinous declines before.

These girls are kept in place by fear of Adiba's fists and the Great Unknown outside the *kotha*'s walls. Maybe Meeta will have a child and all will be well, Ginna hopes. A child is a sort of insurance policy for pimps like her. They are a bother, of course, but a whore with a crying, open mouth to feed is most pliant.

But wait, that's right, Ginna recalls: Meeta has an inverted what's-it, a faulty some such, a cystic thingy. A child she cannot, not ever, not a chance, bear. And since the Great Unknown doesn't appear to deter her, evidenced by the other evening's flight, the fists will have to do.

Come here, Francis. Don't worry – no one is indecent. Meeta is just stirring, checking her swelling in the mirror. She dresses.

Rifat is already up and steeping tea and baking chapattis while smoking a 502 Pataka bidi, certain not to help her health. Meeta eats two pieces to settle her stomach. Rifat gently warns Meeta not to be too disappointed if her investigation does not progress today. Meeta huffs, thanks her for the food and returns to gather her things.

Ginna blocks her at the door. Meeta wears a salwar-kameez, the same from the other night, and sunglasses that hide her blackened eye. Not a trace of make-up. It surprises Ginna how she resembles an upright citizen – a university student, a bank employee, a housewife, someone from a good family. The inability to see her eyes through the dark lenses unnerves Ginna.

Be *back* by midnight, the old woman says.

Of course. Meeta holds out her hand. My advance, she says.

Ginna smiles, places 500 rupees in her hand. Added to your debts.

Meeta rolls her eyes.

Adiba is already on his feet but looking tired; he didn't sleep, choosing instead to watch a *Predator* film marathon followed by a few hours on *Grand Theft Auto III*. Meeta is already down the stairs.

Hold *onto* her arm, Ginna tells Adiba. Like a bitch on a *lead*.

He nods, follows Meeta down the narrow passage and is delivered into the world of light below.

Come on, Meeta urges, tugging against his meaty grip. Don't slow me down. Adiba sniffs, snorts, blows his nose on his sleeve. He continues at his same unruffled pace.

Meeta feels her senses sharpen. The air is clearer than in the *kotha*. The light gives her vision a new acuity. If only it could sharpen her *plan*. Despite much reflection, it is undeveloped. She decides to start asking around.

There is a pair of older touts at the base of the staircase. She checks if they saw a man in a black suit the night before last. She hoped the rarity of the sight would have stuck. The women are surprised Meeta is even on the street, but Adiba's looming presence explains it. They answer with slight incredulity: hundreds of men have come and gone in the last two nights. To the best of their recollection, no suits.

The road is already crowded with men. A few go up and come down, but mostly they visit the respectable shops on the bottom level to find a motor gasket or a spool of wire, or pause in the shade of a nearby peepul tree and talk with the chaat vendor. She knows the shops would have been closed when Ram appeared on the road so the owners would be of no help; she also knows they wouldn't talk to her even if they *did* know something. They have a gift, treating the parallel disreputable trade as if it is invisible.

The pair continue up and down the block, Meeta checking with other touts and pimps. Nothing. After only an hour she wonders if the evil eye is fixed squarely upon her in these pursuits.

What if someone had *seen him?*
Does she think they'll just hand over an address?
What a stupid girl, thinking she can right this wrong!

She reaches the spot where she and Ram climbed into the rickshaw. The memory of their flight is already blurring. Standing there for a moment, eyes closed, she replays everything that happened. The pursuer. Ram was troubled as they rushed from G.B. and jumped in the rickshaw. She pictures Ram's face. He was terrified, but not of Adiba.

She steps back to the first night Ram found her some four months before. He wasn't dressed differently than any other men then, though he was more courteous. He was tentative. It was a slow week-night and all the girls were bored, assembled in the *kotha* entryway and listening to All India Radio, waiting for the next customer to arrive, line them up, look them over, and make his selection. Ram entered alone – many times customers came in pairs or groups. Ginna greeted him warmly from her chair, inviting him to choose among 'her *choice* gems, her beautiful *daughters*'. Each stood there, with wide smiles. Their act was not because they wanted to sleep with a customer, but because this one was young and handsome and well-kempt, and, in a word, uncommon. 'Prime boyfriend material', as Deepti would say: a young man who might become a regular and patronize his favourite and buy her phone credit or make-up or biscuits and maybe, just maybe, stoke her dreams into a flame.

Ram said that he had come looking for the *mujra* dancer. He heard there was an accomplished one here.

Of course, Ginna smiled.

Meeta swelled with pride and stepped forward. He looked awe-struck. Ginna whispered into Ram's ear and he scrounged around in his pocket for the price without looking away from Meeta. When Ginna was satisfied, Meeta spoke.

Come with me.

She led him to her room. Flicked on the tubelight. He was momentarily stunned by the collage of posters, unsure where to focus. The pair did not speak. Meeta seated him on her floor. She took off her outer salwar-kameez to reveal a full-bosomed choli. She resembled the women in the images lining the walls. Going to her CD player, she pressed play. A *thumri* burst from the speakers. She was transfixed, taken up. He paid, and she danced, and he paid more, and she danced with more fervour. Finally, she ended and left the room with a grand flourish, as if closing a performance before a grand Mughal audience. Ginna came in and explained that she would return after a brief rest. The anticipation made Ram's skin tingle. Ginna opened her palm. He paid.

Though there was sex, no intimacy was exchanged that night. Meeta did not offer him her name. He did not offer his.

Meeta had no reason to expect him back and was bemused when he came. She had not tried to bait a hook and wasn't looking for a new patron; she was already juggling three other men, two of obvious means. But there he was the next night, ready to pay a sizeable sum of money to pass the night with her. After a short-lived passion (on his part), they settled into a conversation that lasted hours. Timid Ram had disappeared. She was introduced to a new, Confident Ram with dreams the size of her own.

Meeta hears a husky whisper in her ear. She is pulled back to where she stands in the present. Looking for some excitement?

Meeta opens her eyes. It is Latika, a didi from the neighbouring *kotha*. (You remember her, right, Francis?)

Get away from me, bitch, Meeta mutters. I'm in no mood.

Latika gives a mocking laugh.

He's dead. Ram is dead. So shut your mouth.

Latika freezes. Shock touches her face, but gives way to a wry smile. Is that so? Come and go, they do, come and *go*. She pinches Meeta.

You never touched him, you whore!

Ha! I gave that poor fool the best nights of his life. Must have been – she looked up, trying to recall – just last week.

He wouldn't. Not so recently.

He *would*.

He didn't.

He *did*. Ram told me all kinds of things he said he couldn't tell another soul.

Meeta lunges at her, scratches her face while spewing invectives. Latika shrieks and gives her a punch to the stomach. Adiba soon steps between them and subdues Meeta in his flabby arms.

He went to Pinku, Latika says, panting. After a fight. Asked him for – another girl – a *better* girl. So Ram came to me.

I'll kill you if I see you again! Meeta shouts. A tittering crowd gathers and gruff shop owners tell the pair to stop disrupting business. Latika makes an obscene gesture at Meeta and climbs the stairs. Meeta wriggles out from Adiba's grip and wipes tears away as she rushes down the street. Adiba trails close behind.

Only a week ago? She tries to remember, but evenings blend together so easily and the days of the week seldom matter but for the TV schedules they herald.

There was an argument, she remembers. He had come to her, as he did every few days, but was troubled. Very drunk. He hadn't brought her any gifts, had called her selfish. She baulked. What happened next made her realize she was not particularly good at talking things over. The volume escalated. Quickly.

Get out! she told him. *For good!*

Once he was gone, she feared he would do as commanded.

He returned the next night in a cloud of gloom. She assumed his guilt was regret over the fight; maybe it was because he had gone in to Latika. Maybe it was something else altogether.

That his eternal vows of love had so quickly unravelled and he slipped into another's bed disquiets Meeta. It isn't the sex itself – that has almost no meaning. It is his discounting one of the only things she is able to give. She turns to blaming herself, for all of it – his drunkenness, depression, death. In a moment of unusual clarity, she worries she cannot help but spoil good things.

She kicks that thought to the curb. She needs to find Pinku, the tout Latika mentioned.

Don't let her get too far ahead of us, Francis. We don't want to lose her. It shouldn't be too hard to find Pinku; he has quite the reputation.

Up the staircase at his favourite *kotha*, No. 158? Meeta frowns after checking. Apparently not.

Despite Pinku's young age and small stature, he is notorious, a product of G.B., made in, made for, this place: he harasses, promotes, drinks, assaults, robs, gets high, whenever the inclinations strike. A fish in water.

Hmm. Nor is he taking chai at his usual dhaba, either.

Pinku is often treated to free sessions with girls in order to incentivize his touting, but word was he has paused for a time after contracting a nasty venereal disease. I can only imagine what new strain of virus is breeding in that boy, and I don't think it's wrong to call him that even though he's reached the age of majority.

Meeta enquires again. The other young male touts, preoccupied with their mobiles, tell her to get back to her *chodai khana kotha* before they make her. She curses them and continues on her way.

Our young thug is known for his memory, rather extraordinary, in fact, and he maintains a complex catalogue of customers and their preferred *kothas* and girls with remarkable clarity. Meeta hopes it will prove useful for her needs, should she find him.

Achcha. Good. It appears Meeta and Adiba have found their man. No, no, you must look *down*, Pope. That's right. Blending into the refuse at the edge of this fetid trash hillock.

Meet the illustrious Pinku.

Meeta nudges him with her toe. He stirs, grudgingly.

What?

I need your help, Pinku.

Pay me now. In a few hours maybe I can do something for you.

It's just a question I'm having.

He tries his best to avoid the light, but the sun is at its peak and bathing the streets without mercy. She offers her sunglasses and he puts them on, giving an appreciative grunt.

Meeta? What are you doing on the street? Trying to run again?

Her eyes flick to Adiba and back. No.

Your eye. A customer been to work on you?

Her fingers rise to her bruises. Again, an unconscious glance at Adiba. The lunkhead is poking a scabied dog resting on the heap.

Pinku yawns and puffs his cheeks, blowing out a noxious blend of booze and garlic. How're things going?

I need help. Your help.

Ginna let you out? His non sequitur annoys Meeta.

Haan. Yes. Look. Two nights ago, Ram was here.

That your guy? He closes his eyes tightly as he tries to recall. Your dead guy, right? I heard. Yeah. Him I saw. He arches his back, throws his arms out, stretching, gives a hoot. He and I almost got into it when the *chodu* bludy fucker brushed me off. Dressed like a prick, coming down here like he's something he's not.

Meeta stares at him for half a minute, his grimy sweater and hair's curls cemented in place by dirt and God-only-knows-what. She rips her glasses from his face. Pinku rolls his eyes as he moans. A hand over his face, he says, What do you want? I have important…busy…things.

Meeta flicks his nose. Did you see anything else? Ram was scared. I realized only later. I thought it was nerves, due to this lump of ghee – her thumb points to Adiba – but we were running from someone else. Whoever it was chased after and… killed him. I know it.

Pinku's interest is kindled. There was a *gaandu*. In a suit. Around the same time. Gods above, I hate pricks, but ones in suits? *Especially.* I thought he was your guy. That same puffed, stupid hair, like Salman Khan. But this one wasn't so good-looking. A part of said *chodu*'s ear was missing. He had a scar on his cheek. I almost got in fighting with him, too. Nothing I like less then someone rejecting my most kindly-offered services. Staring at his scar, eh, maybe didn't help so much.

Meeta's forehead screws up, her lips purse. The description matches no one she can recall, nor anyone Ram talked about. Picturing him in her mind's eye, the description conjures a bristling thug in a tight-fitting suit hardened by a hundred fights. Of *course*, Ram – her gentle, soft, sensitive Ram – would have been scared by a villain like this.

You've been a help, Pinku. Thank you. Now fuck off back to your rubbish.

Be careful, bitch, or I'll send a fatty, flea-bitten *chodu* your way, Pinku says. Another Adiba!

He smiles. Meeta smiles too. Adiba grimaces, leaves the dog alone and lumbers off towards the mouth of the alley. Meeta soon overtakes him.

Progress, no? she says, maybe to Adiba, maybe to no one. Her mind races, her feet follow its pace, and it is a half-minute before she stops amid the pedestrian traffic and realizes she isn't sure where she is going.

The police. The idea isn't new, but everyone knows the police on G.B. are as dangerous as the mafia. Still, they could know things impossible for her to ascertain. Maybe they would have Ram's property taken for evidence. Or maybe his address.

Ram never let her visit his home, even on the few nights when she was permitted to leave. He said it was too far, all the way in Gurgaon.

Gurgaon, if you aren't familiar, Francis, is a newish city to Delhi's south where foreign companies set up shop, the very hub of rising India's telecom and Business Process Outsourcing (BPO) industries. Correct, Pope: India's famous call centres. Ram bragged about his place in a new army of 900,000 employees heeding the call to, well, take calls. To Meeta, Gurgaon might as well have been a bounteous land out of Vedic myth.

Out of nowhere comes the image of the train resting atop Ram, the multitudes huddling around hoping for a splash of gore. She shudders.

The decision is made: Adiba, she says, we go to see the police.

He tenses, but she is already off, aimed at the tiny blue and maroon police post near Ajmeri Gate.

She knocks first to no answer. The wooden cabin is window-less. It has a loudspeaker. Painted along its top, in English, is the unsettling police motto: *With you For you Always*. Meeta wonders if it is even occupied. She pushes the door. To her surprise, it creaks open.

The Constable (Singh is his name, if you recall) sits in the dark watching a small TV. A desk fan blows directly on him but he sweats straight through his green and khaki uniform. Adiba waits in the doorway, turned towards the street.

What is it?

Singh says this without pulling his eyes away from his programme. She does not know this squat man by name, but recognizes him from when she looks down on G.B. from the window in No. 201 and he creates as much conflict as he ends.

I'm here to lodge an FIR, she whispers. To open a police case. Her wandering eyes skip past three garlanded portraits of gods on the wall and land upon the large stick resting against his desk.

I'm eating.

This is obvious. His fingers, pulled out from a Styrofoam container, drip with curry. He forces a wad of dipped nan in his mouth. Meeta doubts anew the wisdom of coming here.

It is a murder. I know who killed a man, sahib…

Singh, he says, running his tongue over his teeth. He finally pulls himself from his *Dadagiri Unlimited* quiz show to run his eyes up and down Meeta. He takes up a soiled rag from his feet to wipe his right hand, then sweeps away the detritus caught in his handlebar moustache. He takes up a pencil.

Name?

Meeta.

Victim's name?

Ram.

He looks at her impatiently. Surname?

She blushes. I…don't know it.

The body?

Already gone. Picked up. He was killed at the railway station. N-night before last.

Singh scribbles a little then looks up. The one cut up by the train? Is that who you mean? A *mess*, that was.

Meeta scowls.

Why are you coming now?

I just heard information about the one who did the deed. And I need the victim's – Ram's – address.

Constable Singh picks at his teeth with his pinky's long fingernail. He shrugs. Relationship to the victim?

We were to be married.

His look turns to scepticism.

Girlfriend, Singh writes, chuckling. And you do not know his name?

She doesn't appreciate his mocking tone.

Ahh*hhh*. Why would you report anything here? You're one of *them* – he signals with a grand sweep towards G.B. – aren't you? Take your sunglasses off. That's right. Let me see your face. Nice bruise! And who's this sad sack with you? Your new boyfriend?

Constable Singh tells Adiba to turn around. Adiba does.

Why, that's – Adiba! He turns back to Meeta. You're one of Ginna's? Hey. Hey! He throws a chicken bone at Adiba, which he sidesteps. Did I tell you you could turn away from me, you imbecile? Did I?

Adiba's eyes narrow. He closes the door and stares into space, just above Constable Singh's head.

Idiot, Constable Singh says. Fool, he curses. With just the flickering light from the TV lighting the room, Constable Singh's eyes glint. I'm sure a file has already been opened about this case. Let me call. He holds out his hand.

What? Meeta asks.

Rupees. Give them here.

For what?

For the phone call to our central station. And the case-opening fee. And the paper and file folder you've already made me waste if there's another FIR open. There are expenses for everything. I'm not given shit to do my job. So you need to pay.

Of course he'd say that, she thinks. How much? She reaches for her purse – her very small, very *light* purse.

Costs too high. Bureaucracy, he says, shrugging. What can be done?

I only have a little.

His eyes narrow, then widen with the birth of a new idea. I feel for you. I do. Losing your betrothed. I've not once heard a sadder story.

Her heart leaps. He stands up and goes to the door, opens it, shoos Adiba out, and us too. Constable Singh locks the door from inside. Meeta watches all this with deepening dread.

Sick man. If you must listen, Francis, if your curiosity simply overwhelms you to know what happens next, put your ear up against the wall.

…I can make the call, you can hear Singh say. Find out anything and everything about the case. Hand it over to you. They'll have his address, most surely. No fee. Waived. But for me to do my job, you'll just need to do what you do best – he glanced at his paperwork – Meeta. Do your job, Meeta. Do what you do best…

VII

I'm sorry to pull you away, but you didn't need to see what followed and I didn't need to show it to you.

This world, Francis, this *world*.

Please. Walk with me. I detect you need a rest. Lord knows I do.

Lodhi Garden is a refuge. I am not able to come here often, so every chance to retreat here, I take.

It's an oasis in the heart of Delhi's madness. We've missed the morning rush. The yoga class devotees and past-prime men in tracksuits discussing business. Note the children from the elite international school at play on a field trip. The strolling old Sikh couple, hands held circumspect behind their bodies. Just look at all the greenery of this place, new life, new flowers, amid the ruins of tombs hundreds of years old, built by Muslim rulers and graffitied by generation after generation. 'Abdel #1', 'Yogesh +

Priyanka'. A reminder of permanence and decay, life and death.

Ah, note too the marauding pack of macaques. The monkeys have descended on a loaf of white bread a guest intended for the colour-flecked pigeons of this place. Spectators encircle them at a safe distance, watching the mothers share with babies, males fight with males. Look! Look! They eat only the white centres, leaving behind the crust! The pickiness of God's creatures!

They're stirred up now, making too much noise, growing too wild. This is unacceptable. Monkeys are a curiosity, but there are always stories following them of rabid bites and stolen possessions. A man was reported to have been frightened off his balcony by his illegal pet monkey. Dead!

A laughing matter until they're not.

The partners arrive. You hear the motorcycle before you see it riding along the park's concrete paths. How is a motorcycle allowed in the park? A special dispensation. Note the passenger behind the driver, and it may help explain. That's right: an enormous monkey.

In a flash, before the bike is even parked, our monstrous langur friend leaps off and dashes at the pack of smaller monkeys. The driver pulls out a long cudgel and is soon reinforcing his companion's efforts to terrorize and scatter the pack. They are an elite team, this pair, and know their work well.

Once dispersed, they return to the bike and strike calm and collected poses. Another call comes in: a trio of monkeys has infiltrated a megamall. The mercenaries are back on the bike, a treat passed to the langur, who looks self-satisfied, as if to say, 'Nothing to see here, all in a day's work'.

Showing you this may seem a simple amusement, Francis, but you will see this is no monkey business. At such a time, and such a place, this duo will reappear, and lives will never be the same.

But it is not only for a bit of foreshadowing that I introduce you to Lodhi Garden. I wanted you to see this place, Pope. To take in its obvious beauty after we've been exposed to so much rot. To find momentary rest amid the rows of little flowers in their silent praise of the sun. To look over at those benches where an important scene took place not so long ago.

In 2007, in her 68th year, Sister Shanti encountered Ram in his prime.

She arrived in Lodhi Garden and sat right there. It was a Thursday morning, the day normal MC routine is broken for rest, prayer, and confession. She rushed through her individual meetings with the postulants to keep her appointment with Ram: she shouldn't have. Though Sister was here at Ram's invitation, he was late as usual.

She shivered, tucking in her cardigan-covered arms against Delhi's winter cold and wondered if she was wasting her time. On seeing Ram approach, all frustration vanished. He smiled, and she smiled in return, pride swelling within her. She hugged the boy, really a man now, pinched his cheek. They dispensed with normal greetings, barrelled through small talk.

Before you say anything, Sister said to him, I have something to tell you.

Ram listened.

She said that there was still hope. She had heard the headmaster's version of the story, and convinced him to allow Ram to return to his job as a janitor at St Xavier's School. What had happened, regardless of the culprit, had been smoothed over, she told him. They knew he was not involved.

Ram smiled. Thanked her, patted her knee. But I've already found a better opportunity, he said. At a call centre in Gurgaon.

Sister was mildly surprised. His English was only so-so. It was only then she noticed his elevated style, his new look. He went on to describe living with a co-worker in a nice apartment, the surprisingly good pay, the 'high life' he now led.

Not sure what to say, she defaulted to half-hearted warnings against vice and its dangers. He accepted the admonitions patiently.

It dawned on her. There was something more beyond the outward. An air of contentedness. You've found someone, she said. A young woman. I can see it.

He smiled, looked as if he'd say something, then kept it in.

I only want the best for you, Ram. You can tell me all. No judgement here.

I know. They watched a gardener toiling at a flowerbed. I know, he repeated.

Ram finally broke the ensuing silence, telling her why he asked her here. It is not so unrelated to St Xavier's, he said. I wanted to tell you myself. I want you to know you can trust me now. Really. He looked far off at a pair of tombs amid a hovering cloud of mist.

She touched his arm and urged him on in his telling.

He said he reported for work one afternoon about a month ago, about two months into his new job as janitor. It was difficult for Ram because he was just barely older then some of the boys at the school, and they were from some of Delhi's most privileged families. They treated him like scum.

On the day in question, he was in the rear part of the school with Mr Bannerjee, the prematurely grey-headed custodian, who was explaining how to reset the electrical system in the event of a surge. They heard worried shouting come from a recessed corner at the back of the school grounds, not far from the circuit-breaker box. Mr Bannerjee and Ram ran towards the commotion and found an underclassman on the ground, apparently unconscious amid a group of five upperclassmen.

It was apparent there was a ringleader, Krishan. He told a stupid story, 'utmost nonsense', Ram said. The boy on the ground, called Kapoor, had tripped and fallen, Krishan said, and the group was there to help him. Mr Bannerjee approached Kapoor and realized he was bleeding from the head. In a rage, Mr Bannerjee said he would report them all to the headmaster. Krishan turned dark. He threatened Mr Bannerjee and Ram with all manner of problems if they reported what they saw, and explained how his father, a government minister, would see they lost their jobs, and find the police at their backs. He reached into his wallet and gave them each 1,000 rupees before telling them to leave. Ram watched all this unfold in shock, and followed Mr Bannerjee's lead.

At the moment, I took the money, because that's what Bannerjee did, Ram said. If I'd told the truth, Krishan would terrorize me. Bannerjee might turn on me. I know how these things work, how those of us at the bottom are blamed for the sins of those at the top.

So you quit.

I did.

Sister sat with this for a time. Have you heard what happened? To the Kapoor boy?

Ram shook his head.

A week ago, the poor child died. A cracked skull. He was pushed from the second floor while at school. Mr Bannerjee was arrested on an anonymous tip. Beaten by police and ultimately released, but he lost his job. Twenty years service, wiped out.

Ram skipped a breath. That's – terrible. He turned inwards. What was I supposed to do, Sister? What was I supposed to do? he asked again.

Sister shrugged. Make another way, she said.

Ram left soon after, clearly rattled by the news. Sister waved farewell as he disappeared into the mist, burdened by what he had just learned. After he was far off, she chided herself for once again forgetting to ask his phone number, and the far more significant omission, telling him she loved him and was proud of him. It was already too late to follow.

*

Already too late.

Sister feels foolish wandering the streets with a small suitcase bumping against her leg with every other step. She glances over her shoulder periodically, scans her surroundings. To you and me, this is a curiosity: no fellow nun accompanies her.

She reads the business card in her hand and asks yet another person to direct her to Shah Jee & Sons Antiques and Metal Recycling. The man, a tailor, sits on the ground cross-legged before a sewing machine. He points down the lane.

You promise you know? You're the fifth person I've asked. My ankle can't handle more misdirection.

Most assuredly, he says. Go until you arrive at the tea shop. Just two stalls down and you will find it.

She gives a grateful tight-lipped nod and pushes on.

Weariness tugs at her limbs. Sleep eluded her last night. Sister Neepa made a fuss when Shanti didn't eat after returning home from the crematorium. Sister forgot to run the nebulizer to treat little Bhimrao and his asthma. When trying to play music for the children, she could summon nothing. They all sat in the piano room as she stared at the keys and sheet music, her mind bouncing between pain and sadness: caught in that crematorium, under the Kashmere Gate flyover, her childhood home, a recital hall, the imagined Vatican office that was the source of her other letter.

When she finally did play, no joy ensued. She needed a new song, but improvization was not her gift. The 88 keys before her and their infinite potential combinations were overwhelming.

She rose this morning as she always did, mass and breakfast and newspaper and coffee and small tasks in the office, but it wasn't long before she stole away, packed her case, wrote a brief note, and slipped out the front gate after despatching the watchman on an invented errand.

She looks up. A sign above the shop proves the tailor was right:

SHAH JEE & SONS ANTIQUES AND METAL RECYCLING
Where Metal Antiques are Recycled

An eyebrow does Sister raise.

She sets down her case and leans against a Mercedes of recent provenance parked obnoxiously in the middle of the lane. She has a small hanky tucked away to dab just below the edge of the sari across her forehead. Collected again, she takes up the case and steps into the shop.

It is dingy. A bulky electronic scale rests on the floor. Incense burns. A radio in the corner belts out Quranic suras. There, amid the clutter of dust-covered, lustreless pitchers and pots and bells is an old, bearded man wearing a skullcap and kaftan, happily asleep.

Are you Shah Jee or one of the sons? Sister blurts.

He starts in his chair, though not at all perturbed. Madam! He smiles as he stands. Madam! I am Shah Jee himself!

He looks her up and down: Head covered? *Yes.* Muslim? He notes the small crucifix pinned near her shoulder. *No.*

Buying or selling? he asks, still smiling.

Neither.

His visage clouds, but only for a moment. No matter, no matter! Guests are most welcome, especially one of distinguished age matching – or slightly younger than – my own. He passes her his chair and she obliges.

Out of nowhere he claps. Of course! Your sari! Your affect! You are one of Teresa's?

She gives a curt nod.

I knew it! I've always appreciated your example. Your care for the poor. We may disagree about Allah, but your devotion, it speaks to me. He says this as he digs in a back room for another chair. Your name, madam?

Shanti. Sister Shanti.

Would you like tea, Sister Shanti? Surely. He pokes his head out into the street and hollers. Two chais! He turns back to her with a pleasant smile, eyes alight, and takes a seat, knitting his fingers in his lap.

Nearly her entire adult life she has been met by one of two reactions: bemused confusion, or excessive praise. This man knows nothing of her, really. In this particular moment that appeals greatly.

Mr Shah Jee, I thank you for your hospitality.

It's nothing. My pleasure. The foundation of my businesses.

Right. A 'subsidiary' reads your card. She produces it, all creased and dirtied. You have other businesses?

I do. Antiques and metals are only one of my trades. Pharmaceutical manufacturing. Software development. You look sceptical, Sister.

Forgive me. Picturing this small shop sandwiched between those ventures…

Achcha, you're correct, of course. The 'Sons' of Shah Jee & Sons share your opinion. They run the show nowadays. I'm in retirement. I am keeping this shop for purely sentimental reasons.

The chai arrives, brought on a tray by a small boy. She takes in his grubby face – his wide eyes, scarring from a cleft palate – but he immediately hides from her gaze. He reminds her of Ram upon their first meeting, timid and afraid. She takes a sip of the tea too soon and scalds her tongue.

I'm boring you, Mr Shah Jee says.

No! Forgive me. My mind travelled for a moment. For purely sentimental reasons. Go on.

This was my first shop. My family left the Punjab during Partition. Came to Delhi with just the clothes on our backs and faith in our hearts.

Not so different from my own story.

Is it now? Well, my father started this shop though I was the one who saw it grow. Too difficult to part with. One can only sit at home for so long unoccupied. All of those crying grandchildren and squabbling daughters-in-law. Better to nap here. Quieter. He smiles.

Are there customers?

Few. But profit isn't everything, is it? A nun would surely agree there!

Sister nods out of politeness.

I love my family. Of course! Though I worry what our wealth is breeding. The opposite of virtues.

Vices, Sister Shanti says.

Exactly. Ah! But look what I've fallen into. What do you Catholics call it? Confession?

She nods.

So…now that I've told you my story, and since you're not buying or selling, may I ask what brings you here?

Sister sips again from her glass despite its undiminished temperature. I wonder if you knew a young man. He mattered very much…to me. Ram, Ram Kumar. He is…no more.

Mr Shah Jee shifts in his chair. Ram? I…know him. Knew him, I suppose. A good boy. Tricky, but a good young man.

The conversation lapses. The droning of the Koran fills the open air. Mr Shah Jee's mobile rings, mercifully, and he pulls out an expensive-looking brick of a thing. Not now, he says, brusquely. A visitor. He hangs up, gulps his tea. What happened?

Sister's eyes glisten. Someone threw him onto the railway tracks two nights ago. He was crushed.

Mr Shah Jee is horrified.

First, I wish to know why this happened, Sister Shanti says. Second, I intend to see whoever did it held responsible.

I am…most appreciating this news, Sister. Mr Shah Jee leans in. But I am lost. How…did you…come to be here?

Sister puckers her lips. I went to his cremation. The two items they were able to turn over to me were a crinkled ticket with the name of a girl – Mr Shah Jee looks at the name on the proffered paper and shrugs – and the business card of this establishment.

A mystery, Mr Shah Jee says. Ram was a simple delivery boy. I hired him on a day I was in the shop. Another had just absconded with the goods and I was most vexed. And then he came around. Ram. Looking for work. In my anger, I was going to tell him to bugger off, but his eyes held something.

An intensity.

Yes! An intensity. I knew he was a serious one. That he would do what he said he would do. I liked him right away. Trusted him. It was back in…I don't know…March? February? I didn't see him much since I'm not here so often. But he did well. On time, responsible. Though he quit, abruptly. Strange. I've not seen him in, what, three months? Maybe four?

I hadn't heard from him in a long time, Sister Shanti says. The better part of a year. When I last saw him, he told me he was well, that he had regular job…

It was so.

With a technology firm. BPO.

Ah *ha*. Most strange, Sister. Trying to impress you, I suppose.

I was, she continues. He looked well. Past boyhood, a step into manhood. Understand, there were so many moments in his growing up where I feared for him.

Mr Shah Jee sits, unsure what to say.

Did you have any information about his whereabouts? Sister finally asks. Where he lived, I mean. If my search comes to nothing, I'd like to at least find the girl he was involved with, in case she doesn't know what's become of him.

Specifically, no. Mr Shah Jee strokes his beard, closes his eyes, lost in some deep concentration. But my driver! He picked him up once or twice! Call him, I will! He can take you there, you can ask around. If he was still living at the same place, maybe you're in luck.

A bright smile comes to Sister's face, before she dims it. She finishes the tea as Mr Shah Jee commences an animated conversation in Punjabi over the phone. She steps into the street, and looks at the shop. She can picture Ram rummaging through this old metal, coming and going, finding dignity in his work. Still, she wonders why he felt the need to lie about what he was doing, to be someone he was not.

A tear threatening to drop pulls back. She blinks it away, notices they have had a visitor all along: the tea boy, lingering just out of their view. The pair stare at each other for a moment before Sister's face softens.

Hello, she says, in Hindustani.

The child wishes to speak, but holds his tongue.

The chaiwallah steps into the street and shouts for the boy. The child looks into her perplexed eyes with fear on his face. He rushes back up the tea shop's steps and the chaiwallah gives him a slap. He scowls at Sister Shanti, and she scowls in return. As he goes back to his perch over the street, Sister wonders at what has just transpired.

VIII

In 1995, in her 56th year, Sister had something to say.

Looking back, the years with the MC felt both an eternity and an instant. Shanti changed along with new India. Communist rebellion. Wars with Pakistan and China. Religious riots. A State of Emergency. Political assassinations. Open markets. What would come next?

Sister Shanti, one of the MC's earliest Sisters, had aged as the community flourished. She had been away from home since the beginning, served as mistress for postulants, led catechismal classes in Italy, learned nursing skills, taught street children, even spent a few years in Nepal, and now worked in a home for the dying in Mumbai. If this sounds like part of a recruitment brochure, it's not. There was discipline to mete out. Serious infighting among overburdened Sisters to moderate. Searching for the rare runaway postulant. Even occasional physical abuse masked as penance by over-harsh superiors. The truth of any institution is different from its public face; it is the same with individuals, so why should the MCs, comprised of people, be any different?

The weight of this began to accrue. During the wide open hours of prayer and sleepless nights, she pondered over it. Long periods of disengagement came. Ever on the cusp of more senior leadership, internal and external doubts abounded, and her superiors took note. She had grown tired of the plainest interpretations of the starkest commandments. Felt suffocated by the structures that governed her life. Confused by many of the forms the MC's theology of sacrifice could take. To feel a spark flash inside her soul was a wonder, and she feared the fire was truly dead. But hope that things might change and fear of the Great Unknown kept her in her place.

Of course, she had told no one of these struggles, and yet, everyone knew. Her single sigh could reveal decades worth of discontent.

This day was a special opportunity, for Mother Teresa was visiting Mumbai (called Bombay in those days). Mother's presence was not uncommon. She lived in Kolkata (called Calcutta in those days) and travelled often to the other MC homes in India and around the world. The stamina she demonstrated at 85 years of age was remarkable and Mother was venerated even then, not officially, of course. The mystique of a living saint surrounded her, especially among the members of the MC community she birthed.

Private audiences with Mother were also not uncommon and Sister had been worrying over what she would say for weeks. When it was her turn, she entered the small room darkening in the late afternoon and sat across from Mother on a small stool.

Mother was hunched and looking her age. Sister tried to smile and joke a bit with the playful Mother; they were old friends, and she was still unsure if she could unload her burdens in this meeting.

Something is the matter, Mother finally said, definitively. She saw right through Sister's veneer.

Sister took a whole minute to speak. I…am not who I want to be, she said.

Speak louder, Sister.

I have regrets.

Mother changed in an instant. You are who God wants you to be. That is more important.

Sister wondered if the conversation was over before it started. She tried again, terrified at what her words might bring. I love to love, Sister offered. I feel like myself when serving. But I struggle, Mother, I struggle terribly. I wonder what it means for me, if I might—

You are here, you have taken vows. There can be no question you are meant to be here.

Mother sighed.

You've known this since your aspirancy, Sister. Obedience is simple. Keep the Rule, the Rule will keep you. Obey the bell. Confess. Pray the rosary. Return to the basics and quiet your troubled mind. God will show you. Mother sat up straight. It's not so complicated.

Sister retreated into herself as more admonitions were supplied. They passed the remaining time in conversation but Mother was tired and retreated into a mode that left her relying on practiced phrases Sister had heard, had repeated herself, over the years.

Mother suddenly sat upright and looked deep into Sister's eyes, took her wrist. You are a beautiful creation, Sister. I am giving saints to Mother Church, and you are one of them. Don't forget that. You may feel you are so far away from him now, but you are closer to holiness than you know. Don't be deceived.

Sister Shanti nodded slowly, her eyes drawn to her toes.

Please send in Sister Naomi now, Mother asked.

She rose to follow Mother's instruction.

Oh! Mother exclaimed. I nearly forgot. You're going to Delhi, Mother said. Sister Bernice is ill. You will head the apostolate for street children.

Sister was stunned. I will be a superior? Until Sister Bernice is better?

Mother darkened. Barring a miracle – which we will pray for – she is not expected to become better.

Sister stepped into the hall and signalled to the waiting Sister Naomi. As she descended the stairs she braced herself against a wall, unsure of her feelings. On one hand, Mother had not supplied a word that spoke to her confusion and doubts. On the other, she wondered if a return to Delhi might restore to her something she had been missing a great many years.

The driver presses play on his CD player, adjusts his hanging *hamsa* charm. Sitar flourishes sweep through our auto. Not a problem. We can speak more freely, Francis. You never know when these drivers, quick to feign disinterest, gobble up their passengers' every word in search of exploitable opportunity.

Indeed, what I am about to say may strike a scandalous note.

Mother Teresa was no Saint.

Before you gnash your teeth and throw yourself out of a moving vehicle: hear me out. What seems a slight is actually a compliment.

Yes, I know what canonization requires. A person living a heroic and virtuous life of faith. Posthumous miracles, usually inexplicable healings through the intercession of the holy person. Note my capitalization of the word. I'm not so interested in 'Saints' as I am in 'saints'.

A Saint is impenetrable, uncomplicated, singular.

A saint embraces weakness and transparency.

A Saint is rarified, distant, unattainable.

A saint is of the same flesh and blood as you and I.

I have no interest in Saints. Their narratives are too often exaggerated myth, as boring and mystifying to me as Western superheroes. I want my saints to be lesser creatures. In a word, human beings.

I believe Mother was that kind of saint.

We all know Mother has her detractors; we MCs have prayed for them. We are not unassailable, nor was Mother. (Don't tell my superiors I'm saying this, but that's precisely where my affection for the woman has grown.)

Think of this. For decades, Mother was a rather obscure nun with the Sisters of Loreto in India. She taught in a convent school, and heeded a call within the call to love God as deeply as her frailties would allow and pursue a vision to love the least of these. At the age of 46, after 10 years of prayer and rejection of the idea by her spiritual leaders, she was able to build this new religious community and change the world.

Now, there is much that can be made of her spiritual darkness. Sister's letters to spiritual advisers revealed a woman who felt alienated from the love of Jesus for years. A DARK NIGHT OF THE SOUL that stretched to decades. Her antagonists paint her as a thoroughly depressed and disbelieving old woman. Her proponents say her spiritual desolation over these years was a sign of her remarkable faith and perseverance, that she still clung to God even though she felt utterly abandoned.

I cannot know the mind of God, but I live Mother's legacy. I'm of a different generation of MC that knew Mother only after her death. Sister was in fact the first MC that I knew and my real introduction to the faith. You can imagine the laughter when, during aspirancy, I asked who the shrivelled old woman was with her face and statues all over MC homes! I have grown a great affection for Mother since coming to the MCs, because she was frail, and fallible, and chose to love.

Not the kind of saint the world wants, but certainly the kind it *needs*.

I make you nervous, Francis.

How can I tell? I can read you as a book. Your jerking knee, a twitchiness in your otherwise serene self, furtive glancing at the street markets and traffic as night descends and we breathe auto-exhaust and bump-bump-bump along.

What's that? You wonder at our destination? I see. A change of subject. You could ask those two in the rickshaw in front of us.

That's right: we've been following Meeta and Adiba this entire time.

I'll bring you up to speed.

Their ride to Ram's apartment has been quiet, though Adiba's stare is wearing. Finally, she speaks. I did the needful with Singh, Meeta says. Only that.

The rickshaw hits another pothole and bounces. The afternoon's grease-laden pakoras Meeta ate nearly exit her stomach.

She frowns. She did not give Constable Singh anything not given to a hundred other men before. What causes discomfort beyond her current dyspepsia is the vague notion, renewed occasionally, that she gives nothing in the performance of such indecent acts, but that something is taken from her.

Adiba still stares. She massages her stomach, prompting a small burp.

Arrived! barks the rickshaw driver.

She pulls a vinyl curtain aside. Through the light drizzle she sees a decrepit building. Confusion. The trip wasn't nearly as long as she expected. There are no glass shopping malls, no high-rises, nor brightly-lit signs. Only decomposing veggies for sale by a teenage girl, a trio of very bored dogs, and a row of rundown apartment buildings known as chawls.

This is…Gurgaon? She puts the slip of paper Constable Singh had written on before the driver's nose.

Gurgaon? What are you talking about? This is Sunrise Estates, Jahangirpuri. Just like the paper says.

She looks at it again but the words still fail to make sense. But we need *Gurgaon*, she says. There must be another Sunrise Estates. But in Gurgaon. Take us there.

The driver takes a long, final puff on his bidi before casting the butt into the street. *Gurgaon, Gurgaon, Gurgaon.* Are you stupid, *naah*? Just get out and pay me.

I pay nothing if you—

Adiba pushes her out. She reaches into her purse and hands over the agreed upon price. *Sisterfucker!*

Ah, her usual eloquence on display as their transport putters off. Alight, Francis. Pay our own driver, will you? I haven't a rupee to my name.

Meeta lifts a scarf to shield her hair from the damp, and she runs for shelter under the covered walkway. This is surely a mistake, she thinks. Was Constable Singh wrong? Did he make something up? Maybe a different Ram lived here?

She sighs. Her regretful afternoon meal and paying for the ride had used half of the rupees Ginna advanced her; the return trip would eat up most of the rest.

Adiba looks at her with expectation. She squints at the mostly nonsensical writing on the paper, spins it around. 4-B, it reads. Numbers and letters she knows at least.

Let's climb, she says to Adiba.

Let's climb, I say to you.

The tenants in the building's darkened hallways track the pair as they stumble around. Meeta summons salutations but is unable to meet their hounding eyes. Sounds blare from behind poorly-hung doors: a sizzling stove; a baby crying; a man singing; TV jingles. She rounds a corner and all but slips in a standing puddle. A pair of men loiter in the stairwell, chewing paan and expectorating red goop on the floor. They see her and catcall, but lay off when Adiba appears. For once, she is grateful for the hovering bloated fellow.

The fourth level, once reached, is unlike the others: quiet, more deserted. Whole apartment units are abandoned, their doors actually missing. The empy rooms tell stories of their former tenants. Adiba waits in the stairwell as Meeta searches for some sign of apartment 'B'. Of the doors that remain, they have pink spray-painted letters. Finding her door, she knocks.

No answer.

Shouting breaks out downstairs, a man and a woman caught up in a terrible row. Her skin prickles. She swallows; her throat is a furnace.

Anyone there?

With no response, she tries the door handle. Surprisingly, it is open.

An odour assails her; something rots. There is no window, only a small vent, and no visible light switch. Adiba's lifted mobile casts a blue glow sufficient to make out the shape of the two-room apartment and a wall-mounted fluorescent bulb. She tugs its hanging chain and gasps.

Utter disarray. She steps in further. This is no mere bachelor's untidiness, though there are signs of that – insect carcasses galore, a grimy film on the walls, dust in layered strata. Movie posters – *Sholay* and *Lagaan* – moulder in the damp. Phone chargers left plugged into the sole wall outlet. What finally grabs her attention are the drawers and their contents spilled over two sleeping mats. And then: dark marks abound, flecking the cracked concrete floor, shirts, pirated DVDs, everything. On closer inspection: possibly blood.

Adiba sits on a crate, folds his hands in his lap, and falls into a nap.

Meeta rifles through the room's detritus. Fear gives way to disgust. Oil coats everything surrounding an electric hotplate. A pair of dishes appear encrusted with days-old potato curry. She cannot tell which clothes are clean and which are dirty.

She lifts one of the loosely hanging posters. Her hand leaps to her mouth. A hollow, in the wall. Chipped away. But nothing of value is there – just a school child's exercise book rolled, scroll-like.

She opens it. Pen-drawn lines. Someone – Ram? His roommate? – had carefully partitioned the pages into stacks of boxes. Lots of notations, English mostly, with Hindi script popping up here and there in a different-coloured ink. Each box is numbered, in sequence, never rising higher than 31. Tucked into the book's centrefold are additional papers. She opens one note – handwritten, all in a different hand than the writing in the exercise book. Unmistakeable pen-drawn hearts near the signature are the only things that stand out.

Adiba could at least read Hindi, but she hides the book and notes in her bag. She doesn't want to share them, not just yet.

What could have happened here? Could the killer, wounded at the station, have actually rushed here afterwards in search of something? It would explain the blood. Also the disarray.

Possible – probable – *likely*.

She continues turning over the rest of the apartment. There won't be a chance to return. She rifles through a cardboard box. Mostly clothes, but at the bottom are five pairs of golden earrings. They look familiar; in fact she wears a similar set right now.

Ram gave them to her the third time he had visited her, and the first he arranged to pass the night with her in the outside world under Adiba's supervision. He didn't tell Meeta the price, but she knew it was steep. The gesture made her proud. She thought they would go somewhere conspicuous where he could show her off, and she was right. They went to Connaught Place, Delhi's estimable shopping district comprised of gleaming whitewashed lines of stores with enough columns to connote stability and high class even though it was overrun with touts selling carved knickknacks and Indian kitsch.

They ate at Nando's Chicken and had a feast suitable for a raja. They shared an ice cream cone. He bought her one of those mass-produced stuffed animals, a white bear with an embroidered red heart.

They sat for a time on a bench purpose-built for young couples to *Ohh!* and *Ahh!* Told her all about life working in the call centre, about employee trysts, Americans and their dumb questions, nights out drinking with friends, and how she was prettier than all their girlfriends.

It was at that moment as Ram nattered away that a change occurred.

Though she lacked language to describe what Ram offered her, it was a taste of respectability. No one knew her here. No pimps joked at her expense, nor did shop owners act as if she did not exist. It was intoxicating.

New hope sprang out of her like lines of rope and began to tie her to this image of Ram. Understand, other such dates with customers were purely opportunistic. A bit of show, a good meal, leading a man on to extract a few more rupees to buy some sweets or make-up down the road. Part of the job was all Ram had been until now. But as they strolled under those lights, breathing in Delhi's heavy air, she felt new freedom. She looked at Ram's eyes as often as she could. They were filled with immense pride.

She wondered if her heart was turning towards Ram.

Sex came later that night – but she knew it wasn't of primary importance to Ram. He wanted something deeper. He wanted love. He told her as much. She received professions of love all the time, literally, and brushed them off until customers became so annoying she had to have Adiba scare them off. When Ram told her he was 'in love most certain', she accepted the words as she always did. But he passed her a gift, left behind by his departed mother, he'd told her: golden earrings.

Meeta accepted them. 'Love most certain', indeed.

And so you see the difficulty of what lies at the bottom of that cardboard box in a dirty chawl in a slummy corner of Delhi. Just two days after his death, the gleaming image of wealth and prosperity Ram put across has lost its lustre.

She covers up the earrings, tells herself to forget she even found them. She forces her eyes closed, breathes deeply.

He is dead. That is what matters.

He loved her. That is what matters.

They were on the cusp of new lives. That is what *matters*.

She stuffs the doubt and mistrust away as best she can. All of this is explainable and she will find those explanations.

Foolish, *foolish* girl.

What could not be so easily tucked away in an unseen corner of herself were new fears, what Latika and Ginna and Pinku and Constable Singh and everyone else in her small world believe: that Meeta is a fool. She interrogates her hope:

You're going to find his killer? *I'll do all I can.*
What then? *Contact the authorities.*
What then? *They will arrest him.*
What th—

73

The sound of three slow knocks on the door makes her heart leap. Adiba and Meeta look at each other in horror. He springs from his crate with previously unseen dexterity, killing the light. The door opens, and Adiba grabs the closest blunt object, an unwashed pan full of congealed grease. He lifts it, ready to strike whoever enters.

The visitor, of course, is Sister Shanti.

IX

Will you hear my confession, Francis?

I am not supposed to be writing this.

The religious life doesn't lend itself to the drafting of long missives. You would not believe the relish some of my Sisters have in turning me in to the Mother Superior! I've had to hide the pages of the manuscript in dusty financial reports and train myself to wake up at midnight and sneak away to a gardener's shed on our grounds, pass my pages surreptitiously to a boy who works at the Net café down the street to retype. I trust grace will extend during these lapses of obedience. The good news is I'm fully covenanted now and made my final profession not a month ago. It's settled: God wants me in, and I want to be in, so I'm in.

Still, this writing is taking a toll beyond the corporal penance assigned whenever I'm found out. Dwelling on this story is not an easy thing, for I know the pain it will bring all involved. It's contemplation of suffering, much like looking at Christ on the cross. But I know the suffering is not the end-purpose: Love made the cross a salvation. Not the torture. Not the pain.

I struggle through the day after a night of writing. The lack of sleep is one reason, but I find myself living the scenes I conjure here. Walking around Delhi I feel like I see Sister walking past. I hear Ginna in the voice of my Superior. I look in the mirror and see a glimpse of Meeta. All impossible! Tricks of the mind or religious revelation, I know not.

I've tried to explain to my confessor, but writing this is proving a form of prayer. This is important because I struggle in prayer.

The spoken kind, I mean. I rattle them off. Of course. That's how we show off our nun-ness to the world! For those who grew up in the Church this is as second nature, but for me, it's all too conscious. For me, prayer is not so much the speaking. It's more like waiting. Opening myself, is it? A small hole in my mind where images just plop down when the forced riling of words isn't enough. You have no idea how, when I am struggling with some task, some disturbing call that's been placed on me, if I open up like this I can feel the Spirit wash over me, allowing me to love as I could not on my own. Now, as this pain and heartache resurfaces, as I stir these people up from the emptiness of the blank page, I put them all before God again and remember: Love makes the story the salvation that it is. Not the torture. Not the pain.

Oh dear.

If you'll excuse me for a moment, this is proving too much. I must pause. And I must pray.

*

I'm back.

Sister Shanti has just entered Ram's chawl. She glares at Meeta, and Meeta glowers back.

What are you doing here? Sister Shanti finally asks in Hindi.

Who are you? Meeta spits back. The landlord?

Sister Shanti chortles. That's what I look like?

Meeta looks to Adiba. He has lowered the pan, and his face settles into its comfortable, dispassionate state. He sniffs twice, shrugs.

Get *out*, Sister says. I'm sure you looters have been waiting for your chance to swoop in and take what you can.

Meeta does not appreciate this. You accuse me? I have every right! We-were-engaged-you-stupid-old-woman-and-if-you-think——

Sister slips her hand up to Meeta's mouth to quiet her. Engaged? She exhales the word.

Meeta is disarmed.

75

Were you with him? The night he…expired?

Meeta struggles to nod.

Then you're Meeta?

Another nod.

Where is the light? Sister asks, running an urgent hand over the nearest wall. It's Adiba who pulls the cord.

Sister slides her glasses down her nose and squints, taking in this girl in the new light. Her bony fingers delicately touch around Meeta's bruised eye; Sister's habit for seeking out injury. Only then does she take in the pleasant symmetry and proportion of Meeta's face. Unexpectedly, the old nun smiles, her crow's feet catching small tears.

Are you alright? That injury…

An accident. Meeta can't help but glance at Adiba. A fall, she says. How is it you know my name?

A ticket. A railway ticket. I am called Sister Shanti.

Shanti. Meeta feels tenderness towards this odd, old woman well up. She shifts the milk crate from near Adiba to Sister's feet. You may sit.

Sister does, setting her suitcase down. Thank you, Sister says.

The two pause, taking stock of the situation, its improbability and consolation. Each feels their own measure of suspicion, though. Adiba is − not surprisingly − consumed scratching a mosquito bite.

How did you find the ticket? Can I − have it?

Sister nods, unlatches her case, produces it.

Meeta looks the rectangle over in her hands. Its written contents are inscrutable but magical all the same. We were leaving, she says. That very night. Running away…

From what?

Meeta is still enraptured by the creased paper in her hands. We were going to marry.

Eloping?

Meeta doesn't know the word. She whispers yes anyway.

What was the problem?

What it always is, Meeta says, eyes snapping to Sister's. Caste, religion, money – a dismissive wave casts these social determinants away.

Your parents didn't approve?

Meeta snickers. Our parents didn't approve.

Our? But Ram had none.

Meeta gulps – besides the mention of Ram's dead mother, the subject had never arisen. Sister stiffens. Meeta sidesteps the question. What was your relationship – to him?

I met him on the street. In my duties as a Sister. I've known him since he was a child.

His sister?

Shanti cocks her head, confused. A Catholic Sister, she says, signalling to her dress. From Mother Teresa's society. The Missionaries of Charity.

Meeta looks to Adiba for help. These names are a meaningless litany.

I'm a Christian, Sister says, and Meeta finally understands, at least in part. This woman is some strange, shrivelled religious creature, like the crones who live near temples or widows who beg at mosques. Meeta frowns. The only Christians she knows are Ginna and Adiba, and the only thing she knows for sure about the faith is that its followers eat pork *and* beef. Extrapolating from these Christians, she holds the entire lot in low estimation.

Christian. Yes, she says.

Sister Shanti rubs her temples and withdraws her rosary. Meeta thinks they are Muslim prayer beads, only confusing things further. Please, forgive me, Sister says. It's been a long day. I'm sure you're as…saddened…as I am by Ram's departure.

Oh, much *more* sad, Meeta says, and watches Sister's eyes flash. A realization dawns on Meeta. Before her sits a woman who:

knew Ram for so long;
could unlock his life unlike anyone else;
would commiserate like no other;
would *want* Meeta to succeed in her mission.

Tell me about yourself, Sister says, again a bit teary-eyed. Ram and I last spoke a few months ago. He didn't mention you. He also said he lived and worked in Gurgaon.

He told me the same, Meeta replies. We only knew each other for a few months.

Sister expressed no disapproval. Where do you live?

The Old City.

Are you from Delhi?

No.

Are you a student?

No.

Where do you come from?

Meeta appears at a loss. I'm from a village in U.P.

Uttar Pradesh. Hmm. Sister reflects. *Feudal place. Likely worked in fields. Low-caste, surely.* And you came to Delhi for…

Work.

What type?

Meeta swallows, struggling for an answer. Dance. I'm a dancer.

Adiba, who had all but disappeared, snickers. Meeta wonders how best to kill him.

Sister demonstrates a new iciness. She clears her throat. I'm rather adept at detecting when someone is lying to me. It comes from years of experience with young Sisters who try to hide their mistakes.

I *do* dance.

What style? Where do you perform?

Words escape Meeta.

And this lout? Who is he? A brother? A 'cousin brother'?

He's…he's…

You stay near here?

Meeta is panicking. Not so far. Over near Connaught Place.

Oh Lord.

Silence.

Where? Sister asks. Don't tell me it's G.B.

Meeta looks down: her anger and shame are in stiff competition to express themselves.

I know your type, Sister says darkly. You're a bowl of honey.

You had Ram's whole mind and body tied up in knots. I've seen it before!

Meeta speaks very quietly. You don't know a thing. *He* came to me.

And *you* invited him in. *You* spread your legs. Making him waste his money. *Dance. Mujra*, I'm guessing? Ha!

You're terrible.

You should speak.

Sister's whole person shrinks, as if the flame animating her has just been snuffed out. A moment. A new grimace. And she's back.

What are you doing here, Meeta? Go to the homes of all your boyfriends? Eh?

She looks hurt. I'm trying to find the *truth*. I'm trying to find who *killed* him. To take *revenge*.

You sound like an actress delivering lines.

Meeta first takes this as a compliment. Once the insult dawns: What about you? Why do you have the right to be here?

I suppose – Sister sighs – like you, I'm looking for some… explanation. I…keep thinking about what I might have done. To prevent it.

Emotion finally cracks through Sister's exterior. Her shed tears seem a surprise to both of them.

Meeta lifts a mildly-soiled shirt from the floor for Sister to wipe her eyes. They look at each other, wondering what comes next. Adiba belches.

You're doing the right thing, Sister says, softening. The right thing, she repeats. She surveys the room, taking it in. I suppose you didn't up-end all this.

Meeta shakes her head. There's not much here.

I see two mats, Sister says. Who lived with him?

Meeta shrugs. He never said.

Sister's eyebrow peaks. Do you think his killer rooted through all this?

Who else?

The roommate, perhaps? Maybe he stole everything of value and got out when Ram didn't come home. Sister begins to poke about the room. Blood, Sister says definitively. Spread all over the floor. She kicks a propane tank. Flips over some clothing. Frowns at Adiba as his eyes follow her. Her fingers run over the rosary beads and her lips form words under her breath. She looks so very frail to Meeta.

You say you found nothing?

Meeta hesitates, then proffers the notebook. There was this. Sister takes it and flips through the pages. A calendar, she says. With many meetings scheduled. One even – she looks up in the air, counting days – for tomorrow afternoon, by the look of things. 'Tourist Hotel'. What a stupid name, she remarks. In the Tibetan Colony, 3 p.m. 'The Bogan', it says beneath.

Really?

Sister highlights the entry. Where was this found?

Hidden. Meeta lifts the poster.

Achcha. What a thing. And these folded notes?

I...can't read.

Of course you can't. Sister begins scanning them, three in total. Meeta waits expectantly. Could these be for Ram?

Or his roommate.

They're love notes, Sister says. Florid things. And a bit dirty.

His roommate's, then, Meeta says grimly.

Sister explores the room again and a glint catches her eye. It is a tea biscuit tin that looks utterly familiar. *Could it be?*

She walks towards its place on the shelf and looks inside, turns it over. A collection of trinkets falls into her hand. A plastic figurine of Rama; a polished stone; a chain of paperclips; a toy car. A number of other valueless, invaluable knick-knacks.

What are those?

Small gifts, she says, her voice shallow. Each given to Ram, when he was little.

By whom?

Me.

Sister holds up the can to peer inside. There's a...photograph. Meeta approaches to see.

It has Ram, and someone else, another young man. Their smiling faces fill half the frame, each one's arms around the other's shoulders. Meeta looks closely and gasps.

What – what do you see?

He has a scar, down his cheek. Part of his ear is missing too.

So?

Pinku – this young thug I talked to – he saw who was chasing Ram and me that night. Who must have killed him. He described his scarring *just* so…

Sister grimaces. The papers had none of that.

It occurs to Meeta: the man at the station said the killer had been stabbed in the leg. The blood spread all over…it's his. The killer's.

Could it be? This one in the photo, the killer, could be his friend? Even his *roommate*?

The composition book…

The roommate's!

He came straight here from the railway station, looking for something, turning the room over.

Ram was nervous when he arrived in my room that night, Meeta tells Sister. Skittish. Normally nothing would surprise him. I thought it was just nerves. He must have known he was being pursued. But why?

It's as if Sister has just recalled Meeta's role in all of this. *The honey bowl.* Her flash of excitement is past, her steeliness returns.

Meeta looks at her feet. I thought no one else in this world wanted to know what happened to Ram. I…also know I cannot do this alone.

Sister still frowns.

But maybe the two of us?

Sister looks to her suitcase as if it contains all her hopes and fears. She sighs. I think we should.

Meeta's heart swells and she tries to contain a smile.

We'll need to talk to the landlord, Sister says.

Yes, the neighbours, too.

And the meeting tomorrow. Maybe our killer will appear if this is his notebook.

Maybe this 'Mr Bogan' can tell us more!

Sister gives an assenting bob. It's already late. After making enquiries we'll part ways. We can meet again in the morning.

Are you travelling? Meeta gestures towards the case.

No.

Where will you stay?

Sister shrugs. Here.

Here?

I was thinking I might. I have no money to waste on accommodation.

But where do you live?

In Delhi. At a home for poor, disabled children. In Shahjahanabad.

That's not far.

Sister considers her answer. While I look…into…what happened to Ram, I'm… staying away from my home.

It is Meeta's turn to cast a suspicious glare. Then, out of nowhere, a plan springs to mind fully formed. Despite Ginna's permission to leave and not work for this entire week, Meeta knows it will be a hollow promise.

So goes Meeta's resulting calculus:

$$Ginna = \text{Christian}$$
$$Sister = \text{Christian}$$
$$Ginna + Sister + kotha = \text{A brothel full of Christians}$$

You can come with us, Meeta declares. Adiba's mother, my employer, is a Christian herself.

Adiba has nearly fallen off his crate.

Sister cocks her head. Considers the offer. I accept, she says. Come. There's much to do.

X

Walk with me down G.B. Road, will you, Pope?

Over the din of honking horns, that truck's exhaust pipe spuming black, the chowk's bright signs, the chaatwallahs advertising paranthas and sabzi wrapped in little newspaper packets, the clinking of utensils and pots drowning out conversation.

I can see you're looking a bit confused. Doubtful.

You ask: *Isn't it unlikely, these two meeting in such a way? Joining causes?*

I answer: *Yes.*

But it happened, just so.

Overcoming astronomical odds and crossing paths are as two wild atoms crashing about, happening to connect and bond – it is what it is. Seemingly impossible until you realize that's all life is. Chance encounters of unlikely attraction that shape everything.

As for the decision to throw in together, let us look at the psychology involved. No, no, I'm no expert in the mind and its ways, but I have reflected long and hard on these events. Anyone can see this begins as a relationship of convenience and mutual purpose. The degree to which it is unlikely they would ever yoke themselves together is diminished by several mundane factors:

They are grieving – the other is consolation.

They are hopeless – the other is a hint of the impossible.

They desire truth – the other travels the same path.

And so you see, this most unlikely pair, is rendered, well, *likely*. A Likely Pair.

Let's continue our stroll down G.B. I can see your eyes travelling over different wares for sale, trying to avoid looking at the women young and old as they watch you, call out to you, from barred windows above. Burlap sacks brim with colour overflowing: brilliant red peppers, blindingly yellow marigolds. The spice shop makes your eyes water, makes a cough climb up your throat. Ah, I see your eye captured by the frozen-fruit vendor's chopped melons. I warn you, your stomach will revolt by morning. Cholera in a cup, they say.

Will some chai do? Let us stop at this dhaba and drink up. I need you alert. Our Likely Pair will arrive shortly. I can tell you what's happened while we sip.

While Adiba couldn't be bothered to leave Ram's apartment, Sister and Meeta canvassed the hallways. They were an odd sight. The neighbours – old aunties, young men from the countryside

– were unsure how to greet them.

Sister did the asking. Age commanded respect.

They were quiet boys, said one neighbour. We never spoke.

Both around the same age, said another. I had difficulty telling them apart.

Been there since the New Year, said a third. That's what I think. But these people, they come and go.

Piss off, said a fourth. Meeta replied with an unkind gesture.

They ultimately found the 'landlord'. She was an older Jain woman – Sister noticed the poster with the sect's 24 ford-makers gracing the wall. She met our pair with immediate suspicion.

Sister explained all. Ram was dead, they were looking for the roommate to see if he could explain more, and, by the looks of things (and of most concern to the landlady), no additional rent would be forthcoming from the young tenants.

The landlady said she didn't know which one was which. Is the dead one with the scar or without?

Without, both Sister and Meeta replied.

Eh, doesn't matter. They paid, but spent most of their time elsewhere. Come and go. Mostly here to change clothes only. Up to something.

They tried to ask her further questions but she demurred, answering with a raised hand. Nothing else am I knowing, no trouble am I wanting. She closed her door.

They reclaimed Adiba and proceeded to G.B., packed tightly into a single autorickshaw. They did not speak for a while.

Your tea is finished, Francis? You may throw the cup on the ground. Worry not, it will be cleared up by a sweepress by morning. There is an order to things, even when it appears there isn't.

What luck! Here is our trio rolling up. Couldn't have timed it better.

Sister Shanti is the first out of the auto and pays the way. Thank you, and God bless you, she says to the driver. As she gets out, Meeta wonders how his wild driving merits such a benediction.

G.B. is alive and doing monstrously well tonight, devouring souls it has lured in and trapping them in its dark belly. Meeta breathes deeply once, standing on the road. Whenever she is

84

away from G.B., there is a keening feeling, as if on unfaithful ground. Here, all is level.

Sister Shanti watches all the activity. The men walking hurriedly, going up, coming down. The touts, the music, the orange lights that bathe it all. On one side of the road is a wall that bounds the railway shunting yard. Cars are parked all along it, and groups of young men congregate in circles under light poles, tittering. There are solitary men, too. Those just off the trains or heading towards the trains, stopping off to try and fill the aggressive emptiness that gnaws them from within. Like eating days-old bread these visits are; utterly unsatisfying, just to fill the space.

Meeta is taken by *how* Sister seems to observe. It is as if she sees past the surface of things. She is distant, and Meeta, tired as she is, is willing to indulge her.

Where do we go? Sister finally says, snapping out of her reverie.

Meeta signals.

Sister collects her case and steps up off the road and onto the raised cement walkway, past a sitting vendor's idols of Lakshmi and Ganesha. Pinku is there with two other young pimps. The bottle of Jalwa Spiced Country Liquor they pass around is down to the dregs.

Found your man yet? he asks, louder than necessary.

Soon, Meeta says. Pinku, meet Sister Shanti.

Ginna's new girl? Hoping to attract different customer demographic, is she?

Unfortunately for you, Sister says, I'm taken.

The three young men's mouths drop before they explode in drunken laughter. Pinku raises his bottle in salute.

God bless you, Sister says, a smile at the corner of her mouth. *Chalo*, Meeta. Let's go up.

Meeta and Adiba take to the stairs slowly, tiredness weighing upon them. The warning 'BEWARE OF PICKPOCKETS AND PIMPS' greets Sister and she sighs. She sets foot to stair, and suddenly the Profound Sadness is there again, rising with her. As foolish as it sounds, what she looked for on the road a moment ago was

Ram. In so many of the young men's faces, in their affects, she saw hints of him. She indulged the strange hope that maybe one of them might actually *be* Ram, walk right up to her with a smile on his face, a treasure in his hand. The Profound Sadness gave way to another: that so many youths were on the cusp of being lost with no one to scoop them up and rescue them. Not enough Sisters to go around. Not enough hope.

She rises, one step. Another. And another. She pauses, needing a rest. She has not eaten a thing since breakfast and is lightheaded. Adiba, already up to the door, comes back to her level. He takes her other hand, helping her. Thank you, she whispers.

Now, at the threshold to No. 201, a thought strikes Sister: she enters hell by climbing rather than descending.

In her many years of witnessing the infernal on the earth, she has not once entered a brothel. Yes, she has consoled a child whose mother was just murdered before her eyes by her drunken father. She has come upon a dead and abused infant on the edge of a dump, found by street children while picking through the garbage. She has been held at bay by police while their colleagues raped a young girl she tried to love, whom she hoped would become an MC herself.

Hell upon *hell* upon *hell*.

There is shouting from within. A woman's voice.

Ginna, Meeta says the name like it's a curse. She eases the door in just as a man throws it open. He is like a beaten dog, longing for a look of kindness but finding none from the three who stand before him. He sidles past.

Ginna transfers the balance of her rant to Meeta:

Coming back *so late*, I *didn't* give you permission to—

And then to Adiba:

I had to kick out *two* perverts—

And then Sister:

Who the hell are *you*?

Sister, of tight lips and lidded eyes, steps in.

My name is Sister Shanti. There's no need to yell.

Ginna is reduced to her girlhood self. Her eyes dart between the three. Rifat and Anu, unoccupied, poke their heads out from down the hall.

A n-nun? Here? Ginna's words leak out of her pursed lips. She signs a cross, a vestigial reflex.

Adiba pushes his way between them all, grunting, and locks the door to his room once inside.

You've brought a nun? Ginna asks.

Meeta nods, failing to suppress her glee.

You are welcome, you are welcome, Ginna says, forcing a smile. She offers her chair to Sister and mutes the radio. In its place they hear a customer making all manner of sounds.

Adiba. A-*diba. Adiba!*

He opens the door. His full belly on display distracts Sister from his frown.

Free up Deepti, *would-you-please-thank-you-very-much*. She is currently, uh, *entertaining*.

Confusion. Adiba makes a throwing motion towards the *kotha* door. Ginna nods enthusiastically, her eyes daggers. And so Adiba trudges down the hall and pulls aside a curtain. He works to eject the man despite his protestations.

Sister's displeasure remains through it all. So you're running this place? she finally says.

Ginna looks down in shame.

You should stop. Sister gestures towards the illustration of Jesus framed on the wall. I see you invite Christ's presence here.

Ginna's eyes are still cast low. They remain so for the duration of the customer's removal. Meeta is near bursting with pleasure.

Can you bring the women out? Sister says. I would like to meet them.

Girls! Ginna calls. Anger is beginning to overtake her surprise.

They come out, Deepti last, and stand beside Ginna, unsure where their eyes should rest.

The hot disapproval she received when Sister learned of her occupation worries Meeta. Her first doubts about bringing the nun here rise.

I am Sister Shanti. She paces in front of the women, like a diminutive colonel inspecting her troops. I shall be staying with you for a brief time. I am grateful to this one – signalling to

Meeta – for inviting me here, and to this one – signalling to Ginna – for giving me the opportunity.

Meeta's mouth drops. These are not the words of an imperious commander. They are punctuated by…*tenderness.*

Sister approaches Rifat first and takes her chubby cheeks in her hands. Rifat is frightened.

You are lovely, Sister says. She brings Rifat's face low and kisses her forehead.

Next is Anu. You are beautiful, Sister says. She accepts Sister's kiss.

She steps up to Deepti, who strains against the touch. Sister forces nothing.

There is no need for shame.

I'm not ashamed, Deepti mutters.

Sister smiles. Of course you aren't. She strokes Deepti's forearm and moves on to Ginna. The old woman looks as if an executioner looms.

You are my sister, you know. Adopted into the same family, we two have been. Sister takes Ginna in her arms, raises her up, kisses her cheeks in turn. The old woman braces against the table to keep herself from collapsing.

I am very happy to meet you all, Sister says. It's rare I'm out these days, and rarely in new places.

The room is silent, pregnant with the ineffable. Meeta, meanwhile, wonders whether Sister has forgotten to come close and kiss her.

A knock at the door just before it swings open: Ramesh, a regular. All eyes shoot to Ginna.

What do you think you're doing, Ramesh? Barging in without any politeness, like some randy street dog? Get out! Out!

Ramesh, dumbfounded, then offended, slams the door, rattling its hinges.

Ginna's phlegm-filled wheezing is the only audible sound. Adiba, Ginna finally says, stand outside the door. Tell other customers we are closing for the night.

Sister's expression is inscrutable.

Are you hungry? Ginna asks Sister quietly. You must be tired.

I am both.

I could make some dal, Rifat volunteers.

Oh, I don't wish to be trouble, Sister says. I saw a somewhat clean-looking restaurant on the way here. Let's have them bring us a meal. And drinks. And desserts! A real feast. I've not had restaurant food in some time.

Ginna's eyes widen as she counts the mounting expenses.

I will pay, I will pay, Sister assures Ginna, wrapping an arm around her shoulders. Turn on the music, Sister says, some good, classical stuff.

Meeta comes close and hisses: *I thought you said you had no money!*

I have funds, Sister says with a grin. They were entrusted to me to spend on others.

Realizing the withheld kiss was not a mistake, that Sister was not some force to be marshalled by Meeta, is unsettling. While the others are finding their defences breached, Meeta's heart hardens towards this strange, otherworldly woman.

XI

In 1959, in her 20th year, Sister Shanti was surprised by joy.

Heera, Shanti's name by birth, if you recall, was in her university years, ticking off assignments given to her by others when the joy arrived most unexpectedly. She lived at home, and was enrolled in Delhi University's law course when not many women were. Her father and mother were both happy. Heera was not.

Still, she remained faithful to her lectures, which were mainly built upon the vagaries of mouldering British jurisprudence. She went to the *mandir* with her parents for hours-long pujas and recited *Om Bhur Bhava Swaha* time and again. She continued playing the piano with the meagre passion she could muster. But change was brewing. Miss Winthrop, an old British marm, Delhi-ite, and church organist, had been Heera's piano teacher all through the girl's childhood. Failing health finally sent the old woman home to Cornwall. A new teacher was necessary, and the search commenced.

All the while, Heera, so given to dutiful obedience and guileless openness, felt she lived a lie. Why, you ask? Hidden in her bag was a rosary she carried everywhere. She had long since begun toying with the Catholic religion, testing it. It was the first real secret she had ever kept from her parents and friends alike, but the secret's life-changing power took her breath away every time she ran her fingers over the beads.

Her parents might have been alright with a stashed rosary, but it was really much more than that. During occasional visits to her alma mater, Heera met Sister Angelique who always greeted her with a smile to dwarf the sun. Their aim: to further discern whether Heera was meant to reject the world and its glittering, false attractions and become a Sister. There were short visits to different religious communities about Delhi. Prayers and Bible study. Heera secretly read the biographies of saints instead of case law. As she was driven around in her Ambassador, she saw the impoverished on Delhi's streets, the waves of migrants arriving from the countryside with nothing, and her heart went out to them. She had given the abounding misery of the world hardly a thought growing up, accepting the order of things. But now, every time she played the piano she put her hands before her and wondered what it would be like to instead see them heal wounds, care for the sick, bind the broken, set the oppressed free. To see things change: for them, and in her. Heera was equal parts terrified and thrilled at the heady prospect of it all.

And all of this spiritual tumult was kept bottled up inside.

Meanwhile, her parents had begun discussing Heera's marriage. Though she had been enamoured with the idea since girlhood, now she only played along. Nuptials would not come for another two years, 'not until the degree is finished', her father said, full stop. Meanwhile, Sister Angelique believed Heera could do well in her own community, The Sisters of Our Lady of Loreto, but she could see in Heera's eyes that the familiar order that had provided Heera her education was not so attractive. There was a recent offshoot she might be interested in, Sister

Angelique told Heera. Started by a charismatic European nun, a former Loreto-ite herself, just a few years before, right here in India. This religious community was dedicated to the service of the poorest of the poor while living outside the cloister and in a poverty that matched those served by its members. Heera began listening for the name of the new community's founder, and heard it echoed all over: Mother Teresa, Mother Teresa, *Mother Teresa*. At Sister Angelique's recommendation, Heera wrote to Mother with a set of interrogatories that would make her law professors proud. The response, received two months later, simply said: 'Come and see'.

Through this period the search for a suitable piano teacher continued without success. Finally, to her parents' satisfaction, an accomplished older professor at Delhi University was prepared to offer private lessons, although, not so satisfactorily, at a significantly higher rate than old Miss Winthrop's. Her parents baulked, but Heera's playing was seen as an investment when searching out a husband. 'Necessary, with her so-so looks', her mother said quietly. 'Not a stunner', her father concurred. And so it was settled. But, just two days before starting lessons, the professor excused himself; too busy, simply too busy, he said.

Heera smiled.

But he could offer a recommendation for another teacher, he said.

Heera frowned.

A visiting American professor was willing to do it, and at a lower rate. And so, on the appointed day, a young American appeared at the door to the family home and Heera's life changed for good.

Walter Simmons was lanky and walked as if on stilts. He wore a well-appointed coat and tie but suffered for it in the heat. He was a Fulbright scholar, from Philadelphia, recently minted with his doctorate in ethnomusicology, and he also taught at the university. Piano was his first instrument, and his most accomplished, and he could play in a variety of styles, though they could stick to classical if that's what Heera wanted, he explained to her wary parents. Heera stole glances as he said this. She was shocked at his youth! Not conventionally handsome, he did have a clean-cut confidence and appeared like a rising US politician seen in grey-inked newsprint photographs. Relatively new to the country, and not particularly bothered with cultural sensitivity despite his academic discipline, Walter shook her hand in greeting. After a brief interview about her musical preferences and aspirations (she couldn't meet his eyes), the lesson commenced.

He put Heera through her paces. 'Good', he said. 'Excellent', he said, offering mild correction here or there. He tutted at the pieces she was so fond of playing, and vowed to bring some new, 'glorious' modern sheet music to the following lesson, 'Some jazz maybe', he said, scratching at his pomaded hair. 'God knows where I'll find it though'.

'I am not so sure I would be able to play that', she said after a pregnant pause. 'I have attempted the rare piece before and found myself ill-suited to its style and manner'. So very anxious, she spoke as formally as she was capable of while her nose was practically wedged between notes on the page.

'Heera', he said her name so forthrightly: 'Anything worth doing is worth failing at. This is my philosophy in all things. We'll give it a try'.

She nodded, hardly believing Walter – her teacher! a young man! a young *foreign* man! – sat so close to her on their shared bench. They reached to turn the page at the same time and their hands touched again; with the touch came the spark of a mutual idea that inexplicably, and immediately, caught flame.

He smiled at her, and she smiled back.

*

Meeta sulks, resting on her haunches, apart from the others, unsure what she'd hoped for as the feast unfolds. It certainly wasn't this.

There is much laughter this evening as they eat Rajasthani food – dal *baati churma*, *pyaaz* kachori, *gatte ki* sabzi – and sip mango lassi before teetering on the edge of diabetic comas with nigh-bottomless balls of gulab jamun for dessert. It took two deliverymen to bring their order, stacked high in six plastic bags stretched to the limit.

Ginna regales them with stories about her childhood in Goa and her stupid husband. Adiba listens to word of his father as he plops more sticky-sweet morsels in his mouth. There were OK times with him early on, she says. They were both from good families, same caste, same faith: their arranged marriage made sense. The ceremony took place, and though they tried to love each other, he began drifting, and began drinking, and began hitting, and soon she was living in a distant land even when sharing the same bed. Adiba's birth helped nothing, she says. She casts her adult son a tender look, though one full of resignation. He remains focused on his dessert.

There were chances along the way, Ginna recounts, for them to reconcile and form their marriage into something new. She hoped the move to Delhi would change things. Then her husband invested in the brothel with some garrulous acquaintances. He had actually managed to keep the true nature of his work secret for years! They had been living in relative comfort and she didn't ask questions, but the ever-widening chasm between them was enough to end the marriage even though there was no formal dissolution. It wasn't till these Delhi years that she finally stopped attending Mass.

What happened to him? Anu asks.

Heart attack, Ginna says. With his beak inside of one of the girls. Can you *believe* it? All manner of debts, and only a brothel's business to pay them. Her eyes are glassy. She opens her mouth but doesn't speak.

You could sell it all, Sister interjects. A clean break from the past is sometimes necessary.

Ginna's mutterings evaporate into the air. All I know is…no one to take care…

Everyone in the room is quiet, contemplating tomorrows unlike today.

What about you, Sister? Rifat asks. Why are you here?

God, I imagine.

Which? Anu asks.

My God. The one I serve. Sister looks slightly troubled by this statement. She decides to change the subject. Meeta has told you about Ram?

We all knew him, Ginna says. Poor Ram. He was here often.

Sister darkens. Yes. Well, I have known him since he was a young boy. I saw him through many difficulties and troubles, and when he was still little I saw a vision – just so – of who he… who he *might* be. She pauses – do her eyes glisten? Have you ever had that experience? Sister asks. A vision of who someone is made to be? She turns to each woman. It's easiest with children. Not a view of what they *will* do in the future. But who they *could* be with all of the hurt and fear stripped away?

They all look mystified; chewed food actually tumbles from Adiba's gaping mouth.

Sister simply smiles, shrugs, saddens.

You are exhausted, Ginna declares. These hours we keep are not yours.

We Sisters don't get so much rest. Even less these days for me. Since Ram, especially. Still, maybe it would be a good idea…

A tear escapes Meeta's eye. It is followed by another, and eyes slowly turn to her. Ginna goes to Meeta, wraps her arms around the girl, and makes her involuntarily tense. I'm sorry for having Adiba…*discipline*…you the other night, she says. It wasn't good of me.

Meeta clenches her jaw, bites her tongue, longs for Ginna to never touch her again.

Sister will have your cot, Meeta. And Adiba will give you his mat.

He moans, shovelling another samosa in his mouth as consolation.

Come with me, Meeta says to Sister, not without tone. She lets her tin plate clatter to the ground.

Sister budges but has trouble standing. Oh, my body.

Meeta extends a hand. Lifts her up. Leads Sister. Flips the switch. Deposits her case.

Sister is assaulted by the room they enter.

The union of smells: sweat *perfume* incense *sex*

The obtrusive sights: *posters* magazines *mirrors* stains

She meets all with a grimace. She inspects the posters more closely.

They're beautiful, Meeta says, indignant.

This…this is not beauty. She moves from one manufactured pose to another, overwhelmed. It's…*glamour*. Only glamour. Beauty is something else. She turns back to Meeta. Something else entirely. This is where you stay? Where everything with Ram…happened?

Meeta sours. That's the cot, she says, gesturing.

Sister nods and sets her creaky body down.

This doesn't do anything for us, Meeta blurts. You being here. Maybe you're here for a night. A week. Maybe a year. This doesn't help us. Rifat, Anu, Deepti, and me.

Sister can only muster confusion.

You're going to leave, Meeta clarifies. That's what we're all thinking. This night is just, just putting off what's to come. But after, it will be even worse. Meeta pauses, clearly reflecting on events earlier than tonight's, perhaps involving Ram. It's better to never know a thing like love, she says. So you don't know what you're missing.

Sister looks at her hands, traces the worn ridges of their surface as she speaks. I'm doing what I can while I can. Small things, with all the love I can muster. This is the only defence Sister can summon.

Meeta doesn't understand, doesn't care to. She slides her nail under loose paint flecks on the wall.

Would you care if I clear that nightstand? Sister asks. And can you find me a candle?

We have light. They aren't load-shedding.

I need to make an altar.

The thought of observing an odd, foreign ritual actually appeals to Meeta. She retrieves a candle from the kitchen space and plucks a match from Rifat's things and the sleeping mat from Adiba's room.

Sister pauses from her unpacking and gives a thankful word, takes the candle, lights it, pours the melted wax on the night stand and sticks the candle into place. She rises from her knees to turn off the light.

Meeta steps back into the hallway and hears Deepti tell a joke, something about a talking penis. Laughter erupts again, and Meeta feels the hatred of this place grip her. She recites a nursery rhyme she learned in her first brothel from one of her mother's cousins and breathes deeply. This keeps her from screaming.

Reclaiming herself, she watches Sister through the cracked door. Sister, softly lit, absent her sari, has donned a clean set of white nightclothes. Meeta almost gasps at the sight of the nun's head. Her hair is cut shorter than she's ever seen a woman wear before. She looks like someone, an adulteress, maybe, who is shorn and trotted out among the village to be shamed.

Sister leans a wooden crucifix that must have come from her case against the wall. Before her is a folded sheet of paper, a letter, and Sister puts it at the feet of the small, carved man suspended on the cross.

And then Sister slumps, on her knees, listing to one side. Then there are small movements; Sister shakes with quiet sobs.

A foreign feeling registers, but Meeta doesn't know a word for it – something floating between compassion and empathy. She is tempted to go in and kneel beside Sister and ask if she needs anything. She ends up leaving her be and retreating into herself, sliding to the floor of the darkened corridor.

The pain of Ram's loss, so gnawing, so acute this morning, is already blunted by the day's discoveries. New tears seem impossible to muster. And yet – there is one!

But Francis, be not mistaken: this teardrop is not an offering for Ram. A momentary urge to be a thousand miles away, anywhere else, takes hold. She breathes deeply, until the invisible hand around her neck loosens.

She looks in on Sister again. The old woman's crying has stopped, but she remains hunched. Possibly asleep where she kneels? Meeta's eye travels to the nightstand again and notices something new laid at the foot of the crucifix.

A key.

A small key.

A small key that undoubtedly fits the small lock on Sister's case.

Meeta pushes in the door with a clearing of her throat and Sister starts. Meeta offers an exaggerated yawn. It's late, Sister. Big day tomorrow, this meeting and all that we have to do in the Tibetan Colony. Rest is needed.

Sister sighs. Yes. I suppose so. She blows out her candle and staggers to Meeta's cot in the dark. She gives a sort of grunt, a wince, whether from pain or the odours or the creak of the cot that reminds what this room is used for, Meeta knows not, and does not ask. She just strips her outer clothes off, unfurls the rolled mat, and lies down, struggling to find a way to repose that doesn't press her bruised, bony edges.

Within a minute Sister is asleep, and, unfortunately for Meeta, snoring. Meeta shifts. Instead of her mind slowing and succumbing to its weariness, it only moves faster, and faster.

That key...that small key...

XII

By revisiting these events, a rather startling thought has come to me, Francis: the brothel and convent aren't so very different.

Confined space. Regular schedules. Lack of sleep. Work with members of the community. Poor pay. Poverty. Non-marriage. Passions. Fear of being trapped for the rest of one's life. Suffocation. Bad food. Discipline, corporal or otherwise, meted out by superiors. Survival through the fostering of a sisterhood. Hope for eventual salvation.

Both are places of worship, though to very different ends.

I can see you're not pleased with my comparison. It has hints of the provocative in it, I'll admit.

Let me say it differently.

Suffering takes place in both, but where it is *directed* makes all the difference.

We the religious stare at Jesus, suspended on that cross for all time in a moment of his greatest pain. Mother, for all her eccentricities, understood that identifying with Christ's sacrifice was a form of love for him. The poor of the earth are being crucified daily, she'd say, and so we work to relieve that suffering. We all know, as we do unto our suffering brother, we do unto Jesus himself. And so we MCs prepare to serve and seek Jesus in all his distressing disguises: impoverished, cast out, miserable, hungry, tired, desperate, exiled, lost, and…trapped.

And so I turn to my final point: we inside the religious community dream of being what we are *not*, namely, saints. The woman trapped inside the brothel lives out of the same place, until she is so pushed into the ground that hope is lost and she cannot imagine being something different than she is. The nun is not worthier than the prostitute. Till the day they die, it is God's grace they both need.

How do I know this? Because, to this day, I know Meeta very well.

I'm sorry if in knowing that Meeta will not die I've robbed my story of some of its dramatic effect. No, I am most sorry to relay that she lives much as she did before, a bit deadened, a bit dense, tending to show up at the most inopportune moments: when a child is inconsolable, a thief has stolen from our house, or a brawl breaks out in the street. It can almost be counted on that she will make herself known. *Such* a needy soul.

I've sat across from Meeta many times, but often for only short visits since, I am sad to say, we make poor company. Though I tolerate her little, I still love her like myself.

How could I not, knowing all she's been through?

Ah, here she is again. She has risen to take in the morning sun, just as we have. I'll tell you more later; it would be impolite to carry on in her somewhat dimwitted presence.

Delhi is brilliant from the rooftop, isn't it, Francis? The blue, smoggy sky. The tickling breeze. It's like the heat and humidity conspire together, saying, Just a few more minutes we will give them before we descend! And then – POW!

Look at how light breathes into the city, and shadows cast over the streets begin to give way. You almost feel alone, except for your poor neighbours poking out of the million *barsati* hovels erected on rooftops all over the city. Look how those below can run about their business with not a thought of who watches from above! Unschooled children at play. The knife sharpener who calls out for customers as he rolls his whetstone. And look at that! Would you believe it? There go our monkey chasers on motorcycle, surely off on an early-morning mission!

Meeta notes none of the world's waking. She stretches out and accepts the sun's caress.

I've always loved how in the groggy first moments of waking, whatever was experienced the night before fades. Like the Lord has reached in and pressed a reset button, granting us some distance from ourselves and what bedevils us. Of course this is fleeting, but those few moments in the in-between are a grace.

Before I became a nun, I can't tell you how they sustained me. Now it is bells ringing and jumping out of bed at four in the morning, superiors bearing down on you if you indulge in the least bit of extra rest. If I am ever Superior – God above, what a thought! – I shall let my Sisters enjoy their waking.

Likewise, let's relish the here and now, this moment of fleeting calm and simple beauty. This day will unfortunately not hold another like it.

Meeta descends. So must we.

Hungry? Some indigestion from last night's feast? I'd say let's check the leftovers below, but the amount of oil and fat and salt and poor refrigeration are not what you need at this moment. You've avoided the dreaded Delhi-belly thus far, and we can't have you bowled over when so many happenings have yet to happen.

Parathas. Let's get some. There's a vendor close by, and his are wickedly good, not like Rifat's leaden pancakes.

Hold the chain while you head down the stairwell; I won't be responsible for the Holy Father taking a tumble! How is Sister this morning, you ask? She's well. But you hear that distant, tubercular cough behind closed doors? Rifat, you remember, is not so well. That's her, nearly expelling a lung.

I'll spare you the scene while we take some nourishment. Sister, back in her sari, glasses in place, crucifix pinned to her chest, is up and tending to Rifat. The others are all trying to sleep a little more.

Ah, if you squint, you can see Sister coming down the stairs with her arm around Rifat. And there's Meeta, tearing down after them – sans make-up! in quite the hurry! – shouting. Don't worry, Pope, you're really not missing much.

Meeta says Rifat starts every morning this way, no big deal.

Sister says Rifat is very sick.

Meeta says that there's no time for taking her to the doctor, investigation needs to continue, it'll take hours, there's no money, etc.

Sister says Meeta is a selfish girl if that's what she thinks, that her friend is suffering, that Sister will pay, let the dead bury the dead, but this one is not yet dead, etc.

Rifat says nothing, just stands there, mouth agape, forgetting to cough as this argument over her takes place.

Ginna is on the street now, too; I see you're not as impressed by this as Meeta, Rifat, and I are. Ginna has not descended to the street in at least three years. She gives her blessing that Rifat be taken and orders Meeta to go along.

The conclusion? You can see for yourself: Sister ushers Rifat into the waiting autorickshaw, and Meeta begrudgingly joins. Off they go, while Ginna waves.

Ah, Ginna. So happy in this moment. Last night felt like years of vileness and kilograms of pain were shed under Sister Shanti's brief care. That Ginna just supported Sister taking Rifat to a clinic shows an untapped seam of compassion was opened. It makes me sad to think how short this interlude will be.

Come, Francis. There are potato parathas to be eaten.

The enlightened thinking of today is that these whores or prostitutes or hookers or tarts or streetwalkers or sluts or comfort girls or girlfriends or tramps or floozies or women of the night or sex workers should not be stigmatized for being in this line of work. That it's a woman's choice, her right, to decide what she does with her body. That this is better than starving. That if she consents, it's fine. Work has dignity, whatever it is, and selling one's body is no different than selling the labour of one's hands. That...

Sorry, I'm holding up the line. Yes, that's the menu. Too many options, I agree. Let me order for you. I think I know just what you'd like. Put the rupees in the man's right hand. That's right, they are a real bargain. Take a seat, I'll bring the chutneys.

Where were we?

Right. I'm past anyone who wants to celebrate and condone this life. We live in a twisted age. Look at these women. No, they are not powerless. Not hopeless, helpless waifs. Some accept their lot and face it bravely. But the human dignity these advocates purport to protect by advocating for the existence of – *this* – G.B. Road – is trampled on no matter what they say. Think of the children who grow up in these environments! They are the broken outcomes bred by such advocacy!

But I'm also past anyone who condemns these women for what they do. I imagine you are too, Francis. I tell you, I've spent time working in these brothels, with these women, men too (who can forget the eunuchs?) and I love them all. If given a chance to make a life elsewhere, a real chance at a livelihood, not a one would remain. We can't abandon them to sloppy compassion. They need love. They deserve it.

And there I've gone ranting again. Impressive, Pope! Are you planning to eat the Styrofoam plate they are served on, also? Another round? Why not! Lalloo! Another one for the Holy Father! Who knows when you'll find another chance to have the choicest aloo paratha on G.B. Road!

Right. Maybe that's a dubious distinction.

Lean in close now. Take in the others here out of the corner of your eye. All men. All customers. Labourers, coolies. Filling their empty stomachs after nights trying to fill their empty souls with drink and sex and false intimacy. I have my ministry to the women of G.B. Road, but who can forget these sad, pathetic, wrongdoing men?

I sometimes stop here and strike up conversations. There is always one who pretends he has stumbled here by accident. 'G.B., you say, is here?' They're standoffish at first when a young religious woman in white dress comes to chat with them in the red light district. Lalloo, the squat cook behind the counter in undershirt and flip-flops, doesn't understand why I keep coming. I shrug. I'm a sucker for what my faith sells.

Oh, Jesus!

Foreign God among gods! On the cross and off, how I love you!

But how do you make any sense in India, Lord? In a land of Hindus, Muslims, Zoroastrians, Jains, Hindus, Sikhs, Buddhists, Muslims, Jews, Marxists, Capitalists, and Hindus, a land already teeming with 36,000,000 gods, why add a dash of the Good Lord and a shake of his followers into the mix?

The answer: Why not?

Because he's an Imperialist Imposition! A Colonial Relic! A Foreign God!

And yet I was found out by Him. Called. Made Whole. Those arguments, while valid, fall apart for me.

A mystery within the mystery.

How I love him, nonetheless. I am even a *missionary*, telling others to love Him too. *What* a thing!

What a *thing*!

And what would Jesus do? we followers ask ourselves.

Visit the prisoner.

Clothe the naked.

Heal the sick.

Unbind the bound.

Converse with the slobby john. (That last one is my own addition.)

And so I return to my earlier point. G.B. is a vicious trap. For *everyone*: buyers, sellers, and the products themselves. I can see the value of the customers: poor, trapped, fools who are ground down by their poverty and empty lives, devoid of hope. Sure, a number test my patience, but you'd be shocked how many, in their tiredness and shame, will open up and share their deepest secrets, sadnesses, fears. It's easy to say you care for the poor prostitutes of G.B., but to care for the little pricks who keep this whole enterprise running? To try to love *them*? That's an uncommon grace, and my stomach to love them, let alone tolerate them, is a credit to Sister's example, and God's movement.

Here's a napkin. You've got some grease on your chin.

Ah, right on schedule. There's our man, Constable Singh, ambling past. We need to see this.

Up he goes, climbing those stairs. You can see he has a certain spring in his step. I'm afraid of the reasons why.

He taps the door to No. 201 with his steel-tipped lathi once, twice.

It is Ginna who hollers an answer. Closed today: *syphilis* outbreak! *Most* unfortunate! Come back *another* time!

Not closed to me, Singh says, bemused. Open up, Ginna, I'm here to see one of your girls.

That's what they all say.

Not all of them are police.

In an instant, the door opens a crack. Ginna's slitted eye is visible. What do you want?

Constable Singh rubs his belly, scratches his balls. He peers above the short woman's head, looking down the hall. He finally meets Ginna's glare with a wide grin.

Meeta in?

No.

That so? He pushes the door in further with his stick.

Ginna huffs. Leave me be. I've already paid this month. Besides, business has been shit. One of my girls is out of commission going on two weeks.

As I said, I'm here for Meeta. He twists one tip of his moustache with his thumb and forefinger. I have some information to share. About her dead man. When does she return?

Later.

Maybe I'll just wait.

Pervert, she says under her breath.

All part – Singh barges in – of an investigation. Ginna topples over.

You can't do this! Ginna hollers. By now Singh sees the rest of the *kotha*'s residents are all hidden behind the door.

You – he points to Anu and orders – get me a chair. Anu obliges while Adiba helps his mother up, refusing to look at Singh.

An hour or so passes and Constable Singh relishes making them squirm like worms pinched under his heel.

There is sound in the hall; they can all hear Meeta's familiar high-pitched nattering as she ascends. Rifat steps in first, followed by Meeta. Meeta freezes on seeing Singh.

Y-you? Meeta raises her hand to her mouth.

Singh nods: a tight smile, a small wave, a clearing of his throat.

What's the hold up? Sister says, pushing in past Meeta. Oh. Who are you? Sister looks around. She doesn't like what she sees. Seems you've put everyone on edge, she says.

Constable Singh, he replies. You are?

An old nun, she says. You are wanting something?

Here on police business. I need to see Meeta. In the back. I have news to share. With her. Singh's lasciviousness practically radiates off him. About Ram, he adds.

Meeta unconsciously steps behind the old nun. Sister Shanti clears her throat. Ah, then tell us all. Air it out. We're all looking into the young man's death. Aren't we?

The rest nod reluctantly.

Constable Singh's eyes narrow. I must insist.

Sister walks up to him. Looks at him. Leans in close. She smiles, nearly face-to-face and looks him in the eye. *I* must insist.

Who are you to talk to an officer of the law like this?

Sister turns, begins pacing. Singh, your name is? I take it you're stationed down here?

Constable Singh folds his arms.

Three yellow stripes on your shoulder, is it? A head constable. That's a very nice rank. A low rank, but at least not the *very* bottom. Climbing your way up the chain. Hoping not to be at G.B. much longer! But then again, this is a very lucrative posting. So *many* illegal activities! Just a bit of selective enforcement here, a little application of justice there, and your admittedly pitiful salary grows by leaps.

Constable Singh forces a smile.

My dear Constable. Your deputy commissioner of police and his lovely little wife and three precious gems of children come once a month to share food and care with the disabled children in my orphan's home. We always have such lovely conversations. The next time I see him, I'd be so pleased to tell him how you selflessly shared your information without a second thought for yourself.

Constable Singh swallows.

I can't imagine how disappointed he'd be to hear the opposite, Sister said.

His colour drains.

How *incredibly* disappointed.

His erection flags.

What information do you have to share with us?

Constable Singh assesses his options and decides to share. I have a name, he says.

A name? Sister suddenly darkens. What value is that to us?

The name of the murderer.

Sister's eyebrow arches. Give it.

He's called Manoj. Manoj Bajpai.

And how did you come by it?

Security cameras. At the railway station. Got a good look at the one who started scuffling with Ram on the platform. Did complex analysis of the footage, cross-referenced in police databases, interviewed bystanders—

Nonsense you're giving me. The deputy commissioner is no fan of lies.

The policeman sighs. The man's identification was left behind in his suit-jacket pocket. It was found at the scene.

A murderer was kind enough to carry a proper ID?

It appears so.

Sister tuts. An amateur. She turns to Meeta. So we have a face, and now a name.

Meeta is still avoiding Singh's predatorial eyes.

That's right, Sister says. So what are you police types doing to catch him? Running all over? Canvassing neighbourhoods, radio bulletins, wanted posters...

It was Singh's turn to snort. None of that! If one low-level criminal wants to kill another—

Watch your mouth! Sister snaps.

How dare you speak ill of the dead! Meeta shouts.

The room falls into complete silence but for Adiba scratching his dandruff-laden head. Even he eventually stops.

Look, I'm assigned to G.B. There's no motivation to seek out this goonda, this thug. The amount of time and energy for a guppy fish like Manoj is beyond the dignity of our inspectors!

What if we do the work? Sister asks. We find him. We trap him. We deliver him. You get to arrest a murderer. Get a commendation from my mouth straight to the deputy commissioner's ear. What then?

Constable Singh lets his smile shine forth again. That would be something else. It would be my duty to assist. I of course have my doubts this one – he points to Meeta – and you –

Sister Shanti of the Missionaries of Charity, Sister butts in.

– will be up to the task. I can't be held responsible if you're injured while attempting police business, you know. Against my highest recommendation, it is.

Thank you for your concern. Pass your number to that one over there. I have no use for those mobile phones. We'll call you if we need to see you again.

I'm happy to be of assistance, Sister Shanti of the Missionaries of Charity. Whatever is needed.

With a turn of her head, she dismisses the policeman.

As soon as Constable Singh is out of earshot, Meeta cannot contain herself. She whoops, lifts and lowers her arm in a phallic sag. The room erupts in laughter.

Rifat clasps her hands together in front of her, genuinely touched by what Sister shared. That's so wonderful that someone as important as the deputy commissioner does such a thing! Visiting the children every month!

Sister reaches up and lays a maternal hand on Rifat's shoulder and pats her twice. She smiles impishly. My dear, I've never met the deputy commissioner in my life!

XIII

In 1969, in her 30th year, Sister Shanti visited her parents.

She rang at their gate at precisely 10 a.m. and a middle-aged woman answered. This unrecognized servant did not believe Sister was the Chayns' daughter, and Sister understands why. Nine years have passed since she was last at home.

In her various 'home letters', the rare missives she was permitted to write to her parents during her formation, Sister Shanti tried to ignore what had come between her and them. She shared about her aspirancy in Calcutta, her postulancy, her novitiate, and finally the tertianship that carried her away: to Italy! To Rome! She tried to convince them of the meaningful experiences she'd had, working with lepers, comforting the dying, and teaching street children. She had a multitude of encounters with Mother Teresa, whose celebrity and respect among many Hindus, especially those in the elite her parents belonged to, was on the rise. After all of these years, Shanti was finally professed, and back in Delhi. Blue lines bordered her sari. Even though that meant little to her parents, it meant much to her. She attempted to convey that these details were MEANINGFUL THINGS of GREAT SIGNIFICANCE and SPIRITUAL DEPTH.

She never received a response, which, in a way, was a response.

And so she had decided to visit.

It was Daddy, prematurely retired, who met her. He had traded his stuffy suit for a Nehru cap and kurta-pyjama and sandals. He smiled on seeing her – the weight of memory came crashing in – then he saddened. He wobbled a little as he guided her to their drawing room, hid a bottle with a peg or two remaining in a planter, and slurred when calling for tea. They sat, sipping and conversing in pleasant terms, until Mummy came home.

Presumptuous, was the first thing to leave Mummy's lips. She eventually sat down next to Daddy. Her distant stare made it seem as if death had settled in.

Chatting eventually commenced between mother and daughter, full of false starts, clipped middles, aborted endings. Daddy tried to mediate but was in no state to do so. Sister soon realized

Mummy had never read her letters, not a one, and Sister did not know how to cover so much complicated ground in a matter of minutes. Mummy did, spanning the last near decade with blinding speed:

Loss of Daddy's job at ministry, poor investments, recurring illness, need for her to take work, just the old home preserved, only *one servant.* Mummy was breathing deeply by the end, reinvigorated by her anger.

Sister felt shame rise within her.

Do you still play?

Sister was confused by Mummy's abrupt question. Finally: A little, she said.

Mummy came close, lifted up Sister's hands, inspected them. The things you could have produced with these. Such a waste.

I'm spending my life well, Mummy.

Betraying parents? Heaping humiliation on us after what you did? Now, just showing up, unannounced, uninvited?

Sister faced this head on. I came to say what my letters said all along. I am sorry for what I caused you. I was a girl. I erred, grievously. Though I cannot be sorry for what I've become. This is me and...

Mummy left the room and did not return.

Sister stared at the floor, re-living the swirl of crooked experiences and unlikely choices that brought her to this moment.

Her father eventually pulled his chair up to Sister Shanti's, and warily cradled her head in the crook of his neck. They sat that way for a while, simply letting the clock's tick-tock, tick-tock, tick-tock testify to the indefatigable march of time and the loss that accompanies it.

*

I see you tapping your foot, Pope. I'm sorry for the wait.

The hour plods ever closer to the fated meeting: 3 p.m., the Tibetan Colony, Tourist Hotel, The Bogan.

Sister meanwhile rests in the other room, or prays, Meeta is not sure which. Meeta prays too, in her own way, eyes tight and lips moving, asking whatever god is in charge to use everything he or she's got to help the Likely Pair pin down Manoj before he gets away.

Manoj. Ma-noj. *Manoj.* She focuses on the two syllables, crushing them through gritted teeth. Ever since Constable Singh uttered his name, Meeta can hardly help but repeat it, overwriting her memory:

$$ManInSuit \neq ManInSuit$$
$$ManInSuit = Manoj$$

In the intervening hours she and Sister had pored over the evidence laid out on the floor: the composition book, the photograph, the letters. Sister had read them in the night when she failed to sleep. They were love letters, of a type more lewd and licentious then romantic. There was nothing to indicate the sender besides that it was a woman, owing to the frequent references about what she desired Manoj do to her anatomy. Sister censored some of the contents as she read them aloud to Meeta.

These aren't helpful, Meeta said.

Sister hummed in agreement. Still, maybe the unnamed sender will provide a lead should today's meeting go nowhere.

The notebook, curiously, had no other future meetings scheduled. Most past entries lacked much detail. There were a few geographic references to Delhi and its well-off neighbourhoods – South Ex, Vasant Vihar, GK1 – but around a few months back, the entries became vague days and times. It seemed a miracle that the details of today's meeting would be so explicit.

Meeta sits cross-legged before the items for a long while, meditating as if before her own altar. It takes much concentration to ignore yesterday's dissonance. Ram was Ram. He lied, about any number of things, but he must have had good reason. *Surely.*

She picks up the picture of Ram and Manoj, looking so pleased with themselves, and channels her hatred towards Manoj. What kind of monster would throw his friend before a train? She studies the ugly scar on his one cheek, planning how to give him another scar on the opposite.

She checks the hour for the fiftieth time on Ginna's clock radio. Written words may be foreign things, but numbers she knows! All 10 digits!

Sister. Sister! The time is arriving! We must not miss our man!

Sister exits the room and paws at her reddened eyes. When she replaces her glasses they only exaggerate their puffiness. I'm ready, she says, her small case in hand.

Sister had already asked Adiba if he would come along today to offer protection and he leapt at the idea like an overeager puppy. He dozes on the floor, shirtless. Ginna rises from her chair and prods Adiba with her toe. Up, up! They're on their way and you're still a puddle of fat. He rises, surprisingly quickly. He combs his hair! Brushes his teeth! Washes his face! *Buttons his shirt!* All with heretofore unseen resolve and purpose. As he moves about, one could even describe him as…animated!

It's as you say, Francis: Adiba is made new by a mission.

Ready at the door, Ginna takes Sister's shoulders: Go well, Sister, she says, and gives her an embrace. We will hope for another celebration tonight. Upon your return.

Sister musters a small smile. And this door will stay closed to all comers? No one looking to impose upon one of your girls will enter?

Ginna raises her hand in a pledge, as if to solemnly say, I would *never*.

Meeta exchanges surprised glances with the other girls who are all hanging around in the wings. And then they are off. The nun, the man, and the girl descend. And so do we.

By the weighty mid-afternoon light, you can see the worry on Meeta's face as she casts furtive glimpses at Adiba. She reflects: they need a true bodyguard this afternoon, not a bloated toad.

Sister. Sister. *Sister!*

Y-yes? Sister Shanti is already steps ahead, her mind a few steps further.

What if we were to engage some extra…muscle? It might be dangerous today.

But Adiba…

They look him over. His protruding gut and chubby calves

and shuffling gait and surprisingly thin arms inspire little confidence.

Ah. Sister ruminates. More muscle. Yes. What about – she snaps – that young man? The one with the stupid haircut and bad smell!

Pinku?

Yes!

Probably passed out in an alley. Though he *does* have a knife.

Just the type! Let's try him.

Wait here, Francis. No need to follow as they fan out in search of a smelly boy with a dull knife.

Let me tell you about our destination, Majnu ka Tila, otherwise known as the Tibetan Colony.

Ever heard of it?

It's not so very far from here, up near the old, colonial enclave of Civil Lines, and almost on the banks of the Yamuna river. Tons of Tibetans came here around 1960 when the Indian authorities graciously granted land for those fleeing their homeland. Now it's full of homes on top of homes and a whole generation of exiled Tibetans having been raised here in the administrative heart of India. Certainly, it has the feeling of many other lower-middle-class Delhi neighbourhoods, but with a lovely Buddhist temple at its centre and Tibetan food on offer, it's the closest I've made it to our small occupied neighbour to the north. Since the colony happens to be very close to the MC home for the abandoned disabled, it affords us Sisters the chance to occasionally go in, beg for supplies, care for urchins, and the like.

But we are not there yet.

Just look at Sister as she makes her enquiries after Pinku: an unstoppable force. But since I can peel back the sari and peer into her mind, I can tell you she is afraid. Not owing to this foreign-sounding brigand, The Bogan, but of each new step into the great cloud of unknowing. What if the meeting has been changed or cancelled for one of a thousand different reasons? Answers come to her in a litany of resigned clichés: up in smoke; out of luck; end of the line.

Sister tries to think past her pessimism, but another thought plagues her, and that is passing so close within the MC home's orbit near the Tibetan Colony. But why would the religious community she has called home for all her adult life entrench such a fear in her heart? Yet another mystery…

There he is. Meeta drags Pinku into G.B. by one of his prodigious ears. Sister greets him warmly.

He winces.

Meeta releases him.

Sister asks him to button his shirt, tighten his belt, show some respect.

He obliges.

She makes an offer.

They haggle.

He accepts.

They shake.

But only after Pinku wipes a mysterious substance off his hand and onto his pant leg.

There. Settled. Time for us to catch up with them, Francis.

We're too many for an auto, Meeta says. Onto the bus?

The bus, Sister replies, definitively. She picks up her case again.

I can carry it for you, Pinku offers.

No! Sister snaps, immediately recovering herself. It is light as can be. You're our muscle, along with Adiba, not some coolie. Eyes peeled, Pinku! Eyes peeled.

Pinku doesn't know this expression but feigns understanding.

Meeta takes a look at their odd, shuffling group and feels apprehensions rise. Sister is clearly troubled, mulling over a thousand different things, the contents of the case included. In Sister's fractured state, can they really trust her to guide them well? Meeta has spent so little time in the outside world she feels she has little choice.

Before long we're down the road, scrambling to jump on to a decrepit bus. Run, Pope, run! Just elbow a bit through the crowd! Make way! Hold on to your zucchetto! Whew!

It looks like we all made it on, though Adiba is practically dangling on the outside. And look, just as people make way for aged Sister Shanti, they glimpse you and me in our white robes and give up their seats, a perfect position for observing Sister and Meeta.

Catch your breath and pay attention, Francis.

Sister stares out the window, watching the streets and bundled, black powerlines sweep by in peaks and troughs, creating an undulating motion that all but hypnotizes. Meeta fidgets, looking warily at the case on Sister's lap. Pinku antagonizes an older Parsee man about his beliefs. Adiba is again deep in thought; or, rather, hungry.

The bus is up and over a flyover before it comes in for a landing, lurches, then stops.

Traffic.

And so the beggars descend. Children, the infirm, the able-bodied, the deformed, swarm. Bang! Bang! Bang! on the sides of the bus. They stand on a narrow platform separating lanes of traffic that let them look at passengers at eye level, hands outstretched.

Money! I need money. Grandma's eyes are no more!

I have no food! No food!

Med-*i*-cine!

Please*please*please*please*please…

Passengers' heads turn inwards to avoid the embarrassment of not giving. The pounding only increases. The driver is shouting at a legless little boy pushing himself on a wheeled cart, Get out of the way! Out…of…the…*way*!

Only Sister continues to look at each beggar squarely. Just ignore them, Meeta says to her. They're all liars. I have seen so on TV.

A small girl approaches Sister with an outstretched hand. She is waifish, and her puffy, blue princess dress is soiled and torn.

Crooksters make them that way, Meeta goes on, explaining. Break the kids. Blind them. Use them…

The girl keeps her hand held open in front of the window. Sister doesn't look away. The girl is uttering something in Marathi.

…More money in their pockets, Meeta says. Guaranteed fraud…

The girl plants her open hand on the smudged glass, letting

her small fingers tap in turn. Sister lifts her gnarled hand and places it up against the window's glass with splayed fingers. She looks the girl in the eye. Despite the glass, they touch fingertip to fingertip. And Sister smiles. She starts talking quietly to the girl, and Meeta hears words of benediction. The little girl smiles back.

The bus starts to move and their united hands come apart and the little girl waves.

I wasn't so much older than that little one when I was brought to Delhi, whispers Meeta quietly.

Sister turns, eyebrow arched. The joy that touched her face has disappeared.

A small village, Meeta says, unbidden. Nat Purwa.

Maybe it's not the time…

Heard of it?

Sister shakes her head.

It was a wonderful place. A perfect place. Besides the hunger. Hardly had a thread to cover me, too. My neighbour had a cow with painted horns he let me feed. I *adored* that sick and bony animal. Meeta pauses.

Sounds lovely, Sister said, perfunctorily.

My mother was a whore. All of our mothers were. Meeta says this with a hint of pride.

What…do you mean?

It is our business. Our life. Our varna.

You grew up in a brothel?

No. In a home.

There were no men? You had no father?

No, I did. Two parents.

Yet you're here.

Sent here. It's most common. My friend is in Emirates. Living the high life. While I am in Delhi rotting. I mean, look at me! Stuck in a place like Ginna's. Bottom-barrel. Low-class. Like burying a gem in trash.

Good Lord.

Too many mouths to feed. *Bip, bop, boop.* Here I am.

Sister sighs. Trapped in this life – she looks to Adiba who

114

stands aloof as Pinku cracks crass jokes to himself – since you were a girl.

Eh. Not so very trapped. Look at me! Not a week goes by without some sloppy customer offering marriage. Ram wasn't the first. I could always accept another. Could be in films. They all tell me so. I just needed a new start. And I finally decided that Ram was it.

You mean you feel no shame?

Meeta snorted. Why would I? Is it my fault I'm here? I'm doing work. I'm getting by. Fortunes will change. When they do, I'll be ready.

Sister shudders, clutching the seat in front of her. Meeta doesn't notice.

Why not escape earlier? And be free of it all?

Sister-ji, understand. I am *good* at what I do. Other girls can't dance like me! They're always getting pregnant. I don't have that flaw. I can't! Some problem down below. If the men don't want to use a rubber, it's OK with me. Sure there are the diseases, but I've got debts——

You're an idiot.

Meeta is ShockedStunnedSilenced. She can hardly breathe, Sister's harshness so surprises her.

I can't – believe – you were – don't even – Ram. Sister speaks only in stops and starts, her whole body trembling.

You *judge* me? Where I am, my caste, my karma, my family, is fated and I'm doing the best…

Silence between them. Sister cannot look at her.

You think I have to be here? Meeta says. With you? I'm doing it because I loved him. I didn't know him as long as you, but I loved him. Brightly. Like a thousand suns!

Such a *fool*, Sister mutters.

Meeta falls into an embittered silence. After all she had witnessed in the last day, she had imagined Sister to be very much as a sister: a friend, a listening ear, a confidante. All Meeta wants, all she ever wanted, was to put up her hand like that little girl to have it met, and instead she was met by cold, calloused rejection.

Bip, bop, boop. Like so, we've arrived at the colony.

Be wary as you alight, Francis. These buses slow for no one. Here, you go first.

We'll need to cross at that steel overbridge. Indeed, the one that passes directly in front of the red gates of the MC home for the disabled. Sister Shanti does all she can to not look at it, and the rest of her party think this strange. She walks ahead of the other three, quickly, passing the children who beg on the overbridge steps without a glance.

With THE REJECTION still fresh, Meeta stews in her mind as she walks behind Sister and Pinku and Adiba. She likens her relationship with Sister to a new and difficult dance, one where she is unsure of the steps. Any regret about actions that may or may not have taken place the prior night involving her, that small key, and the case in Sister's hands evaporates.

Cresting the overbridge, Sister stops. The broad gates to the MC home part and a pair of Sisters step out. Their trained eyes snap to Sister's bleached-white form and they shield their eyes against the sun.

They immediately know her. Sister Shanti! they call.

Sister, dreading this exact possibility, begins to run, or the closest approximation she can manage. The pair of nuns take pursuit.

Soon, Sister is off the overbridge, feeling a spurt of adrenaline not experienced in years. She recognizes her pursuers: short, familiar Sister Neepa, and a towering Filipina woman, Sister Suzie, who lopes ahead of Neepa with ease.

Not entirely sure why, Adiba and Pinku and Meeta take flight too.

Sister Shanti cuts past the shop specializing in illegal DVDs and other curios; the travel agent advertising SPECIALS; outdoor restaurants selling fresh *amdo balep*; has a near brush with a monk contemplating his shadow; threads through a gaggle of Indian university students with mild moustaches and poofed hair and obnoxious laughs; bumps a toddling child and chokes out an apology to the small girl's shocked mother.

Superior! Shanti hears. Sister Shanti!

Though the colony is familiar to Sister, this intersection, its narrow lanes darkened by tall, helter-skelter buildings, are momentarily foreign. Always a victim of concerns over decorous self-restraint, Sister fears how she appears to all who cross her. Pinku runs into view and Sister nearly leaps out of her sari before categorizing him as a friend. She clasps her case to her chest and looks down unfamiliar alleys, choosing a route away from the shouted *Sister Shanti, Sister,* Sis-*ter!*

She wheezes. Her body hasn't experienced exertion like this since her days in secondary playing badminton. She's slowing down when a consolatory thought lands: she was *captain* of the badminton team! A top athlete with excellent endurance and…

Her sandal's lip catches an uneven paving stone and she stumbles to the ground. Her case is thrown to the side.

The moment brings a catalogue of regrets:

This is madness. Running from my sisters!

Pursuing a lead to find a killer.

Such callous, foolish, stupid disobedience!

OW!

Her knee smarts as she attempts to stand. She can't rise! A spasm originating in her left calf paralyses her, and new panic ripples as the pursuing footsteps echo, growing closer, closer, *closer.* The thought of facing the nuns and its attending shame proves too much. One more attempt to lift herself and…

She cannot.

Meeta pops out from a perpendicular passage. *Ai-o!* she exclaims, and then scowls. Despite THE REJECTION, she still helps Sister up, ushering her into a dim wedge of space between an abutment and a wall. Sister leans on her uninjured leg and does all she can to trap and keep her breath. Meeta whips out a hand mirror and preens herself as the two white forms snap into her view.

Did you see a Sister pass by here? Sister Neepa says through her panting breaths.

Meeta looks up, distracted. What? I don't have any sister.

No, an old woman, in white, dressed like us, says Sister Suzie. She crosses her arms.

Naah, Meeta says, lifting a wisp of her hair behind her ear, further examining herself in the mirror.

What's that case? Sister Neepa asks. It's familiar.

Ow! Meeta shouts. Sister Shanti has just kicked her from behind. That's, er, mine, Meeta says. Don't touch it! I left it there.

Sister Neepa stoops anyway.

I said don't touch…

But Sister Neepa, smiling, restores it to Meeta's hand. Better in your hands than in the middle of the passage where others might trip and fall. Blessings on you. If you should see an older woman in white, tell her we miss her. Tell her that, please. And that I will find her.

Meeta, hesitating to meet her eyes, gives a nod. She follows them with her gaze as they flutter away.

She needles Sister in the side, and the old woman is genuinely shocked. That's what you get for kicking me, you old crone.

Sister looks down.

Why are you hiding? Meeta asks. From your own people? Huh? *What* are you hiding? Watching an elder run around like that! Shameless!

Sister looks up. She adjusts her glasses. You're right.

You could have killed yourself. Who's the…

You're right, Sister says, cracks manifest in her composure.

Meeta stops ranting. She is embarrassed now, and returns to her mirror to escape Sister's pleading eyes.

I've not been honest with you, Sister says. About my being here. About my search for Ram's killer. And I am a fool.

Meeta looks up, feigning disinterest. Her attention is rapt.

In my house, I'm a Superior…

A what? Meeta interjects.

A leader. A guide. A mother. For the other, younger Sisters. I…direct them in their spiritual journeys. Help them grow in love. Grow closer to God.

Meeta forces a yawn.

It is this I have left. One of the chief values of my order – my life – is obedience. Above all else. Obedience to our superiors is obedience to God. Even if we disagree completely, we are not to go along with our fickle hearts. We are not to trust ourselves.

That sounds terrible, Meeta says.

Sister smiles, sighs, grows morose. Nonetheless, it's a vow—

A what?

A promise. That I made. But more than a promise. She leans against the wall and looks up to the muddy blue sky. It meant a rewriting of who I am.

Meeta looks at her impassively.

When I got news of Ram, Sister says, I took the liberty of going to the ghats with one of those young nuns who just went by. I was given permission for this by the Superior General – Meeta cocks her head dumbly – the chief leader of my religious community. But, you see, everything *after* that visit has been of my own will.

So you're not supposed to be doing any of this?

Sister shakes her head.

That's why you don't have a place to stay?

Sister nods.

So you're being disobedient. Meeta smiles.

Sister sighs, nods again, and not without shame. Sister's lips crack, as if there is something else to confess, but nothing comes. All of this nonsense, and we're already late, she says. Let's hope they are not being punctual. *Arre*, this pain in my knee. Give me your shoulder…

And off the Likely Pair goes, Francis, Sister begrudgingly leaning on Meeta, Meeta begrudgingly providing her support.

XIV

In 2005, in her 66th year, Sister came up short.

She had been up late into the night, puzzling over her books.

Money was missing.

Much money was missing.

Much money for which she was responsible was missing.

She took this seriously, as she took everything. God's money wasn't to be frittered away. Her mind turned to questioning: Who had access to her office? When could they have entered and pilfered it? It took a day before it finally dawned on her after morning prayers: so obvious, but impossible for her to see.

Ram had been coming around lately.

She had treasured the visits from the adolescent. He was familiar with her daily schedule and always appeared just in time for a hot meal. While she disliked being seen to be taken advantage of her position of authority, she hated the thought that Ram needed her and she wouldn't help.

He had been doing well, he said on his last visit. Staying off drugs and drink, attending the school in which she had secured him a place. He was staying at a home for boys run by another religious community. She had smiled at him. He wore a school uniform when he came, and she thought he looked brilliant in his crested pullover and grey trousers. She had struggled that most all of what she did in this life was of no permanence, but with Ram it felt different. She felt like loving this boy well and that seeing him grow and develop was proof she was meant to be where she was in life, doing what she was doing, even as she felt heaviness weighing upon her soul.

That day, she asked permission by telephone of the Superior General to visit Ram at his school to enquire about the missing money. She was reprimanded, 'This is the Lord's money, meant for his poor', and 'We must not throw pearls before swine', and 'You, of all our sisters…' and she accepted this with her head hanging down like a guilty schoolgirl before a headmistress. The permission was nonetheless granted.

She went to his school. Ram wasn't there, the headmaster told her; it turned out he had not been there for some months.

And so commenced another search, albeit brief, sending Sister right back to where she had most recently found the boy in a dire state. He was at a bus station, scamming passengers for their money.

She sneaked up on him, a great difficulty in her garb. You lied to me, she said from behind him, disguising her hurt.

He tried to respond, but tripped over his words. His eyes looked clouded again, and a twitchy, manic air claimed him.

I would like an explanation, she said.

His composure regained, he offered one. It involved his indebtedness to a one-eyed bearded man, the one who taught him to deceive these passengers. He learned to use just enough detail to make his dire situation sound plausible to the harried passengers, and passed his days here under the man's threat. There would be consequences if he did not bring him enough money at the end of the day.

She asked about the missing money.

He confessed, told her the money he had stolen was gone, taken by the same one who exploited him now.

Come away with me, she said. I'll keep you from this predator. I'll protect you.

Ram simply shook his head.

And what of school? What of your future?

I'm working hard for myself.

Please. Come.

He shook his head. Cannot do it, Sisterji.

She could not bear waiting there another moment and left him among the station's bustle. He watched her go, almost calling after her, but not quite getting to it.

Over the following weeks, she felt such guilt over abandoning him to his ways, until it dawned on her one morning while doing paperwork: there likely was no shadowy one-eyed man, that she was just another mark to be separated from her money, and Ram was weaving another web of lies. She lay down her pen and sat there for a time, feeling a great shame, and sadness, and told no one of the turmoil within her that this boy so easily created.

*

Standing before the Tourist Hotel, Adiba and Pinku find the Likely Pair. The men have ice cream bars melting in their hands. We got distracted, Pinku says. Amul brand. The *best*.

Sister stares him down as he takes a final bite. Don't let it happen again, she snaps. We may have missed our chance. Fifteen minutes late, we are! This is dangerous. *Really* dangerous! A murderer is *very likely* in the building.

Pinku drops the wrapper on the ground and licks his chocolate-stained fingers. All this – talky-drama – I only need a dark corner – and my knife – and I'll *murder* him.

This Manoj is to be *punished*, Sister says. We will see to that. *No* Murder. *No* Killing. *No* convenient, coincidental manslaughter. This one will see the courts, and the prison. Final word.

She turns to Adiba. You watch the doors and hallways. Block Manoj or this Bogan if they try to run. He gives an affirmative grunt. Pinku, you're with me.

Meeta again stands shocked. She is forgotten. And what are you wanting *me* to do?

Watch our backs, of course. Keep the eyes peeled.

And in we plunge into the forlorn hotel's maw, Sister and Pinku and Adiba and Meeta and you and I. Enter the lobby. Note the clock on the wall. Nearly 20 minutes late. See the attendant, half-asleep, a geometry textbook open in front of him. The patchy vinyl furniture. 'Tourist Hotel' written in chipping paint on the pink, pink walls.

One of Delhi's five-star establishments, this is not.

It's 'bohemian', the guidebook would tell you. 'Budget accommodation', 'Populated by colourful characters'.

Euphemisms. It is a love nest, Pope. It is a drug den. Perhaps the guidebook's author would not be able to collect his baksheesh from the owner for such direct writing.

A European backpacking couple – glassy-eyed, unwashed, unmarried – descends the stairs surprised to meet a short nun with a harsh gaze. They slide around her, their laughter ceasing. But it's not for them or what they do that Sister disapproves – it is an acute sense of worry.

'The Bogan'. It's an ominous name. Heavy. Full of danger.

Sir, Sister says to the attendant, whose nameplate reads Venkat. His eyebrows rise, his only reply. I need to know if you have a guest here who goes by the name 'The Bogan'.

We have many guests with many names. Many, many.

I need to give him something.

No.

What did you say?

No. What kind of employee do I look like? Just look at this place! Falling apart. All sorts of dirtiness. And I have to clean up after these animals! Already today – he shudders – no. I cannot even describe it. My shift is almost done. My job is to sit here, and that is what I will do. No deliveries, no showing of rooms, unless you are looking for a room, and then I am obligated.

Sister was taken aback. You are very open with your discontent.

Why do I care what some old lady thinks? You won't stay in a place like this. He looks over her shoulder. But those others look like the kind who would. Are you all with this one? he asks, pointing to Sister.

Adiba and Pinku and Meeta nod. Well, get out of my face. You're not here for some four-way love encounter, I am most sure.

Meeta steps forward. Have you seen a man with a scar come in? Running down his cheek? Like so?

Venkat rolls his eyes. What do I care about scars? The only thing I care about when I see someone enter is whether they look like they will throw their internal fluids across a room and leave them for me to clean up.

Look, you didn't answer my question, Sister says. Is a…Mr Bogan here? It's very important.

Does this gora owe you some money, or what? Is that why you have these sorry-looking 10-rupee thugs?

Pinku pulls out his knife. Watch your mouth.

Without blinking, the attendant pulls out a long-barrelled pistol. Don't mess with me. I have nothing to lose! Nothing!

Pinku drops his knife. All four of our party raise their hands.

(Ah. Francis, you may lower your hands. There's no danger. Not to you, anyway.)

The clock ticks away as Venkat lets his pistol jump from person to person. Sister sees the appointed hour slipping further away.

123

My dear Venkat sahib, this has only been a misunderstanding of the highest order. You're right: we want no trouble for you, and my friend Mr Pinku is only here for my sake, protecting an old, frail woman. You see, Mr Bogan is set to meet someone, someone who has taken something of utmost value from us. We simply need to talk with him. And–

Money.

Excuse me?

I thought you'd have got it by now. He taps the counter, once, twice, thrice.

Your sales pitch is lacking, Sister says. She reaches to open her case.

I can pay! Meeta says abruptly.

Sorry?

I have funds. Meeta is quick to open her purse, rifle through it, and pull out a hundred-rupee note and slip it to the man. Sister is surprised.

He allows his gun to slip back beneath the desk.

Room 32.

Be assured we won't tell him you gave us this information.

Whatever. He returns to his textbook, looking as bored as ever.

As they climb the stairs Sister tugs at Meeta's elbow. Thank you. For that. I don't like spending this money on bribes. That was a sacrifice.

Meeta gives a smile that Sister takes at face value. It is worth it, Meeta says.

Hey, Sister, are we just busting in the door?

No. New plan. Adiba will block the stairs. You'll be with us. If Manoj is in with this Bogan and tries to run, you'll tackle him. We'll call for Adiba, and Meeta and I will do all we can to help.

This sounds like a bad plan, Meeta grumbles. What if they have weapons? He's a killer. And we know nothing about this Bogan.

It *is* a bad plan. But it's the best we have. We're late already. All this drama. Pistols, knives. I tell you, I'm tired of it. She huffs.

The corridor is lit by a single naked bulb. It lights up a car-toonish calendar with a blue-skinned Rama and a monkey-bodied Hanuman in superhero poses. The stairs are uneven heights, demanding constant attention. Sister absently reaches for her injured knee, as if it would help lessen its swelling. Each in our party wipes sweat from their brows.

They reach Room 32.

There's talking inside. Two voices. Sister and Meeta lean in to listen. The words are indistinguishable over a blaring TV and a rumbling A/C unit. Sister tries the door handle. Locked, naturally.

Pinku, Sister whispers. She signals, ramming one of her hands into the other silently, then jerks her head towards the door.

Pinku is confused.

Bust open the door! Sister whisper-shouts.

Pinku frowns. Shakes his head.

Extra money for you! she hisses. I promise!

Despite the dark of the corridor, he puts on his sunglasses, I suppose to channel his inner action hero. He steps back, just so, readying the blunt side of his shoulder and arm to barge in, as Aamir Khan would do.

Breaths are held. Fists are clenched. Prayers are uttered. Pinku dashes into the door.

POW!

Budge, it does not.

Pinku, now on the floor, nurses his newly-bruised shoulder.

Adiba! Sister shouts. Your turn. *Now!*

Without a hint of hesitation, Adiba repeats Pinku's wind-up process, sans pretension. He barges into the door.

POW!

Budge, it does.

With the door nearly blown off its hinges, Sister is in first, shouting. *Manoj, Manoj!*

Manoj hides his face. He grasps a bag on the bed then struggles to open a window. Good Lord, he literally leaps out of it!

Sister is after him while Meeta is looking at Pinku on the floor. Adiba stands, stunned, and a light pink man sprawls on a bed looking impossibly relaxed despite the tempest that surrounds him. Manoj is jumping to another balcony, hanging down. He drops! Drops again! Such recklessness!

Adiba! Pinku! Sister yells. After that man! To the street. He's getting away!

Without a second thought, Adiba is out of the door, nearly stepping on Pinku, and down the hall with remarkable alacrity. Pinku lifts himself from the floor and follows.

Ladies, says the man on the bed, good to see you. He smiles. In the market?

You're The Bogan?

He-he. Bo-*gan*. Heh. How you say it. It's funny. Your accent.

Sister approaches the side of the bed. He is young. His feet bare, shirt unbuttoned, stubble unshaven. A Tibetan medallion hangs from his neck. The room smells as if doused in camphor and spilled Carlsberg.

What is the matter with you? Are you unwell?

Nothing. Nothing's the matter. He grins, tiredly. Can you pass me those rotis? I'm running on fumes here. You're interrupting my meal. He chortles.

Meeta, struggling with his accent, gets him some bread-looking things in a take-out container. He starts to gobble them up. God, these are good. Want one?

Are you some kind of idiot? Sister turns to Meeta. By God, we have an idiot here.

No, I'm just Australian. He chuckles maniacally. Heh. No, I'm at peace. Transcending the plane.

I think he's on something, Meeta says.

Are you on something? Sister asks.

Bogan smiles. I'm *definitely* on something.

What was Manoj here for?

Confusion slips across Bogan's face. Man-*ooj*?

The man who just leapt out the window as we came crashing through your door?

Bogan looks at the door. At the window. Huh. He eats another piece of roti. Are you here to buy?

I'm a nun, you idiot.

He hiccups. Hey, yeah, you are. I'm totally confused right now. Shrugging, he turns to Meeta. Are you here to buy?

Where is Manoj staying? Meeta asks.

I don't know. I'm just a dealer to his dealing. I mean, we'd hang out sometimes. Get high on the supply, as it were. Do you all want my card or something?

He killed someone.

What? Who?

You know Ram Kumar?

Ram! Manoj killed Ram? That makes no sense. Bogan seems to wander back in time, recalling who stood where, who did what. Those two are tight! Real tight! Best friends! Bogan actually looks present for a moment. Gone. I can't believe...

What was Manoj doing here?

Bogan rubs his stubble. Manoj. Trying to buy.

Buy?

You know. Drugs.

The man's just killed not four days ago! And he's buying!

People dying ever'day. Addict's gonna use.

This sits heavily with Sister, Meeta can tell.

He bought?

And sold. All over. He and Ram. Hey, can I take a nap? I'm really feeling the effects of this.

No, Meeta and Sister say jointly.

Focus, Sister says.

Or we'll call the police, Meeta says.

Not so bonzer. This is clouding my energy. Heaps. Bogan suddenly looks very tired.

You're saying Ram sold?

Yeah, he and Manoj. I mean, they had a boss. Small guys like him and Ram can't find the funds to start buying. They were just couriers, ya'know? Errand boys, little-teeny-tiny drugwallahs, running here and there.

They did deliveries? Sister asks.

Yeah. Well, Ram did. I mean Manoj. I'm really getting confused.

They looked alike. Besides the scar.

Like *brothers*. And one bloke killed the other…hea-*vy*.

They remain in silence. Bogan lays his head on a sodden pillow and the pair give him a moment to let out his emotions. Sister looks at him more closely. He has fallen asleep.

Wake up! Wake *up*! She shakes his arm. No response.

Police! Meeta shouts.

Wha–Right. I'm here. I'm here.

Sister is pained, angry. So Ram was selling drugs.

Yes and no. He holds his fingers to his temples, trying to concentrate. Ram gets out of the big business. Swears it off. Just a while ago. Manoj is still going strong. I'm seeing him every couple of days. Ram, not so much. He'd call, sure, turn up, but only to buy a little bit. Just for personal use. Seemed like he'd found another job.

So you don't know anything about where Manoj comes from, where he goes.

Not a clue. If I did, honestly, I wouldn't tell you. Bad for business. Can't go ratting on customers, can I?

Bogan starts to droop again.

Sister lobs a question at him to keep him awake. Why do you work from here? The Tibetan Colony?

Oh, I'm *totally* spiritual. But this whole spiritual thing is kind of an act. I mean, tourists *love* it. They're most of my sales. They think I'm a fucking guru or something. I came to India to tap into the source. Don't get me wrong. I *love* to meditate. To contemplate. To copulate. But I usually need some chemical stimulation to see the face of God, *amIright*?

Sister speaks: You're a fool. You're going to live in a state of despair. You're there even now. I can see it. You'll drift from here to there. Your drugs will let you down. There will be no one to care for you. You probably have parents? Back in Australia? Brothers and sisters wondering what's become of their son, their sibling?

Yeah.

They are grieving for you.

They hate me.

They are grieving. And when you finally overdose alone, or step on some gangster's toes, or make a bad deal, they will not even know you are gone. This is your life, and it is bad, brutish, nasty.

Do you…see the future? Is that, like, a power you have?

I'm old enough to have seen people make decisions that break themselves. And old enough to see people change their minds and be healed.

You're a nun, yeah? Christ, are you going to offer to introduce me to Jesus now? Tell me he's the answer to it all? That he'll save my fucking soul? Make my life bearable?

Sister only looks at him. No.

A flash of surprise.

The Holy Spirit can take care of that business, she says. My job while you are in front of me – pathetic and wretched – is to love you. To tell you there are better ways, that there is hope – she looks around the room – even in this mess. This is all I have to say to you.

Sister turns to Meeta. We need to go. Mr Bogan has helped us very much.

I have, now? Bogan says.

If Manoj has escaped, we need to head to the Muslim quarter. There is a man we need to see there.

We do? Meeta says.

Yes. Let's be off. I don't have time to waste talking to pig-head-ed blockheads like this one here. Mr Bogan, I see your pain. And I believe Jesus does too. It's for you two to work out. Goodbye.

Bogan's laughter follows them down the stairs, past Venkat and his calculations, past new arrivals in the lobby hoping for the answers to life's questions, and out through the poorly-hung lobby door.

Sister stands outside, breathing heavily through her nose. A thousand thoughts run through her head.

Who is this Jesus? Meeta asks. The Britisher on Ginna's wall? He's alive?

Sister looks pained. As if she's neglected some fundamental

responsibility. She reaches to touch Meeta's arm and her eyes have a deepness to them. Her lips purse. A strange hope swells in Meeta.

Another time, Sister says. The day, it is wasting.

And Sister turns, leaving Meeta to feel THE REJECTION's cut dig deeper just before the wound is cauterized by her searing anger.

We need to find that monkey with the knife and his ape friend, Sister says, referring to Pinku and Adiba.

With these words, so begins one of our story's darker scenes. It's possible a more ironic simian-invoking insult has never been uttered.

XV

Follow at a distance, Francis.

Meeta straggles behind Sister, consumed by feelings she attempts to hide. Sister pretends no blow has been struck.

I've had a while to think on THE REJECTION and a story is helpful in understanding it. I also want to stave off what is coming at least a moment longer. Our Father in Heaven knows it will arrive soon enough.

And so my little parable begins.

'Once a man had two sons. The younger son said to his father, "Give me my share of the property." So the father divided his property between his two sons. Not long after that, the younger son packed up everything he owned and left for a foreign country, where he wasted all his money in wild living. He had spent everything, when a bad famine spread through that whole land. Soon he had nothing to eat. He went to work for a man in that country, and the man sent him out to take care of his pigs. He would have been glad to eat what the pigs were eating, but no one gave him a thing'.

You think you know where this prodigal tale is going, Francis. Think again.

'Finally, he came to his senses and said, "My father's workers have plenty to eat, and here I am, starving to death! I will go to my father and say to him, 'Father, I have sinned against God in heaven and against you'".

But the son never gets around to it. On the way home, he has a windfall, falls back in with the same revellers who helped him squander his inheritance, visits the same prostitute night after night who saps him of will and traps him where he is. The son never bows before his father, the father never embraces his son, reconciliation never occurs.

Imagine how the father feels. The slap of the son's initial insult, asking for the inheritance as if it would be better for the father to fall over dead that instant. And yet, the father hopes one day he will look into the distance and see his son returning home, and he will run to his son and forgive him and welcome him back. But instead of seeing his son cresting a nearby hill, it is but a messenger bearing the worst news: your beloved son, who you hoped and prayed and dreamt would have a future, is lost. And not just lost, but dead.

How would the father feel, I ask you?

Fill in the blank: _____

And all because of a damned prostitute.

Ah. I see the creases in your brow. It is a difficult relationship Meeta and Sister share, no? The two are similar magnetic poles, pushing and pulling, wishing to join together but forced apart by the elemental.

So, looking on the Likely Pair as they hurry to try to find what has become of Pinku and Adiba and Manoj, I have chosen to look at it like so: maybe, instead of focusing on Sister's inability to extend compassion to Meeta, I remember that like the father in our story, Sister has a deep well of forgiveness and a desire to love, but also weaknesses, just as we all do. In reflecting on THE REJECTION, I try to instead focus on the many moments of forbearance proceeding and following it, seeing Sister as a bereaved mother made to tolerate the presence of the very one she blames for the death of her child. Not so difficult to understand when viewed as—

Give me the case, says a voice from beneath an awning.

Sister and Meeta forget themselves for a moment, wondering if this man indeed speaks to them.

What is this you're saying? Sister says. Speak up.

He steps into the light. He wears a cream-coloured suit, possibly polyester, with penny loafers that match his suit to perfection. His skin is an almond tone of brown, his hair thin. He wields a generous paunch like a wrecking ball. The only extravagance of colour he affords himself is a lively orange shirt, and, in the fashion one would expect of his type, wears dark aviator sunglasses with gold rims, gold rings on his fingers, and a gold chain about his neck.

But I focus on the inconsequential. Sister and Meeta are concerned only with the man's pistol pointed at them. Despite THE REJECTION, Meeta and Sister clasp one another.

What are you getting at, you goonda? Sister spits. All I have in my case is simple nun things. You want my rosary? M-my undergarments?

The man gives a sly smile. Yes.

You're a fool, a villain, a…

He takes the case.

Just reclaiming what's mine, he says.

Before anything can be proclaimed or protested, the man has already sprinted off; I note your shock, Pope, and feel it too: he's surprisingly nimble for a fatso.

Sorry for the lack of warning, Francis! But follow we must!

Get back here! Sister shouts, but she's lost the race before it starts: age, that swollen knee, and her accursed faulty ankle limit her gait to a limp.

But not Meeta. She screams all the way. Thief! Thief! Catching up to an overweight, middle-aged man in penny loafers and a too-tight suit is no challenge for her. He wags his gun behind him and Meeta trails, trying to dodge its line of sight.

Duck under that clothesline, Pope! Dodge that monk! Hurdle that child!

What a procession we are!

They wind through the narrow alleys of the Tibetan Colony, weaving here, turning there, losing themselves among labyrinthine passageways, doubling back, circling round. Ah! Indeed! The goonda, The Goonda we shall call him in absence of a known name, has paused: he has again come upon Sister Shanti.

She gives him a scathing look. This does not impede him.

Couldn't you have – THIEF! RUNNING! THERE! – done *something* to stop him? Meeta wheezes as she speeds past. Sister lifts her hands to the sky and shrugs.

Despite Meeta's protestations, no one intervenes. This is because The Goonda now waves the gun in front of him. Even a traffic warden springs from his platform and hides, seeing peril bear down on him.

It seems The Goonda finally has his direction. They're all nearing the main road. If he reaches it unhindered and has a car waiting, Meeta realizes, he'll never be caught.

A hundred million questions crowd Meeta's mind:

Who is The Goonda?
Did he have a part in Ram's murder?
Was he here *with* Manoj, or *looking for* Manoj?
Why does he want Sister's undergarments?
Why is she even bothering to help Sister?

An answer hits her just like the child's errant football that speeds through the air and into her gut: *the money.*

Sorry, miss! calls the kicker as he retrieves his ball.

Meeta, doubled over, lets out a breathless roar and the boys-at-play scurry off. Meeta holds her belly, nurses a side stitch, and watches as The Goonda reaches the wide road. Her only consolation is a tiny, small secret.

Instead of taking the SafePrudentWise option of a pedestrian overbridge to make it to the other side of the road and meet his car, The Goonda decides to ford the flowing river of cross-traffic with the help of his gun. His attention (rightly) fixed on approaching cars, he misses the stamp-stamp-stamp of cheap shoe leather, announcing the man barrelling towards him from behind. Using his own considerable girth, none other than Adiba flings himself into The Goonda, and the pair go sprawling to the pavement.

Meeta whoops with delight! Sister has finally arrived and helps Meeta up. They exchange a glance laden with misunderstanding before Meeta rushes off to help subdue The Goonda.

Adiba and The Goonda tussle on the hot pavement like large, unwieldy sea mammals on land; almost comic if there wasn't such danger at hand.

The gun explodes and the watching crowd convulses: everyone ducks.

Adiba looks as if he's hit! But no! The bullet was a miss: he merely cups his deafened ear. Somehow in the grappling the gun has left The Goonda's hand and is flung to the pavement. He still clasps the case to his chest. He sees his waiting car, and, in a bit of quick mental calculus, reasons that if he is to escape injury or police intervention he needs to be in that car IMMEDIATELY. He extricates himself from Adiba's bear hug and runs headlong into speeding traffic, damn all!

Meeta, sprinting again, pauses at the road. She isn't foolhardy enough to throw herself before that speeding Mahindra Scorpio and risk meeting her end, especially when she knows what is in that case, and especially when she knows what isn't.

But Adiba rises. He draws from some previously unseen store of verve to pursue The Goonda.

Dodge left, Adiba! Dodge right! The Goonda weaves and runs as cars hoot their horns and zoom past. But Adiba dashes ahead singularly, not pausing nor waiting nor delaying for anything, demanding that for once, the world react to *him*.

Oh no.

It is upon us. The fateful monkey encounter.

I can hardly watch. As Adiba strains to take hold of The Goonda's flapping jacket, the motorcycle driver and monkey thwacker arrive. Whether from poor eyesight or a disdain of natural consequences, he literally runs into the running pair.

The Goonda turns and the case flies from his hand.

The motorcycle driver remains on his bike while his passenger monkey catapults into the air, only to land with surprising grace.

But Adiba is down.

Pinku is reunited with Sister and Meeta now, and all shout in horror, hands held to foreheads, before rushing into traffic together.

With his monkey now dutifully returned to his perch on the back of the bike, the driver can see no benefit in remaining at the scene. After all, was it his fault two idiots were dashing through the middle of the road?

Agents of Fate, away he and his monkey go, straight out of our story.

The Goonda, though stunned, has a similar inclination. He scrambles to retrieve the case then stumbles into his car. Away he goes, unfortunately to remain at the heart of our story.

As the trio reach Adiba, they see he is unmoving. They check to see if he breathes, if his pulse signals life. They try to goad him back to consciousness.

He is, in fact, dead.

They stand over the body for some time, entangled in knots of emotion.

He was an oaf; a sometimes brutal degenerate who had wasted almost all his time on the earth. But in this final moment of reckless bravery, all would agree that he acquitted himself well, and showed the possibility of a different, better, glorious, man. What might have been if this new Adiba, not bound by a fascist mother's edicts but animated by purpose and concern not for himself, had continued to live? Would he resort to his old ways, or choose a different course? Would he have finally conquered his dandruff and body odour?

Only God can know. Only God can know.

Sister curses her suitcase, bends over Adiba, and prays for his soul. All this stupidity over money and her few personal effects. Because of her insistence to defy the odds and discover what befell Ram, another man is dead.

There is…

There are…

There…

I can't. I can't do it, Francis.

Recounting these events has spent me. I must lay down my typewriter. Besides, I hear the bell ring, calling me to evening compline.

I will take it all up again tomorrow.

XVI

It was a blow to the head, Sister tells Ginna. Adiba fell pursuing a villain.

Ginna has already taken a seat. She was hanging colourful streamers with the girls in preparation for a party as Sister and Meeta arrived back at No. 201.

Ginna does not speak. Rifat silences the radio, '*Kajra Re*' coming to an abrupt halt.

And it is my fault, Sister says. All stand silently. Sister remains stoic, having been the bearer of bad news many times before.

All watch Ginna, while she remains fixated on a window looking outside. It is as if the old woman has become allergic to breathing. The streamers in her hands crinkle. She finally stands up and looks Sister in the eye, and Sister braces for a blast of invective.

The mother – the mother-no-more – begins to weep. To howl. To shake. She clings to Sister, and Sister's arms rise to comfort her.

The others stand dumbstruck.

Meeta sheds no tears. She has borne Adiba's blows and will never forget them. His death is only another postponement; soon there will be work again, sweaty men with grotesque thoughts who press against her, into her. Meeta slips away to her room while the other girls, all moved to varying degrees, lay their hands on Ginna as she falls to her knees and weeps.

Follow Meeta to her room, Francis. Crack the door just so, and peek in.

She quietly packs her things into her oversized purse. She pulls her most favourite poster from the wall and folds it until it slides in easily. She reaches far beneath her bed and removes a hand-held, opaque, plastic case, a gift from Ram. She is most wary about what it contains and slides it to the bottom of her bag.

I'm sure you have guessed what she is doing, and you are correct, Pope.

Sister opens the door and Meeta gives a start. She glares at Sister.

I am going to the morgue with Ginna. When I return, we go immediately to the Muslim quarter.

Meeta nods, all the while repeating to herself, *If I am still here, If I am still here, If I am still here…*

In 1960, in her 21st year, Heera received a note.

She found it tucked in the pages of her sheet music after a lesson, scrawled on a misplaced sheaf of Elgar's *Salut d'Amour*. Receiving a note wasn't a surprise, but this one was written in the minutes between playing the final piece, her fetching tea, and Walter's departure. Its contents stopped her cold.

The young American had taken the pre-eminent place in her mind and heart, displacing music, service, studies, Mother Teresa, friends, God, and parents. His auburn hair. His gentle instruction. His foreign allure. She worried at first, but it was clear her growing feelings for him were by no means unrequited. He had taken to her keen mind and subtle beauty and remarkable talent. It became a question of finding space to explore their attraction.

With every moment of their relationship all but chaperoned, they had lived within others' constraints these past months. Moments were stolen between pieces or when Mummy left the room and they joked like schoolchildren. The relationship's strangeness made it enthralling. What were the rules? Who knew! Every secret felt like a delicious transgression, the sort of disobedience that Heera had indulged in little over her short life.

She spent those days of infatuation in a heady blur, wondering what her life ought to be. The paths were clearly delineated and remarkably different. She loved her music but doubted it would carry her far. And what of her legal studies? Were they only to achieve a university degree and net an older husband with a large bank balance and undoubtably large waistline? Would she even have the chance to apply what she worked so hard to learn? And would the piano, this instrument that meant all the more to her under Walter's instruction, be relegated to a corner of her life, only to be trotted out after dessert for guests' enjoyment?

And then, almost an afterthought, were the Missionaries of Charity. Sister Angelique had paved the way, and Heera had talked via a (very expensive) call with one of the MCs in Calcutta. She was invited to participate in an aspirancy to take place next week, sandwiched in the summer months between academic terms. It would be a chance to taste the religious life. Would she like, as Mother Teresa had put it, to 'Come and see'? But that seemed an impossibility. Maybe next time, Heera thought, doubting her conviction.

Typical Indian domesticity. Life in another culture. Devoted service to the poor. Heera had a decision to make, that much was clear. And suddenly, the contents of Walter's note put her choices in sharper relief:

6 a.m. This Saturday. New Delhi railway station.
Secret destination. Back on Sunday.
Tell your parents a story.

*

The ensuing hours are long. The girls have retired to their mats. Activity on G.B. Road buzzes. They hear feet on the stairs, knocking at the barred door, customers finally giving up. The sounds fade.

The other girls chat a little. Their thoughts naturally turn to escape. Why don't they run? The answers: No money. No family. Homes an impossible distance away. Their fears outbalance their courage.

Meeta is meanwhile caught up in a world oher own:

Sister is worse than Ginna. Telling me what to do. Where to go. So much judgement I receive. So cruel. He chose me, fell in love with me. What did I do? Fell in love in return and hoped to run away. What fault of this is mine? And telling that drug dealer he is loved, while treating me like a soiled rag, to be wrung out after wiping up filth and being thrown away?

But then there are thoughts about Ram and the mounting lies she tries feebly to ignore: living in some dirty chawl, wrapped up in selling drugs. Barely even educated! Enticing her to run off with money stolen from evil men!

She glances at her purse. The opaque case at the bottom of her bag shouts silent accusations. She is burdened, regrets what she's done, has nowhere to confess it. If she doesn't run now, she'll be found out. What then?

When she hears the key turning in the lock, she curses. She may have missed her chance.

Meeta peeks out of her room. In staggers Ginna, aged a decade in an afternoon. The other girls rise and hover around anxiously to meet her.

Ginna walks to Rifat, Deepti, and Anu in turn. She hugs them. She steps slowly down the hall until she arrives before Meeta. Meeta can hardly look her in the eye, knowing she must blame her for Adiba's death. Ginna offers Meeta a silent embrace as well.

Peer inside Ginna and analyse the machine's inner workings: She is a pimp. She operates a brothel. She is afraid and ashamed. Family ties have been cut. She has no one to turn to but the women whose bodies she exploits.

Without another word the old woman lies down in Adiba's room. Anu takes her some dal-roti from over the dying stove and puts it besides Ginna, closing the door behind her.

The burdened soul is a heavy thing.

Sister finally appears, finding Meeta in their shared room sitting cross-legged. This has been a difficult day, Sister says. Well, let's be off—

I can't continue—

That Sister is willing to head back out the door and Meeta is willing to quit their investigation shocks the other.

They stare at each other for a moment.

I've been thinking, Meeta says, about all of this. I'm leaving while I can.

Sister sits herself down, mulling it over. Of course. Her words ring with disappointment. Finally: But you love Ram, don't you?

I do. I did. He lied to me. And you've lied to me, she almost says.

I can understand. But his killer…. Can't you remain? Just a while more? We've lost so much for this to add up to nothing.

Their eyes lock. Sister looks away. Of course I can't ask that of you. I have no right. Meeta notes Sister's hands tensing. Can you hand me that envelope? Sister finally says, signalling toward her altar.

Meeta obliges. Sister extracts the simple letter and hands it to Meeta.

I know you can't read it, but you should know. I need someone to know. Just a few ounces, and yet…

Meeta turns it over in her hands.

It's just…I'm…confused. Right now. This moment. Hardly knowing what is up and what is down. I asked for permission a few months ago for a pause, a time to leave my community and reflect. A period called exclaustration. If I am honest with myself, if I do as I believe I ought, it would be a final break.

'Eks-claws-tray-shun', Meeta parrots slowly, still holding the letter carefully in her hands. What is it?

It would mean the end. The end of my vows.

Meeta is still confused.

My request was refused, on the Superior General's recommendation. I received this news at nearly the exact moment I learned of Ram's expiry.

Meeta thinks she understands. You said earlier you've left for just a few days. That yours is a small disobedience. But – you've run away for good? You're taking off your – she hovers her hand over her head – sari? Unpinning that little man on your shoulder? Her eyes narrow. Why?

It's most complicated. I don't know that I'm having time to go into it with you.

Meeta hears the slant of the words and darkens. Sister grows distant, and her gaze rests on her reflection in the mirror on the wall. She wears a look of surprise. Maybe at how gaunt she is? How aged she's become?

Sister's body contorts. This pain, Meeta. If not for Ram's death, I would have accepted the letter and the decision, I would have. But something, something has changed…

Meeta's hand involuntarily slips to her purse. She lets out a throaty, disbelieving laugh. It cuts Sister, as intended. I see. You think *your* leaving is somehow like *mine*? From what I know, you escape a place where you float around, serve others, sit and talk to your god, eat enough food, drink enough water, have a place to sleep, and never, *never* experience what it's like to take a man you don't want. You're terrified when a couple of white-dressed women – your *sisters*, you even call them! – pursue you on the street? Will the bearded man stuck to a cross come hunt you down in your disobedience?

Sister says nothing, does nothing.

You know what happens if I run? Adiba's gone, but there's an army of Pinkus out there who, for a few rupees, will chase me down and hand me back over to Ginna, bloodied and raped. And she will beat me. Starve me. Lock me away. My family would do the same. How…how can you put these sufferings side by side with yours?

I suppose I can't, Sister finally whispers.

Meeta feels a new satisfaction. She stands and draws her purse to her.

I…need you, Sister blurts out, her whole affect changed. Don't leave me, please, not yet. I must make two other visits, before the day is done, and I don't…I don't know if I can alone. She holds out a shaking hand, grasping for Meeta and appears just as shocked by the gesture as Meeta is. Ginna is in deep grief, Sister says. Whether you escape tonight or tomorrow, it will make no difference. You all will be free, and I'll help make sure of it. I promise.

Meeta feels something new, an unlikely compassion crawling up the walls of her heart. She sees Sister, her tired soul and fragile form. *Poured out* are the precise words that rattle around Meeta's head. Come, she says to Sister. Eat something to give you strength. And then we go. Two more visits. I can at least do that.

Sister brightens slightly.

But then, no matter what, I leave all this behind, Meeta says.

XVII

I see you looking about, Francis, relieved at the sight of the familiar. That's right: we've returned to Shahjahanabad, the old city, and are nearing the heart of the Muslim quarter where our story with Ram began.

Look, just now: the Likely Pair appears.

Sister told Meeta that the Australian idiot sparked a thought, that an old vendor in the Muslim quarter may have some further information. No problem, Meeta had replied.

So why does Meeta walk five paces ahead of Sister, barrelling through a children's cricket practice and cursing them when they protest?

It is because the second visit has just been disclosed: it is to none other than Constable Singh.

We'll need his help if the first meeting goes as I hope, Sister explained.

He'll know you lied about the deputy commissioner if you go to him.

Sister shrugs. I'll find another way to scare him.

But…

Meeta. I know he has wronged you and done evil and that he is not to be trusted. It's all plain as day to me. Please. Give me your trust.

Meeta rolls her eyes. And what about the fat thief? What if he's on our trail?

He wanted the money that Ram and Manoj took from him, nothing more. He will be satisfied with the case he stole and its contents.

Meeta hugs her purse a little closer. Of course. He'll be satisfied...

They talk little the rest of the way.

Sister turns her gaze. Obscene traffic sees them pause and chart a course among the dented, dilapidated cars. Furious drivers curse and shake their heads and make obscene gestures out of their windows in signs of frustration. Her eyes follow a line of worshippers carrying marigolds and coconuts and ghee who step into a blue-painted *mandir* to make offerings and receive blessings from Krishna. At the same time, the call to prayer erupts all over the city, with an especially loud blast coming from the direction of the enormous domes of the Jama Masjid, Delhi's triumphant mosque. She turns away, repelled.

Owing to the practice of a religion not her own? you ask.

No. Any example of religious devotion is enough to inspire fresh guilt. Though still clothed in her white-and-blue sari, it is only due to habit and the fact she doesn't have a thing to change into. The sari is a mess from car exhaust, scuffed knees, and prodigious sweat stains. She would have to borrow something soon, likely from Ginna. It would be the first time in decades not wearing a nun's dress.

She had tried to buffer thoughts of what comes next, but she finds them breaking through her defences. TOMORROW looms large. Where will she go? There are distant family members Sister could impose upon for a bit of financial support. Her parents' old bungalow is, remarkably, in her name, passed to her in the absence of a will, and she has never gone to the trouble of disposing of it even though title to personal property is not allowed by the MCs. There are likely tenants to be dealt with. She skips a breath, fearing the reactions of distant nephews and nieces if she were to attempt to claim the old home and displace them. 'This is what a Hindu who leaves Hinduism looks like', they would say to her, sneers on their faces.

She can scarcely imagine what shape life will take after the MCs. To have so many hours of the day available to oneself, to do what one pleases, when one pleases, as one pleases. Will she still serve others? Remain in the poverty to which she is accustomed? Or cast it all off? Will she be lonely beyond all reckoning? Shrivel away to nothing? She glances at Meeta who still walks ahead, pouting. Like the girl, Sister suspects, she finds herself on the cusp of unknowing, terrified by what it all means.

Back to the here and now. Sister worries that their first intended visit may be a miss if Mr Shah Jee is truly the business owner he purported to be.

As they take another elbow-turn, Sister is reassured to see his Mercedes parked in the middle of the lane, making all passers-by and motorcycles and goats move to one side or the other. This is our place, Sister says. Meeta assesses the street with her arms crossed.

As she walks past, Sister looks in the tea shop, searching for the small boy who had brought her chai and a cryptic message. The shop bustles and the chaiwallah doesn't notice her, at least not at first. He avoids her stare.

A few feet off from the antique shop, Sister pauses and exhales, looking skyward.

Anxious? Meeta asks.

Sister turns her head. Accusations are difficult things to make.

Meeta wonders at this. What shall I do? Wait outside? Keep watch?

A new thought dawns on Sister. Look...upset, she commands Meeta. Yes. Gruff. Sister pulls at strands of the girl's hair to make her seem unkempt. You shall be a dissatisfied customer. I will do all the talking. Remember the love letter? The one we found written to Manoj? You are the woman who wrote it. She is your part to play.

Be an angry lover? Not a problem, Meeta says glumly.

Good girl. Follow my lead, Sister says, giving a wink. And she steps forward, her jaw set and fists clenched at her sides.

Mr Shah Jee, seated, has no chance to speak before Sister opens up with a barrage:

You lied to me about your business relationship with Ram Kumar and sent me on a fool's errand across all of Delhi because of some story you concocted about him being a 'delivery boy', but I know better now that your 'antiquities' are just a front and whether you have 'software' this or 'pharmaceutical' that, I don't even care, because what I do know is that you're moving drugs about this city – and I even have one of your customers to prove it…

She snaps at Meeta; a signal. Meeta gives a stern-faced nod.

…and if you don't tell me what I want to know this very minute, I will share all with my police contacts, including the deputy commissioner of police who is a close personal friend, and would like nothing better than to lock up a drug trafficker, and all I want and need is one address, one simple address to find Manoj, who killed my Ram, and your problems with me and us will disappear and we will never see each other again.

Whew!

Mr Shah Jee is stunned first, then saddened.

Namaskar, Sister Shanti. Good to see you again, Mr Shah Jee says, coolly. Have a seat.

Sister sits, crossing her arms. Another chair for the young lady? Mr Shah Jee asks.

My name is Meeta. And I'll stand, thank you.

All three look at each other for nearly a minute while Mr Shah Jee reflects.

I don't like being bossed about, he says.

Sister grimaces. Another man died because of this foolish misdirection of yours! Today! This very afternoon! I consider you having a hand in his death. If you had not been dishonest, I might have found Manoj sooner and prevented this mess.

Nonsense, that is. I—

Sister protests.

He holds up a hand to silence her. It's you driving after all this, stirring up trouble, feeding beef to Hindus. None of this would have happened without you! So blame yourself.

Meeta looks at Sister. She is quiet. Introspective. Her eyes are fixed on the floor. It is not Adiba she thinks of, Meeta realizes. Sister is tracing lines of causation with Ram further back. What mistake of Sister's might have set Ram on the path he travelled?

I see this is about something else, Mr Shah Jee says. You feel I corrupted Ram. I did nothing of the sort. The boy was already defective when he arrived. There was no manipulation here, no temptation. Delhi is a hard city. And India is a hard country. We're trying to find ways to escape its difficulties, and my 'antiquities' – it takes Meeta a moment to realize he means drugs – help my customers. Of course I don't touch what I sell; drugs are having no place in my home, but I don't blame those who resort to them!

There is no disagreement from Meeta or Sister on the difficulty of life in Delhi.

Mr Shah Jee mutters under his breath, shifts in his wicker seat. Believe at least one thing I told you about Ram: I liked the boy and I'm sad to hear he's gone. I liked Manoj, too. But Ram and he left my employ a while ago. Manoj has not made deliveries for me for some time. He was delving into some other trade, something more lucrative, more dangerous. He wanted out. I let him go.

You seem very reasonable, Sister says, under her breath, almost regretfully. She had been ready for a fight which Mr Shah Jee declined.

He shrugs. We all want villains to hate. I cannot excuse myself, nor take full responsibility. Each of us is a ball – he looks up and into the open air, as if seeing the image he describes – plinking off one another. None of us knows where we'll fall.

Help us then, Meeta says.

Who are you again?

Meeta sees no reason to lie. I was with Ram. His fiancée.

Mr Shah Jee nods. And how would I help you?

Meeta pauses, open-mouthed. She doesn't know. Sister takes her cue.

When I searched Ram's flat, the one he shared with Manoj, letters turned up. For Manoj. In English; florid language. Written in a convent-school hand. I've been asking myself, 'Who could this boy have known who could write such a thing'? It was Mr Bogan who helped put the pieces together.

Rolling his eyes, Mr Shah Jee blurts, That *idiot*…

Yes. 'That idiot' made me realize your part in this. Customers contact you discreetly, your errand boys buy and sell in your name. We *just* missed Manoj as he was buying from Mr Bogan. But for whom? Not for himself. It dawned on me – the woman who wrote that letter. A lover, though I have my suspicions about the nature of their relationship. I need to find her.

Meeta's mouth gapes. She saw none of these connections – not one!

Sister continues. As you said, this 'antiquities' trade is your side business. You know who your customers are. And a businessman such as yourself will keep records.

Mr Shah Jee smiles. You think I would write all of this information down? Make it so easy for the police to clap handcuffs on me?

I'm sure some third-rate copper or tin pitchers are passed around with your drug orders inside. You're not stupid. You have high-end clientele, others who have money like yourself. They're your friends, friends of friends. I arrive at my point: I believe you know exactly who wrote that letter to Manoj. Which woman would carry on with such – *hanky panky* – with a young delivery boy, and who would be willing to help him even if wanted for murder? Your ledger in the corner there would be having her exact address, no?

There are hundreds of customers in there. I don't interact with them at all after initial contact. It's the couriers who meet—

My deal, a one-time offer: give me the address of the author of these letters. We will not disclose the source of the information to anyone. Right, Meeta?

A nod.

He glowers – but reaches for his ledger. You think I'm doing this for you, but be not mistaken. It's for Ram. Even if it's Manoj who did the thing, I'm willing to send him away to prison. He flips open the ledger, lifts his glasses to his face. He sweeps a gnarled index finger over the names inside until it stops.

I tell the boys never to indulge the clients. Many of the buyers are lonely sorts – too much money, too few friends. But these boys are masters of the hustle. Good salesmen. They see opportunities and exploit them. Mr Shah Jee withdraws a pen and a scrap of paper from a small drawer and writes.

Sister takes the scrap and reads: Sharmila G., 25 Falaudi Kalam Marg, Chhattarpur.

I would have thought this would be closer. One of the bungalows in the cantonment or what not. Not out near – are we in Gurgaon?

Not quite. It's a farmhouse.

Sister hands the slip to Meeta to read, forgetting Meeta is illiterate. Meeta nods solemnly for Mr Shah Jee's sake.

One final question. When they left your service, what work did Ram and Manoj take up?

Mr Shah Jee thinks upon his answer. I truly don't know. But I didn't tell you something the last time you were here. I have no reason to hide it anymore. The day Ram died, he came to me. Asked me for protection, told me he was running, hoped I would smooth things over with those he'd wronged.

Sister braces herself on Meeta who braces herself on a decorative spittoon.

I wasn't having it. I said his mess was *his* mess. Not my concern. Sometimes young men need love that feels like discipline and – Mr Shah Jee chokes on his words.

W-who – Sister stutters – did he wrong?

I haven't a clue. I refused to listen. He sighs. His phone vibrates but he lets it ring and ring and ring. I'm sorry another man died today. This work has its unsavoury side. Most unsavoury.

Then *cease* it. Why continue when you have reputable businesses to run?

He cocks his head, eyes squinting, his expression turned patronizing. A reputable business? This is *India*, Sister. Ha!

Sister has no desire to argue. Come, Meeta. We have what we need. God bless you and your family, she says to Mr Shah Jee. As she steps down into the street, she mutters, *but not your trade.*

Look at those two natter, Francis! Not five metres away and they can hardly hold in their excitement at the address in hand: a small victory in a day of defeats. They even walk arm-in-arm for a moment before they remember themselves and the inconsistent rift between them.

We'll wait for tomorrow. My hope is Constable Singh will see the wisdom of aiding us.

Meeta clouds at the mention of Singh. Though she's reluctant to cross him again, she will defer to Sister. There is a tug on her arm from behind. Once turned, she finds no one until she looks down. Before her stands a small, ugly boy with unkempt hair and a strange lip.

I can help you, he says to the pair. Sister, peering around Meeta's side, recognizes him as the tea-stall boy. She leans forward. What's your name, my dear?

Mohsin, he says, timidly. He looks away from Meeta; he's made bashful by her beauty.

Look here, Mohsin. I remember you. A few days ago I saw you.

He nods. Signals for her to bend over. He whispers in her ear.

A secret, is it?

He nods.

And you will tell me?

The boy looks again at Meeta, who tries to contain a smile.

Tongue-tied, I see, Sister says.

He nods again. The boy starts to share, his words coming in a trickle before they gush. Meeta sees Sister's countenance darken until her lips form a fine line. She turns and throws a furious look at the tea shop. Finally, Mohsin finishes his story. Sister rises.

What? Meeta asks.

Take us, Mohsin.

What is it?

But Sister ignores her questioning. She takes the boy's hand and they set off together. Meeta stamps her foot, refusing to follow until she can no longer resist. She takes off in hurried pursuit.

Step to it, Francis!

Today has been long – watch out for that bullock cart! – but we have made great progress – excuse us, Sir; could you move your cow? – and, if I remember correctly, rest for the Likely Pair is not so very far off – how dare you cut off the Pope! These streets are pandemonium! So many close calls close together.

Hardly any of the day's waning light reaches into the crevice of an alley into which Mohsin leads us. At last! We've arrived! It looks like he is stopping in front of...a plank. A large sheet of wood leaning against a wall. I worry this boy may be short a gulab jamun or two. He's signalling to Sister to help him shift the wood, but carefully, as to avoid making a sound. Meeta, still floating in her own world of personal slights and indignities, stands to the side.

I *see*. It is not so much the sheet of wood Mohsin has guided us to, but what lies *behind* it. There is a grate, and they have shifted it just enough to spy inside. A cacophony comes from within, like a horde of locusts, stopping and starting, starting and stopping. Sister gives a restrained sigh. Meeta cannot contain her curiosity. She parts Sister and the boy to see herself. There is one faint light, and the figures inside move like indistinct shadows, hunched over sewing machines.

Meeta is unimpressed. She whispers in Sister's ear: What is it? Just people working, *naah*? Sister looks at her with annoyance, and puts a comforting arm around the boy. Meeta strains to hear what Sister says to him but the noise inside overpowers it. Reaching the limit of her patience, Meeta grabs the boy and pulls him aside.

Tell me what you told her! she snaps.

Sister interposes herself, supreme displeasure rippling on her face. Meeta, you leave him be!

Well, what is it? All of this here and there, and secrets no one tells me!

Sister pulls Meeta to the side while Mohsin gravitates back towards the grate to watch. I'm not sure what to make of it, not just yet, Sister says. But this boy, he doesn't speak so very well, and it's all coming out most confusing. I think he's telling me that Ram…brought him…*here.*

What? From where? Is he confused? Does he mean Manoj?

Sister holds up a hand to dam the torrent of questions.

He says he's from a village called Nadiyami. I asked him where that is. Bihar, he said. He's been in Delhi not so very long. And I think he does know Ram. He listened in to my conversation the other day with Shah Jee. That's when I first saw Mohsin, when he brought us tea. He described seeing Ram again the night he died; he remembered because his favourite programme was on the TV. Three nights ago. Mohsin says he *knows* these people at work inside this room. Some were on the truck with him. And that Ram and a man who looked like him were the drivers and put them in the truck. Ram delivered him personally to the tea shop.

Meeta plunges back into her own memory. She can picture how it went, not from the clarity of the retelling, but because the same remembrances rest within her. Money changing hands. Men with wide smiles and assurances. Quick goodbyes. Confusion for the small girl caught in the middle of it all.

Achcha.

With Meeta rendered speechless, Sister speaks. These people have been tricked and sold. They are like slaves. And Ram and Manoj were not just party to it, but responsible.

The Likely Pair turn to look at the small boy who is lost and alone, perched before the grate and fixated on the shadows of the people trapped just behind.

XVIII

I see you are taken aback, Francis. Not that you are surprised; clergy rarely are by sin made manifest. But maybe you feel shock at the closeness of it? That evil can be so utterly banal, so near the surface of things and yet not be seen?

Can you imagine if Ram had signed a contract with his employers? 'I, Ram Kumar, shall, in exchange for money, but not that much money, take this child from his home/people/culture/family, and deposit said child in a place where his body/mind/soul will be exploited for an indeterminate amount of time, until he shall succumb to injury/death, or escape, and, in the event of the last, will result in his injury/death. If I should steal/lie/deceive/err/dilly-dally, or otherwise fail my employers in any way, I will fear for myself'.

A devil's bargain if there is one.

As for young Mohsin, he fades from our story, pulled back for a time into a numbing life of servitude. No education. No prospects for a future. One of a few billion small tragedies unfolding day in and day out with no one ever standing up and declaring, FULL STOP.

I surprise even myself with this gushing lament. Becoming numb to stories like Mohsin's is the default for me, and I hate it. It's shocking how difficult mustering sympathy can be when one has suffered personally.

Are you hungry?

Let's part ways with our Likely Pair as they grapple with the implications of this new discovery. I can recount what happens next, but I fear, not without ice cream. We rarely get a treat like this in the MC home, so I will indulge as we spiral down the drain into the sewers of this world. Come this way. There's a vendor around the corner who is wrapping up his prayer mat and finishing his obligatory *namaz*. He has hardly had a sale all day. We shall be the hand of God to him.

The Likely Pair, exhausted by the new revelations of Ram's misdeeds but energized by Mr Shah Jee's assistance, push on in search of Constable Singh. There is justice to achieve for Manoj's murder of Ram, but also for the victims of the sordid trade that both perpetuated.

The address Sister holds in her hand corresponds to a farmhouse that is far, relatively speaking, meaning they would arrive at a late hour even if all the stars obeyed the astrologer's command and aligned. She also doubts Constable Singh's willingness to drop everything to come to their aid. No; they wait for the morning.

'Farmhouse', I should explain. To you, Francis, it conjures a pastoral scene from your Argentinean homeland, or maybe a humble, whitewashed frontier home from a cowboy film. Farmhouses in Delhi are nothing of the sort. Decades ago, in what used to be the city's outer edge where agriculture was still common, landowners were allowed to build simple residences to manage farms. Soon the rich saw an opportunity, bought up acreage, and turned the agrarian land into sprawling estates, 7,000 of them by some counts. In the loosest sense that grand mansions are a 'house' and a handful of shrubs and topiaries constitute a 'farm', does the label cover the 'farmhouses' of today.

What flavour of ice cream would God's representative on the earth prefer? Strawberry, is it? Alas, the shake of our poor ice cream wallah's head means no such luck. Chocolate. Aha! My choice too. Here, hand him the coins. I'll give him a bit extra to take home to his family. What's that? Oh yes, I'll interpret. He just said that God would protect you.

Let's stroll back to the main road.

So the Likely Pair will find Constable Singh absent from his police box – '*With You For You Always*' – out on the prowl. G.B., that beast, is waking from its daytime slumber, and its appetite is huge. So many men coming and going, like termites, degrading everything as they sate themselves. As a matter of course, our Singh wields his large thwacking staff with fervour.

Indian Law Enforcement, you are something to behold!

Indian Justice, you are the exception, not the norm!

When justice is actually meted out by our police and courts, how we rejoice! Of course, bribes paid to overturn verdicts on appeal sour our adulation. All while petty thieves and the completely innocent rot in prison because they don't have the money to see their cases advance.

I digress. This cone is melting too quickly.

The Likely Pair *do* find Singh. He is about to thwack a poor rickshaw driver, and that man is grateful for the constable's distraction. They confront Singh, pull him to the side. They reveal the name and general location provided by Mr Shah Jee. Singh is pleased, but demands the address. Sister refuses. She doesn't want him going without them. He shrugs; hearing that it's a farmhouse warms his belly. Even if Manoj is nowhere to be found, he can line his pockets by threatening the rich owner with some made up charges. Singh promises a crack team will join him in making the arrest. Sister knows he'll show up in a Maruti Gypsy crammed with three off-duty policemen and they'll intimidate their way inside with the one gun they share between them.

The Likely Pair will call Singh at 7 a.m. the following morning and reveal the address. They will then confront what they find together.

And that is that.

Your cone is finished. Do you need something else to line your stomach? No?

Considering what's coming, maybe that's for the best.

Meeta and Sister return to No. 201 and try to rest for the night, despite the heavy cloak of despair within.

They will not succeed. Both are haunted by the sight of the motorcycle, the flying monkey, Adiba lying on the pavement, him being loaded into a truck, him disappearing. Besides this, there is the anticipation. Will they catch Manoj? Will this amount to a fruitless step in their investigation? The end of their investigaton? What will Singh do? Can he be trusted? All manner of imagined scenes play out, some ending with success, most ending with disaster.

Sister erects her altar again and tries to pray, but worries crowd out her heaven-aimed words. Meeta, exhausted, eventually falls into fitful sleep after staring at her purse in the corner like it's a time bomb.

You must be tired too, Pope. But there can be no rest for us, not just yet. We must leave these two for now. Our place is back in the belly of G.B.

Here's a chai to boost your strength and fortify your spirit, for our place is with Constable Singh as he winds down his beat and keeps a most unfortunate meeting.

After encountering Sister and Meeta, his mind turned from

his next thwacking target to his son and the TV he will buy him, his wife and the jewellery he will buy her.

What's this? A son? A wife? Like so many of our story's players, Constable Singh is a very real person, with a very real past. He does not float along only to enter and exit our story at whim, or cast a nefarious shadow. He lives in a small, respectable apartment not so far from the Azadpur Metro stop, has a respectable wife, a respectable young son who came late after many years of trying and hoping. His son still loves him because he only sees the uniform and doesn't know much of the man who fills it.

Singh dreams of better things, of promotions, or, better yet, breaking into some new market and cresting the next wave of technological innovation. He's old enough to have seen the last two decades' revolutions and realize his chances at wealth have come and gone, but he pretends otherwise, living in ignorance of the fact he is a middle-aged man sitting in a police box, watching his body slip into lumpiness while his dreams deform like a block of melting ghee.

His abuses of power are a drug that satiates temporarily. When he manipulates one of the countless girls into sex on G.B. or when he extracts a few rupees, his ego inflates and he feels strong, capable, a man of volition. Then he returns home to a wife who knows what he's done without knowing the specifics, and a boy who sees his father as a hero. He can hardly meet his boy's eyes.

And so he drinks, unable to keep up the charade, hoping for that one karmic turn of events that will deliver him from himself. He believes that opportunity may have just been handed to him by a prostitute he lusts after and a funny-looking old nun.

He makes a phone call but the din of the street prevents you and I from eavesdropping. There he goes, on the move again.

Where to?

Who to?

All is soon revealed: to none other than Latika.

You remember her? Meeta's adversary for the affections of our young Ram? Ram was taken by Latika's looks, holding them in higher esteem than Meeta's, but she had an insufferable haughtiness. I won't tell Meeta this, but Ram had initially hoped his flight into a new future was to take place with Latika. He told her his secrets, hoping that confiding would show he trusted her, and win her over. Secrets that Singh himself has learned.

You see, Singh is no fool; merely corrupt! He's acquainted with many of the gangster-types that lay claim to G.B. and its environs, and is wise enough to only extract the margins due him. He expended some genuine effort in seeking out Ram's killer because he perceived it as tied to his rational self-interest. He found Latika. 'Interrogated' her, if you get my meaning. Learned a delightful secret that could give him some leverage to turn this situation to his advantage.

After a brief scuffle with her pimp that ends in (not surprisingly) a thwack, he has Latika in his grip, forces her down the stairs and out onto the street. She struggles, but only enough to register her discontent.

Latika, you may be surprised to learn, had not lied to Meeta. Ram indeed visited her shortly before he died. Worry over some grand problem was eating him up, and Meeta could not be his confidante. To her, he was a hero, a rescuer, Rama to her captive Sita. He had an image to maintain. So he shared what haunted him openly with Latika, about how everything was spiralling out of control.

Constable Singh and Latika wait in an alley that Singh knows to be quiet. You can see the type of place it is as you step over spent syringes and torn *gutka* tobacco sachets gathering dust. Painted on the wall is a public service announcement: CONDOM EK, SURAKSHA ANEK (ONE CONDOM, MANY PROTECTIONS). The residents who live in chawls above close their windows tight to protest what goes on below, and to keep out the distinct odour of evaporated urine.

Singh tries to joke with Latika, goad her for a kiss, but she has a unique power; she is able to make men feel small and weak without uttering a word, and she is using that gift now.

Constable Singh, attempting to take it blithely, blathers on his phone again to round up his fellow officers for tomorrow morning. Latika looks up at the few stars visible through the night haze, cursing Singh, and Ram, for getting her into this.

He's arrived.

Ah, Ravinder! Singh exclaims. He closes his flip phone mid-call and moves to embrace the man.

I see you tremble, Francis. It is precisely who you think it is: the one called Ravinder is none other than our tubby villain, heretofore known only as The Goonda.

Ravinder offers no smile in return. He looks haggard. He has changed clothes, but wears another suit exactly like the one from earlier in the day. Make it quick, he tells Singh.

Of course.

Who's she?

A friend, Constable Singh says. Latika grimaces and – yes, that's quite right – that's her thumb between her teeth, flicked out. I'm sure you can guess what the gesture means, Francis. Singh pinches her cheek and laughs.

Ravinder looks bored. I don't have the money.

You don't? Singh doubts this very much.

All I have are the nun's underwear. They put on a good show, that's all I can say.

Constable Singh rethinks his approach. Well, there's always more money to be found. You seem good at it.

Just tell me what you want, Singh.

I want a partnership. Short-term.

Stop wasting my time.

My friend here has given me some information that concerns you. That concerns your boy in hiding, Manoj.

Ravinder listens.

Singh, emboldened, steps forward. We know about the bodies.

Bodies?

The bodies: 18. Disposed of on the road between here and Lucknow. The press reported, local police have sought the culprits, all without luck. Corpses simply abandoned in a poor farmer's field.

A small tragedy. And?

Your boy Ram liked to visit my friend over here. Liked to divulge all manner of information. He told her things. Ravinder – Constable Singh places his hand on the man – I am going to find Manoj. Tomorrow morning, the nun and the whore will lead me to him.

Oh. What if he's not there?

If he's not there, I and my chums will break heads together until he turns up.

Ravinder reflects. Constable Singh comes close again; Ravinder can smell butter chicken on his breath. Our deal, Singh says. You recover your money. I find Manoj. You tie up your loose ends. I solve 18 – *19* – killings. You are left out of it all.

Interesting.

Ah. Not yet finished. You pay me half of what you take back.

Not possible, Singh. We all have our overseers.

Then you miss out. I'll get my man, and I'll take all of the cash.

You'll make enemies.

I'll be promoted and moved out of this hell hole.

She's the only one who knows about this? Ravinder turns and addresses Latika directly. You've told no one else?

Why would I, *naah*? Only makes more trouble for me. Already I am having to wander around at night with *maaderchods* like you two.

Ravinder gives a half-hearted sideways nod. I see I don't have a choice.

Constable Singh smiles. Excellent. The nun will be calling me to give me the address. I'm going to meet them there tomorrow. They'll surely have the money with them. I can meet you after we have Manoj in—

Constable Singh slumps to the ground. Ravinder has fired a shot. Latika springs up, terror tugging at her features.

I'm sorry. Ravinder fires again, at her. He shoves his gun in his over-stretched waistband and walks over to already-dead Singh to pluck his wallet and take his phone. He sighs, turning it over slowly in his palm and walks back onto the main road, looking both ways before crossing.

XIX

In 1960, in her 21st year, Heera ran away.

Walter's note had urged her to visit a mystery destination over the weekend. She had vacillated about going; she knew this was about far more than an overnight trip. It likely meant committing permanently to one of her three paths: Indian domesticity (a much-travelled road), the Church (mysterious but also mundane), or a relationship with this magnificent American (utterly unpredictable).

Heera, a bit dizzy with excitement, made up her mind.

She convinced her parents she was to travel for the weekend with her friend Anita's family. Her parents said yes. Heera met him at the railway station, and, with a radiant smile, he revealed their destination: Jaipur, a city she had never visited, just several hours from Delhi that brimmed with legendary forts and palaces. She felt peace beyond all understanding as they made themselves comfortable on the train in first-class seats.

That lasted all of five minutes.

She felt judging eyes upon her in the railway car. Guilt set in, and Walter, instead of intuiting it, tried harder to make her crack a smile. This drew more attention. Their conversation remained halting as Heera struggled with her lie, imagining her decision to come as setting concrete, soon to trap her. Walter retreated into himself, possibly dreading the fiasco this weekend might become. She watched Walter staring out the window at wheat fields slipping past, and felt an inordinate amount of love for the man. Suddenly, a sense of surety descended. Damn *all*. She was here. She made this decision. She would own it.

Heera touched his arm. He turned and smiled.

It turned into a day of such beauty and perfection it would haunt her.

They travelled by rickshaw up out of Jaipur to the Red Fort. It was a majestic old thing built into the mountainside, and they rode up the long stone road to the entrance on the back of a bobbing, painted elephant. When around others, she posed as Walter's tour guide, making up absurd historical facts that sent them into fits of laughter. They let their hands brush, and each touch was electric. In a remote corner of the labyrinthine fort, away from all others, they kissed. Repeatedly. There was no getting carried away, no lustful passion, just kind, gentle, respectful kissing.

After a picnic lunch packed in tiffins by Walter's house help, they headed back to the city. They drove past the Jal Mahal, a palace in Man Sagar Lake that appeared to float magically above the calm waters. They wandered around shops famous for their blue pottery, and Walter bought her a small, lidded box, perfect for a ring. 'You might need this someday', he said. She accepted it bashfully. By late afternoon, drunk with love, Walter sprang the greatest surprise of all upon her. Back in Jaipur's centre, they stood before the gates of the remarkable City Palace. It was a grand thing by all accounts, but showed wear in the 13 years since the Rajput kingdom came to an end and the extended royal family fell on hard times.

So unfortunate we can't enter, Heera said, a bit glum.

Let me see what I can do, Walter said, and walked up to the main gate.

He spoke to the guard, but ultimately needed Heera to interpret, ruining the surprise. Walter knew a prince, had become friends with him in Delhi. He and Heera were to meet him and stay here for the night as his guests. Heera could hardly breathe.

The prince, Yashwant, welcomed them with a hearty embrace for Walter and a wink at Heera. As they walked the grounds and Yashwant gave them a tour, Walter took her hand and held it unabashedly. They stared in wonder at the Mubarak Mahal and Chandra Mahal, each new palace inside the walls more captivating than the last. The prince cracked jokes and laughed with them all the way, spouting trivia about the home and his family's eccentricities in his finely cultivated Oxbridge accent.

Not all was perfection. Walter and Yashwant did most of the talking, as Heera felt sheepish in her simple sari and with her Indian-accented English. She perceived more judgemental stares from the palace staff in unguarded moments. Or were these only imagined?

They took a rest and the men enjoyed gin and tonics while they sat in an ornate drawing room. Soon it was time for dinner.

After the meal, for which the prince apologized – 'too simple', he said, followed by a dismissive wave and surly stare (there had been much more drinking on his part) – he urged them to play for him: this was the price for their lodging. 'Pull out all the *s-stops*', was his exact, slurred expression. Heera apologized; she had not brought any music to read from. 'I came prepared', Walter said, retrieving pages and pages of compositions from his suitcase.

The pair traded melodies for a few hours while the prince downed brandies. His look was distant and sublime. The classical stuff gave way to an extended jazz medley by Walter. He sang showtunes and Heera marvelled; she had never heard him sing, and his voice was a lovely instrument all its own. Yashwant proclaimed Walter had 'knocked his socks off'. Despite not wearing any socks, Heera felt it an appropriate sentiment. Her urge to love this man was unlike anything she had felt before.

Yashwant retired in a conspicuous daze, and Walter and Heera were left to climb the grand stairwell and retire to their conjoined bedrooms. Heera unpacked her few things and prepared for bed, touching upon her rosary buried under her nightclothes – she had not realized she'd brought it – and tucked it away again. The sight of it was so jarring in this place of fading opulence. She took it out again, looking at it for a time, and then at the tops of her hands, so tired from their hours of playing. She ran the beads through her fingers and prayers came despite herself. She was breathing heavily, wondering how she would ever fall sleep tonight, tomorrow, or in the months to come.

Deep in thought, a timid knock on the door complicated everything.

I will not go into the particulars. It's not to say they aren't important, or scandalous, or chaste. It's just that I was never told what took place. These were details that only Heera or Walter could reveal.

Here's what I *do* know: the next day, the prince bid them farewell and they boarded the 8 a.m. return train to Delhi. Walter had love in his eyes, had begun talking about their future together with the unrestrained use of the subjunctive. She held his hand all the while, a brazen act, and nodded and nodded and nodded.

When she returned home, her parents asked how her time in Jaipur had passed with Anita's family. 'Lovely', she said with a smile, 'The best'.

She went to her room and penned a short letter before returning to tell her parents an alternate version of the trip.

The next morning, before sunrise, she left that letter on her bed and sneaked out of the house, her small bag packed, ready to begin her aspirancy with the Missionaries of Charity.

*

The hour is early, much like that day decades ago when Sister left her former life behind.

We travel down with the Likely Pair, down an emptied G.B., past Ajmeri Gate, down into the bowels of the Metro station, the same one Meeta ran through with such visions of happiness and joy not a week ago. Buy our tickets (I'll pay for you, Pope). Go through the security line (I can hardly believe the police wanted to look under your cap!). Our train arrives.

The car is full of day labourers from Yamuna Pushta and Nagla Machi, mostly men, but some women too. Meeta and Sister sit together on two seats that a pair of young men kindly vacate. No such courtesy for us this time, I'm afraid. They must have thought the Likely Pair were mother and daughter. Touching.

They sit there quietly for a time. Stations come and go: INA, Green Park, Hauz Khas. Out of nowhere, Meeta asks the question: What if we fail today?

Sister deliberates for a time before answering with words pulled from her past: Anything worth doing is worth failing at. We have done what is asked of us, pursued it to the end. Sister whispers something else to Meeta, and Meeta grunts, a small smirk coming to her face. The train's rumble soon carries Sister off to sleep, but not before she takes Meeta's hand in her own.

Her head slumps against Meeta's shoulder, and Meeta lets it remain as she slips into reverie.

They had left the *kotha* quietly. Just before, Sister had entered Adiba's room to tell Ginna that they would go together to pick up Adiba's ashes later that day. Ginna made Sister promise. 'I will have an announcement once you return', Ginna said. 'Tell the girls, all of them'.

'Most certainly', Sister replied.

Meeta had spent the night adrift. She did hope they'd find Manoj today, but it was not out of loyalty to Ram. She had tried to be forgetful of the facts, but they screamed too loudly. He slept with others. Lied about his home, his past, his work. He was a low-level criminal, dealing in drugs. And what about the small boy with the harelip and his ghastly accusations? For all of her issues with Sister, it is curiosity, and a desire for justice for the victims of Ram and Manoj's work, that saw her rise early and board the Metro, her purse fully packed and in hand. Whatever happened at the farmhouse, she was ready to exit the life she leads for good.

With her head forced to remain looking forward to accommodate Sister, Meeta watches a young family. Each parent holds a small child. All four are asleep. She notices the cracked skin of the father's sandalled feet, the children dressed in clothes with too-long sleeves, and the wife with holes worn in her third-hand *gara* sari. They know every comfortable crook and soft edge to steal just a bit more rest before facing the day. So serene, so gentle they are. It's not very long before the train halts at another station and they rise and exit.

It is almost like a vision was granted her, a glimpse of the hardness of their lives, but then there was also a hope emanating from them. They are *together*; despite all, they have one another. She finds herself praying for them, wherever they might be going, whatever they might be doing, and the prayer simply flows, generously and without hesitation.

Meeta doesn't understand the feelings rising in her as she lifts her arm and places it around Sister. A look of profound worry weighs upon her features. It raises a question: how does Meeta plan to make an exit when such a thing depends on money?

Ah, you're a canny one, Pope. Maybe that *isn't* the question. You've seen the hints.

Ravinder, aka The Goonda, is still in pursuit of the missing money even though he nicked Sister's case. Ergo, the case did not contain the money. Ergo, the money was withdrawn at some earlier time without Sister's knowing. Who had the motive and opportunity?

The problem with Meeta's theft is she has no idea the misery it will bring her. But that's a sad tale, the thread of which we'll pick up later.

More stations: Malviya Nagar, Saket. Little lights on a board flicker out with each stop. The train glides along, delivering them past the great, brick tower of Qutub Minar, so stark against the rolling greenery below. Before long, a voice calls 'Chhattarpur' and Meeta rouses Sister.

We've arrived.

What's this? Sister blinks, adjusts her glasses.

We're here.

So be it. She rubs her eyes, and then takes Meeta's hand again.

Meeta sees how sapped of energy Sister is as they alight. Meeta takes her arm, gives her support. There is a subtle resistance, and somehow Meeta intuits it is not against Meeta's help, but because Sister is being pulled towards what is dangerous and fearful. Can you see what I can see so plainly, Francis? Sister is journeying from Gethsemane to Golgotha: a place of certain reckoning.

Meeta tries to reassure her in whispers. *Manoj may not even be there…Singh will take him away…we don't have to fear for ourselves.*

Sister simply nods, and nods, and nods.

I can see you wish to reach out to Sister, Francis, to bless her, to fortify her with words of hope, a holy kiss, an anointing of oil. You must resist these urges. This must play out as it will. This is the past, after all: fixed, inflexible, immutable.

Here, board this rickshaw just as Sister and Meeta climb into another. We'll arrive within minutes.

The farmhouse's walled gate is a strange sight. The road is mostly vacant, running along a line of enormous compounds owned by rich and sometimes famous individuals. They are all tall walls, well-kept from the outside, perfectly hiding what is behind. But not 25 Falaudi Kalam Marg, the home of Sharmila G. who Mr Shah Jee has led them to. Her gate is marred by flaking paint and its two halves bulge outward from a past collision with a car. Sister takes out Adiba's mobile phone: 6:30 a.m., reads its display.

Do you think Singh will come through? Meeta asks.

Sister dials the officer's number in answer.

We're here, Constable Singh. Meeta looks around a bit as Sister relays the address and hangs up. He says he should be here within the hour, Sister says. He's feeling a bit sick, but he'll be ready.

That's bad for us, Meeta says. We should have called sooner. The sun is already blazing. Nowhere we can wait and get away from it.

This is how I wanted it. It gives us time to talk to Manoj. Assuming he's here and they let us in. I am quite certain they will. I've met the owner.

Meeta is newly hurt by this refusal to disclose. You met the owner?

Sister nods. Ever so briefly. I realized it during my prayers last night.

Meeta stands there, mouth gaping, expecting more explanation. Sister looks about, apparently unwilling to give it. We're partners, Meeta says. You need to tell me such things.

Sister's eyes flash. I only have suspicion and conjecture. No need to bother you if I am proven to be mistaken.

Meeta's temper flares and simmers. She begins pacing as Sister activates an intercom on a nearby pillar. It squawks to life.

Yes? What do you want? grumbles a man's voice.

Sister leans in close. Malhotra sahib, I believe?

The question is met with silence.

The police are on their way this very instant, Sister says. If you have any hope of escaping their visit without being handcuffed, you had better let me talk to Sharmila G.

The man forces a laugh.

I'm Sister Shanti of the Missionaries of Charity and you *will* let us in. We know about your...guest.

The lady is asleep.

Wake her.

I don't know if I can.

Do your best. The sun out here is burning us alive.

The intercom had already been cut.

It takes nearly two minutes. They can hear what sounds like laboured hustling and several commands yelled by Malhotra. A few barks echo in an ill-timed chorus, and Malhotra can be heard inserting keys in locks, sliding iron bars.

I hate dogs, Sister says, maybe to herself, and trembles briefly.

Meeta still stews, considering whether she should take radical action and simply leave Sister behind. As the gates open, she knows this is no option.

Malhotra's turbaned forehead and eyes protrude. Meeta fixates on the impressive bushes of his eyebrows. It's you, he says.

It is. Sister puffs herself up. Take us to your lady. And I would like water for my friend and I.

I told you, she's not well. Especially not this morning.

Sister doesn't acknowledge the remark, simply barges in. She stares at the dogs, grateful they're tied up.

Malhotra gestures. They're gentle. We keep the dogs for their barks alone.

Each German Shepherd rests on its haunches and does an anxious little dance with their front paws, flashing their canines as they pant. They are medium-sized creatures, wear matching red collars, and are glossy and lovely (depending on who you ask). Meeta keeps her distance, hugging her purse. Malhotra's gaze remains fixed upon this newcomer.

Sister looks over the estate as she approaches the main door. Vines crawl over gates and the grass is a yellowed field of weeds. There is a unused swimming pool with all manner of scum extending along its sides. The main house was surely grand in its heyday, but its white had mutated into shades of curdled cream. A small pool house of matching style sits off to the side and looks like a mopey child on time out.

Malhotra intuits Sister's disapproval. ... *Too much work for one person*, he mutters, as he leads the unwelcome guests. The dogs retreat to the pool house's overhang to lie in an ever-narrowing band of shade.

They pass the old Ambassador, the only other thing well-kept besides the dogs. It dawns on Sister: the car's condition is because it is the one thing shown to the outside world.

Malhotra opens the door. It gives a pained creak. Memsahib? he calls. No answer. A ballad, all classical singing and sitar and tablas, wafts from a corner of the house. Meeta takes in the interior – old marble tile chipped in places, grimy hand and paw prints on walls – it saddens her. The home is a fractured dream.

Malhotra tries again. Memsahib? He turns to whisper to the Likely Pair. She is a most-troubled woman, you know, he says behind a cupped hand.

Sister does not.

Mal-hotra! Mal-*hotra*! It is a shrill, cutting voice, how Meeta has always imagined the goddess Kali would sound as she comes to judge. Malhotra shudders.

Sister wastes no time and darts towards the voice. Malhotra tries to restrain her but Meeta steps between them and gives him a look reserved for customers who overstep their bounds.

Sister, inside the doorway, stands in apparent shock.

The room is plunged in darkness owing to thick curtains blocking out daylight. In the centre of the room is a giant TV. Sharmila G. sits entranced in its changing light. She turns. Her jaw drops. What are *you* doing here? Sharmila G. snaps, shouting over the volume.

Turn this racket down! Sister orders. Now!

Sharmila G. is stunned, but fiddles with a remote control. The volume plummets.

We're here for *him*. We've seen *him*. We know you're hiding *him*.

Meeta watches Sharmila G. from across the room. The woman, under a blanket, moves with a certain clumsiness. Some form of illness or inebriation? Maybe under the effect of the drugs Manoj provided her. She still seems distracted by the movements on the screen, an old Bollywood film by the look of things. Meeta watches from the corner of her eye and gasps. The woman dancing and singing in the old film resembles this woman: Sharmila G. is none other than *Sharmila Gulzar*!

Sister goes over to the curtains and lets in the light. Sharmila Gulzar, famed movie actress, screams. You are not answering! Sister declares. You must answer!

Sharmila Gulzar screams again. Malhotra hides his face in his hands. *Not good, not good*, he mutters.

Finally, it is Meeta who speaks into the cacophony. *Mem* Sharmila Gulzar! I didn't recognize you at first.

The invoking of her name is an incantation; Sharmila Gulzar is transformed. No longer the scraggly-haired woman, in nightclothes, transfixed by the past. She is composed. Regal, even.

You are my most favourite star, *naah*! Yes, to be in the presence of the Bengali Rose, what an honour!

Sister is annoyed. Excuse me? What is this you're saying?

Meeta shoots her a look that speaks loudly: shut *up*.

May I approach, Sharmila*ji*? Meeta does anyway, touching the woman's knobby feet. I am your *mostest* biggest fan.

The woman combs her hair with her fingers, sits up straight.

Sister cannot abide this wasting of time. She taps the window frame and looks out the large bay window and out at the grounds. The two dogs appear at play, pawing at one of the pool house doors.

I have wondered what it would be like to be a *star*, Meeta says. To have a life like *yours*. Your dance scene in *Sunset Sunrise*, under the pouring rain – *inspired* me to become a dancer.

The old woman smiles.

Meeta struggles with this woman's reality. They are here because Sharmila Gulzar is likely harbouring Ram's killer, who is her lover and enabler of her drug addiction. Her world seems empty. Meeta continues plying her with compliments and praise.

So was Arjun Mahajan really as handsome in real life?

You know that hair of his? Fake! He started balding by our first picture together. It was all gone by our third! He was a very angry man. Sharmila pauses, staring at her younger self on screen as she belts out a muted song. Malhotra, my breakfast! she cries, suddenly.

Right away, memsahib. Breakfast is coming!

What stories you must have, Meeta says, dreamily.

I've lived well, that's for sure. Look at me! Sharmila Gulzar says, without irony. Just some girl from Calcutta, born to average parents, living a life like this.

Do suitors still call? Sister asks.

Sharmila Gulzar smiles. A few.

Sister steps closer. I remember meeting you not three days ago. Do you remember me?

I meet *so* many fans. It's been a long week with all my engagements.

It was out near Wazirabad Road. On the way to the electric ghats. What were you doing there?

Sharmila shrugs. Passing through.

Malhotra enters with a tray of Western food – toast, pork sausage, a hard-boiled egg standing in a cup – and places it on the woman's lap. All conversation stops. Despite the room's air conditioning, he is sweating profusely. Bon appétit, he says, in the continental manner, before scurrying off.

Do you happen to know a young man named Ram?

Sharmila Gulzar cracks the egg shell with her spoon.

What about a Manoj?

I've known many. She nibbles her toast.

Is there a Manoj here?

Of course not. A sip of chai.

Meeta and Sister agree with each other silently: her answers about Manoj ring with truth. Meeta rises and stands next to Sister, facing away from the woman and out the window. They witness Malhotra go out to the pool house, slip into the door the dogs were pawing at.

There isn't time for this, Sister mutters to Meeta. Meeta nods.

Malhotra exits the building and ties the dogs away from the pool house. He starts the Ambassador.

Leave it to me, Meeta says.

Would you excuse me, memsahib? Sister asks. I need to step out into the hall. Pressing business.

The woman gives her a regal wave.

Sharmilaji, Meeta says, turning around. I am *so* worried for you. The police are coming. They will disrupt your life. I can *see* the newspaper headlines. *Hear* the TV people. All of the *horrible* things to be said about you. Your *legacy* will be forever tainted.

The woman sits still, her fork raised to her mouth. What do you mean? she finally says.

You have a drug problem. Many do. No shame there. But the police will use this to take advantage of you. Only we can help. You have Manoj here. Ah – no need to protest! We know it. You know it. Tell us where he is. We can get rid of him before these bad, *very* bad police arrive.

The woman falls into histrionics. Throwing her tray to the floor, tears leap from her eyes. Get out! Get *out*! You destroyer! You're just another one of my enemies!

Meeta looks over her shoulder. Malhotra is distracted, fussing with something in the car's boot. Sister is creeping towards the pool house door. Despite her efforts to shush them, the dogs begin barking. Malhotra, looking up, sees her and begins to flail his arms madly as he rushes to intercept her.

That's all Meeta can handle. You're *mad*! she shouts over her shoulder to Sharmila as she runs to Sister's aid.

Out the living room, out the front door, into the sun, she runs with abandon. She sees Sister throw open the doorway but has her gaze fixed on Malhotra. He aims all manner of Punjabi curses at Sister. Meeta aims herself at Malhotra until – CONTACT! – she gives him a sharp shoulder and they both go tumbling to the ground. Adrenaline forces Meeta back up. She sees Sister stepping forward into the pool house's dark with her hand held to her mouth.

Shanti, she calls, Shanti! Be careful! Be care—

Meeta finds Sister on the ground, cradling a young man.

A young man without a scar.

A young man who is not Manoj.

A young man who is Ram.

XX

How?

You ask along with Meeta, Francis.

Ram doesn't look well, not at all. Sister releases him from her hold, but her glasses have fallen and she holds her hands to her wet eyes, embarrassed, but not embarrassed. Meeta, stunned, chokes out her question.

I see you struggling with this reversal, too, Francis. All of this coming and going, hither, thither, it seems you were mistaken all along.

Indeed: Ram is alive. Manoj is dead.

Do you feel cheated? That I've disguised the truth from you for the story's sake? Well, you're not wrong. But you must remember that this is as it happened. Meeta had not the slightest idea, and Sister only realized its incredible possibility late last night.

Ah. That's right. She suspected, and yet said nothing.

What made Sister see the possibility when none other could?

Remember, the two looked as brothers. There was the body on the tracks, you say. The face was crushed. Both Manoj and Ram were taken to wearing suits of late. In the scuffling at the station, Ram's suitcoat was left with the body, his ID left inside.

The love letter, found in the chawl and what we believed was intended for Manoj, was actually for Ram. He'd been trying to leave Sharmila behind but she kept on with her obsessive letters. But, with nowhere else to run a day after the incident at the railway station, he came to her. She took him in, despite Malhotra's protestations, on the condition he still supplied her with drugs even if his injuries prevented him from servicing her 'other' needs.

But didn't Manoj flee Bogan's hotel room? Wrong! Expectation and the hurried speed of things played with the mind and its perceptions. Mr Bogan's confused, drug-addled brain was unable to set things straight.

Sister's encounter with Sharmila Gulzar near the funeral ghat was the key that opened the lock. Sharmila Gulzar was there that day for Ram, not for Manoj. Sister realized the letters and calendar could have been Ram's. Sharmila Gulzar must have been shocked when Ram resurfaced, having believed him to be dead.

All of the facts accumulated until they were too much, and the story Sister wanted to believe about Manoj was put into question. These details explain the mix-up, but leave a hundred other questions unanswered about Ram. Just like you, Meeta is ready to demand answers.

Where was the money from?

Who is The Goonda?

Why did Ram bring the little boy and the others to Delhi to work?

And most importantly to Meeta, why did he feed her endless lies?

Ram sighs, unable or unwilling to speak, until he does. With tears trickling down his sunken cheeks, Ram confesses.

Allow me to summarize what became a lengthy telling.

Ram cannot recall his mother. His mother could not recall his father. The man was one of many men to come in for a late night tumble at her Bara Tooti apartment. Ram was her first child, and despite repeated efforts to put a full stop to the pregnancy, Ram came. She left.

This sad episode was relayed to him by the American couple who ran the evangelical orphanage he was turned over to. That strange, strange environment saw him through his principal years and turned him into a crafty little boy. There was eventually a scandal within; the headman liked to do terrible things to the boys, and one day, the police arrested him and kicked the children out, padlocking the doors. Ram was 5.

Becoming an urchin was remarkably easy. The streets, with all their awesome harshness, were a sea in which he easily swam. He was fast, quick-witted, and knew how to play on the sympathies of others. Even though lying came easily, he was capable of sincerity and deployed it well.

And so we turn our narrative gaze upon Manoj. This boy did have parents; he just didn't care for them, their chores, their shouting, or their beatings. One day his father slashed his face with a broken bottle, scarring that would grow with him the rest of his days. Ram, already proficient in the ways of survival on the streets, came upon Manoj in a state of tears early in Ram's own runaway stage. Ram gave him some of his half-eaten paneer and that was that: the relationship status was cemented – BEST OF FRIENDS.

They grew in other ways. They inhabited a predominantly Muslim quarter for a time and were often teased about their Hinduism (all the usual, unoriginal insults: about their misdeeds in prior lives, the red bindi forehead dots of women, eating beef, etc.). They gave back to the Muslims (all the usual, unoriginal insults: about pig genitalia, suicide bombers, blasphemies about the Prophet, etc.). After a close call nearly instigating a major internecine conflict, they considered themselves fortunate when the Municipal Corporation of Delhi decided that to demolish their entire jhuggi colony of 50,000 shacks in Yamuna Pushta was a good idea.

They remained inseparable, until they were separated. Manoj thought Ram was buried, crushed under a bulldozer in the demolition. This was a great sadness, and with nowhere to go, he took up with a band of other children who lost their homes in the clearances. Ram, not dead, but only off taking a leak, came back to find Manoj gone. He too feared his friend was dead. Off they went into new lives, crestfallen, until Fate threw them together again. It was in this intervening period that Sister first met Ram.

I've been careful to present Ram's and Sister's relationship at turns. We have already seen some of the random points of connection and meaning that knitted their hearts together. Ram, despite Sister's efforts, went from one entanglement to another.

There was his employment as a scrawny child beggar until his lack of a handicap put him at a disadvantage; his time as a waste-picker, his snot perpetually blackened by burning trash, his stomach perpetually empty; the old, one-eyed con artist who taught him much; the drunk-as-much-as-sober *mazdoor* who used him to mortar high walls; a stint as an errand boy before he purposefully-accidentally burnt the owner's illegal liquor stall down. There were recurring periods of short-term reform, but they gave way to bouts of mischief: glue-snuffing highs and lows; thievery both petty and significant; surreptitious shit spraying on pedestrian shoes to drum up customers for his shoeshining business; and assorted property damage.

All this before a single hair sprouted on his chin.

Sister never cared to know the details of the harms he caused whenever he showed up in need of a good meal and a change of clothes. She never stopped loving the boy, even though the only constant of his love was that it was inconstant.

The day he was reunited with Manoj changed everything. They were both free-riding on the newly opened Delhi Metro Red Line. He stepped into the car while Manoj stepped out. They embraced and rode the train back and forth between its stops for hours. Their meeting, they believed, was fate, pure and simple. Oh, the new scams made possible with the most trusted of partners along for the ride!

They passed themselves off as twin brothers who had lost their parents in religious riots. They lived a whole year off a benevolent widow on that story alone! Going to the cinemas. Eating in classy restaurants. Smoking bidis. Imbibing the local *tharra* booze until the vomit flowed. The good life! It came to a crashing halt when the widow overheard them making fun of her weight – but what a year!

Then came the brothels. They were itching to get through those doors and get a taste of what every movie and conversation and thought of their pubescent years told them would fulfil them, make them whole, make them *men*. The specifics of their first encounters needn't be mentioned: they were too young, the women too old, and the effects long-lasting and itchy.

174

They lived miserably again before they lived well, and soon Ram's story winds and twists into a familiar shape.

Ram continued to tell Sister and Meeta of employment with Shah Jee, and they told him they already knew.

Ram told them of Bogan, and they told him they already knew.

Ram told them of Sharmila Gulzar, and they told him they already knew.

And so we arrive at the tale of the tea boy with the harelip.

Ram and Manoj reached new heights of success serving as drug couriers, and, in Ram's case, a plaything for a deranged, self-absorbed, retired actress. But these two were entrepreneurs of the highest calibre, and satisfaction remained fleeting as long as they knew they were getting older and larger, ill-gotten gains remained just out of reach. They needed something to be touched, caressed, and poked.

They needed *capital*.

It was a stocky Punjabi man with an impressive moustache who changed everything. Manoj made the initial connection. Ravinder was part of a very lucrative trade and needed responsible part-time employees to facilitate the transportation of his highly price-elastic product sourced from rural India for consumption in the national capital. If they agreed, they were to be the essential links in a secretive supply chain, participating in one of the most dynamic and enduring institutions in world history. Returns *guaranteed*.

That product, as we well know, was people.

Manoj and Ram were enthralled. When asked if they had any issue with this line of work, of *course* they felt no obligation to their fellow human beings! They had been shat on by the world their entire lives. This work was low-hanging fruit that could be picked and processed and transformed into *lakhs* of rupees, catapulting them from subsistence, past mild comfort and security, and land them in the realm of *indulgence*. The thought of all those disembodied Gandhis staring back at them from rupee notes enthralled.

I shall list their duties:

1. Visit places of dubious employ around Delhi. These include

sweatshops, brothels, brick kilns, etc.

2. Make an offer.

3. Collect payment. Owner of business pays, in advance, for the delivery of human beings to his firm.

4. Source the product. Work with local buyers to procure choice stock.

5. Make delivery. Return to Delhi with a truckload of tricked people to be turned over to buyers.

If you asked Ram back then, what they did wasn't as base as *slavery*; nothing so dirty! This was merely *bonded labour*, a practice as old as Vishnu himself. They went to rural communities and found peasants made desperate by their circumstances: land wasting away under the brutal sun, a parched monsoon season, shrinking parcels of property sold off to buy food and pay for prayers by Brahmin pandits. These suffering farmers, these *kisans*, would get a free (to be paid back) ticket to the city and guaranteed (forced) work with an (un)liveable wage and a (leaky) roof over their heads and (maggot-infested) food in their stomachs. In exchange, they would become indebted to the owner of the establishment. Their entire family would work off the debt and eventually be free to own their labour again. This was nothing but reasonable!

That was the sales pitch. Many desperate peasants accepted. *Very* many.

They found particular success. Ram and Manoj were preparing to move out of the chawl and into a middle-class apartment in NOIDA. They were buying nice clothes, watches, chains, rings, phones. They got expensive, movie-star inspired haircuts. They looked like the success they desired. All along, despite the fact they knew they were peddling lies, material comforts abounded. Ram started going to more expensive prostitutes until his life-altering encounter with Meeta. He fell in love with her, truly, and built their relationship with the only bricks and mortar he had at his disposal: lies and half-truths.

No censure came from the spiritual realm. Nominal Hindus, their religious worldview was confused: a hodgepodge of karmic belief tied to Mohammedan appreciation of a monotheistic god with a vague notion that a pink, bearded *firangi* guru once said it was better to do nice things to a neighbour rather than rob him at knifepoint. Their unscrupulous consciences were their guides, with the exception of Sister Shanti's occasional encounters with Ram.

And so we come to the fateful turn of events on which our story has hinged.

Normally the pair would collect the money from business owners and turn it over to Ravinder as soon as possible. This day, a kiln owner named Dharmatma demanded new labour for an imminent deadline. The pair was to drive all night to lawless Uttar Pradesh so that they could get new workers to the outskirts of Delhi by the next afternoon. It was a difficult deadline, but there were two of them and they could take turns driving the lorry and sleeping. They acquired knives in the event of encounters with thieving dacoits. They had to hide and carry the money since Ravinder was vacationing with his family. The thought of stealing the money had once crossed their minds – and that was as far as it went. Ravinder had made it clear during their corporate orientation that the consequences of theft would be severe, referring them to pictures he had on his phone of a bloated, beheaded body floating in the Yamuna river. They took this to heart.

Everything with their U.P. trip was going according to plan. They drove through the night, singing along to the *Sholay* soundtrack as two young men obsessed with the classic film would do, picturing themselves as the rogues Jai and Veeru. It took most of the day to complete the recruitment. The kiln owner was making large demands, so they packed people tightly into the truck's enclosed cargo space. Ram and Manoj magnanimously bought their cargo bottles of water with money from their own pockets and committed to frequent, periodic stops to unlock the sliding back door and allow the passengers riding behind to breathe fresh air. Though the drivers' eyelids sagged, and the sun was setting, they continued on to Delhi.

About halfway Ram parked the truck for what was to be only a few minutes' time. Manoj was already in slumber. It was hours before Ram woke. This mistake changed everything.

In terror, they rushed to throw open the truck's back door. Though the passengers had pounded, screamed, and cried, all 18 had suffocated to death.

Ram and Manoj cursed each other, God, gods, and everything in between. They knew not what to do. They unloaded the bodies in a field under the early morning sky, got back in their truck, and drove off.

Disagreement formed a wedge between them. Manoj said they should own up, tell Ravinder what happened, and refund the money. It was a disaster, likely the end of their work, but they'd hopefully avoid ending up dead themselves. Manoj, growing more loony by the minute, then suggested turning around to try to load up the truck again with people from another village.

Ram refused. The young man went to a curious place in those hours of shocked and angry silence driving back to Delhi. Profound guilt took hold, and it stripped the veil from all of the lies he told about himself and this work. He told Manoj he would take responsibility and return the money to Ravinder. He would accept the consequences. In that moment, he was willing to become the floating, beheaded corpse in the Yamuna.

This soon changed.

When he got back to Delhi, he ran to G.B., not to Meeta, but to Latika. He became so drunk and so high and so sexed up, he hoped to escape any semblance of conscious thought. But of course the guilt remained with him through the night, and he couldn't help but spill the details to Latika.

In a haze the morning after, he wandered the city with all of Ravinder's money on his person. He was ashamed, and scared, and wondered if he could face Meeta again. He wouldn't answer Manoj's calls and SMSs. A last-ditch effort was to go to Shah Jee to ask him whether he could talk to Ravinder and broker some deal to protect Ram. The old man turned Ram down and advised him to flee while he had the chance. Ram, always the planner, already had two tickets to Bangalore in his suit-coat pocket.

And so the plan went into effect. He would run away with the money and with Meeta by his side, hoping to make a clean break from everything he knew and set up a new, forgetful future.

But the money weighed on him like a thousand bricks. He thought of what he could do with the toxic stuff. No prospect of spending it on himself could assuage the guilt. Finally, he thought of Sister Shanti, her enduring kindness to him, and the Missionaries of Charity.

And so he gave it away.

Manoj, Ram's best friend and the ManInSuit, knew where to find him, knew what his disappearance would mean not just for Ram but for himself. Manoj needed that money to return to Ravinder or he'd be dead, too, and it was this fear and Ram's selfishness that prepared Manoj to do what was necessary. When Ram saw Manoj on G.B. Road, all his emotions flared. Ram's flight was a final turning away, a repudiation of his fraternal relationship.

And then they fought on the platform as the train approached. Ram, through gritted teeth, implored Manoj to run too, to join him and Meeta, to forget their mistakes, but it was uttered too late, without time to pause and reflect.

It is difficult for Ram to describe what happened next. He claims Manoj's fall onto the tracks was an accident. Ram was stabbed by Manoj in their scuffling and tried to flee instead of fight. Manoj clasped his coat and tugged, but this was his undoing. The coat slipped off Ram easily, making Manoj loose his balance, and then his footing. Though the train approached slowly and Manoj should have been able to remove himself from the tracks, he had banged his head in the fall. And so Ram watched in horror until he could watch no longer. Then he ran.

To the chawl for some extra money. To the hospital for stitches. To Sharmila Gulzar, who was relieved he was still alive after her visit to the ghat and was willing to provide him safe harbour. Despite his injury she despatched him to get her drugs from Mr Bogan. When Sister and Meeta broke in, it was shame that sent him fleeing once again.

Finally, reaching the end of his confession, he cast himself at the mercy of his surrogate mother and betrayed lover, hoping against hope they could provide an exit from his self-imposed prison.

XXI

Meeta can listen no more. She doubles over, grasps her body, looks as if she will vomit.

I loved – love – you, my flower, my rose, Ram says.

Liar, she chokes out.

I am a liar, but Meeta, you're my light! I chose to run with you. The thought of being with you kept—

You...you think I could want you? I can't...can't even *look* at you! And you – she turns to Sister – coddling him! Don't you care what he's done? Who he has hurt?

Sister tries to speak but cannot.

He killed 18 people. *19! Manoj!* She looks at him with such anger – You know my suffering in that *kotha*. And yet you took children, just like me, and offered us up to be eaten by...by *monsters*. I wish it was you on those tracks!

Ram, staring distantly, looks like he has left his body.

He knows what he's done, Sister says. He understands.

Meeta cringes. How can you even touch him, *naah*? I thought I wanted your love. I see you going all around, sprinkling it, lavishing it. I wanted a taste of it, but – you wouldn't! Couldn't give it to me! You refused me. Why? *Why?*

I was...angry. With you! As each new truth about this boy came to light, I could only blame you!

Meeta lets out a cry.

Please, Sister says. I was wrong! I'm sorry, so sorry. It's only that now, something lost is found. I know the whole lot of this one's sins. I can see them all before me in a heap, but, I can't help it! I still see the boy. I see the boy!

Meeta's colour fades. I can't believe I wanted a thing from you. You're a bitch, a monster, a...

Oh God. Sister clasps her mouth. The realization arrives. The police are coming!

(Or so Sister and Meeta believe. But we know better, don't we, Francis?)

Let them take him! Meeta shouts. We blamed everything on Manoj and wanted to see him pay for it, that this worm has done. He's guilty!

Sister and Ram are QuietDowncastAfraid.

I know. But we all are guilty, Sister says oh-so-quietly. And you, Meeta? What have you done? What money would we find if we turned your bag inside out, even now?

Meeta's eyes widen. N-not true!

Sister speaks softly. I am too tired of lies. She kisses Ram's head. Please, just help me get him out of here before they arrive.

Meeta throws her hands up in the air, experiencing a multitude of competing emotions until her revulsion wins out. She bolts out from the door, pushing Malhotra over from where he listens in, and sprints across the lawn to the front gate, her mind filled with swells of memories and images: dead animals and broken treasures and bloodied limbs and a sad little girl being shipped off alone to a city where she knows no one. She cradles her bag and the bundled money she has indeed stolen as if it's her own precious child.

She is resolute: within hours, she will leave this life and its broken loves behind for good.

I hate to linger here, Francis. I hate watching her walk that empty road with her so overwhelmed and immature to realize that not all can be sorted out, nor need it be.

But I am glad for what she is to be spared.

For coming down that road from the opposite direction is a lorry with a truck full of men who have clubs in their hands.

The vehicle comes to a stop before the gate; the men get down; they enter. At the wheel is Ravinder, watching as they go.

XXII

Doesn't it prick you? While you sit in the Vatican, or travel the world, that HundredsThousandsMillions are trapped in lives where freedom is fiction? In every city you visit, hidden children, women, men live lives written by others.

It's ever so complicated. And yet we're slaves, you and I, aren't we, Francis? To three masters who author our fates: Father, Spirit, and Son. Sometimes religion doesn't feel so different from living under a brutal taskmaster. When faith calls you to pick up your cross and bear it, to share in Jesus's pain and misery even unto death, it is a wonder through the ages all haven't fled the Church.

Why haven't *we*? Because we're also told by Christ that his 'yoke is easy' and 'his burden light', that we journey together as equals in our labour. We are as slaves, but we know we are not. And so we remain in the pews and on our knees and in our vestments, because we feel God in the circumstances. Mercy. Consolation. Deliverance. Old made new. Cosmic wrong righted.

At least sometimes.

I don't mean to scare you off with blaspheming, and you didn't come to this story to wade into theodicy. We're in too deep, anyway. I can see your foot tapping, your fixed gaze set on me, your open, questioning hands: What of Meeta and Sister and Ram and all the others?

You shall have your answers.

First, let's have a drink.

Step past the obsequious, colonially-garbed doorman – *what* a moustache! *what* a turban! *what* a sword! – and into the low lights of the marble-colonnaded lounge we go.

I know, I know, it seems an odd time to seek out a stiff drink or two.

It's not.

Bartender! Two whiskeys, Johnnie Walker Black! I hope you don't mind my ordering for you. I don't imbibe often – usually only a taste of wine during Holy Communion. But between you and me, this is one of the things I miss most from pre-covenanted life.

Here we are! *Haan*, kind sir. Francis, let's take a seat. Pay attention to what goes on around us as we sip, sip away.

The lounge, and this lavish hotel, are mostly empty. Notice the woman sitting at the bar. Her face is painted, her shoes' heels are high. She wears an elegant crème dress with red sensuous splotches, and though the shapes have no particular form, she is a walking ink blot test: see what you desire. An empty martini glass sits before her, and she taps the bar in time with the thumping music, the type common to all luxury hotels aspiring to bland, international standards that appeal to their bland, international guests. She glances at her watch, an Omega, a gift from one of her 'friends'. The alcohol runs its numbing course as her skin prickles into tiny bumps owing to the room's enforced cool.

An older man enters. She breathes deeply, sits up straight, glances his way, but doesn't permit her eyes to linger. Ah, yes, he has seen her, and yes, he is walking towards her.

He is familiar with the script.

She is familiar with the script.

He offers a salutation in English. She responds.

He buys her a fresh drink. She obliges by running her toe along his leg.

He smiles. She smiles back.

They commence with the small talk you might expect. His voice is delightfully full of money. Why is he here? Business. Why is she here? Stood up by a friend.

He plays his part with the lax enthusiasm this production requires, but she goes beyond the bare minimum. Laughs at his jokes. Compliments him. Unsees the wedding ring on his finger. He knows her affect is put on, but doesn't care. He leans forward and whispers something obscene. She guffaws. The bartender brings both their drinks wearing a thinly veiled look of distaste.

Before long they arrive at their most difficult scene, the one that most strains the suspension of disbelief:

He whispers in her ear.

She whispers back.

She places her tongue suggestively in cheek. Raises her eyebrows. Pouts her lips.

He runs his finger along her bare wrist. Too much, he says.

Worth it, she says in a husky whisper.

They both laugh. Having downed his drink, he orders another.

The lobby door opens; her eyes flit; she is distracted: a girl like her always looks to get a higher price.

He is young. In a split-second she registers his overlong sleeves, his cracked shoes, his lack of money. A poor alternative to this tubby business traveller. She tries to fix her attention on her mark, but in glancing she has made a mistake: she has looked at the newcomer's face and recognized him.

He is Pinku.

She has not seen him in seven months; not since Ram and Sister and their disaster.

She tries to hide but he has seen her. He makes a grand wave but Meeta pretends to ignore him. Mr Tubby prattles on, unaware of Meeta's divided attentions, until Pinku is suddenly at her side.

She wants to shout at him, Get out of here! Don't you see what I'm doing! but he lingers. Finally, Mr Tubby notices. He is not amused.

What is it you are wanting, yaar?

This one here.

She's taken.

I need to talk to her. Pinku turns. I need to talk to you.

I'm taken, she says.

I don't care what you are, Pinku says.

Get out of here, says Mr Tubby.

You don't want her. Contaminated goods. Dip your beak in her for a moment of pleasure and it'll burn the rest of your days. I can guarantee it. He points to his own member, feigns displeasure.

Meeta slaps Pinku, and he smiles. Come with me, Meeta. I've been looking for you for an age and a day. I promise this *chootiya* doesn't have a thing to say that can match what I have to tell you.

Mr Tubby scoops up his suit-jacket, slams some rupees on the bar, heads for the door.

Meeta kicks Pinku's shins repeatedly while cursing, in order, him, his whore of a mother, his fat aunties, his impotent father.

184

You know what you cost me, *naah*? He was big time!

Nice to see you, Pinku says, smiling gleefully. He pockets the money on the bar and drinks the dregs of Mr Tubby's whisky. *Mmm*. Johnnie Walker Black Label. Nice, he remarks. He takes her hand and she pulls it away.

Meeta, Meeta, *Meeta*. He looks her in the eye. He has tears of happiness welling in his eyes. She is touched, if only for a moment. Sister Shanti needs us, he says. Come along.

And off he goes.

Meeta watches him, refusing to rise and leave her perch until at last she gathers her things and rushes after, as fast as her heels will allow.

Appearances, as always, are deceiving.

Meeta has the look of a sophisticate: calm, cool, collected, moneyed.

She is none of these things.

The cash she secreted away has been spent. Foolishly expensive dresses, glamourous restaurants, high-end cosmetics, luxury hotel rooms. It is no surprise. She is a teenager, infatuated with the times and their dizzying consumerism. The only reason she is not already on the street is the money of a middle-aged man from Mumbai who keeps her as a mistress on the side and pays for a modest flat and gives an even more modest allowance. Whenever they are together they fight. She does not expect to remain his mistress for long. She spends most of the days watching American action films on satellite TV and eating ice cream.

Though she doesn't realize it, this girl is as trapped as she's always been.

Pinku! Pinku! Wait up!

He turns, his cartoon-character smile running from ear to ear.

You've seen her? she asks. Shanti?

He shakes his head. Come with me.

No. *No.* Give me answers, this minute, where we stand.

Pinku surveys the hotel lobby with its chic silver Ganesh statue, elaborate mosaics, and cascading water over soothing tiles. Ask away.

How did you find me? Why are you here?

I have a new job. Off G.B.

I don't care about that.

I was approached by an organization. An NGO. *International.* They work on G.B. and all around Delhi.

An organization? *NG-what?* It clicks for her. One of those groups that tries to hand out rubbers and teach didis how to sew instead of screw?

Yes, but no. This one is against the trafficking. In persons. Against *bonded labour.*

Meeta crosses her arms. Behind her eyes flicker all manner of imagined scenes and players: tricksters in rural villages, victims clawing at walls as they suffocate. *Ram!* She tenses.

Pinku steps closer, speaks quietly. After Sister came, I wasn't able to do what I did before. I just couldn't. Surely I tried. Sniffed and drank and vomited myself silly. But I had a thing now. A, a *conscience.* That's the word. But I still had to get by. A point led to B point led to C point. I found myself visiting one of those rubber-distributor groups. Asking if they needed help.

And?

They didn't. But they told me about *another* organization. This one wanted to do *investigations.*

Into what?

The human trafficking, *naah!* They use people like spies. Go in, collect evidence, then KHATAM! They bust in with the police and arrest the traffickers. High-end technology. Hidden cameras, secret microphones. CBI all the way.

I don't care. She starts towards the door.

Stop, he says, too loud. He reaches for her wrist to restrain her. The concierge glares over a registering guest's shoulder. *Sister and Ram were taken*, he hisses.

I don't care, she repeats. Wait. How do you know Ram is still living?

Pinku continues as if she didn't speak. I did digging. This Ravinder – the one who got poor, stupid Adiba killed – he did it. He showed up with a bunch of goondas and beat Ram before dumping the pair of them with a villain even worse than the mythical Ravana. Dharmatma is his name. Brutal landlord and man of industry. I tracked the goondas down and they told all.

A look of horror cracks Meeta's exterior. W-where are they? she whispers.

He taps his nose. We sniffed them out. He pulls out a grainy picture from his pocket and holds it up to her face. We have men that pose as traffickers. This is a secret photo from one of the kilns. I was looking through hundreds of pictures and I came upon it. Saw Sister immediately.

Meeta scrutinizes it. It undoubtedly shows the old nun among two other women as they form mud bricks. She is in a colourful sari, starkly different from the holy whites Meeta knew her to wear.

Pinku continues. The NGO – *international* – has been trying to bring this Dharmatma down for years. He runs kilns, many in other states, but also near Delhi. We know where they can be found.

They?

I believe Ram still lives too. I am almost certain hundred per cent.

Meeta is disappointed. She stares at the image of Sister again. I don't understand why you're here then. Just to tell me this? I suppose I appreciate knowing. But I am sad for it.

No! You are missing the point! I am here to tell you to *join* me.

Meeta gives a roll of her eyes capable of unleashing a tsunami.

Listen, *naa*! I am going in to rescue them. To capture evidence of all Dharmatma's wrongdoings. I need help. The Organization has no females trained to go into a place like that.

But you want me to go? Put myself at risk?

Meeta, you know how to work in difficult and dangerous plac-es. You are *perfect* for this operation!

She shakes her head. You do know Ram was involved in traf-ficking himself. That his foolishness with Manoj killed 18 peo-ple. He is guilty of murder, Pinku!

She didn't realize how loud her voice was rising. One of the co-lonial doormen clears his throat and urges them to step outside into the humid dark.

Once out of doors, Pinku can't contain himself. Then don't

do it for Ram! Sister did none of those things. She is innocent!

Meeta begins pacing.

There would be danger, but we wouldn't be alone. At every moment after we are inserted, there are police ready to descend on the kiln. We can call out via mobile at any time. Yes, you would free Sister, but Meeta, there are over a hundred more people trapped in that place. Some kiln owners are better to their workers than others, but this kiln exists to cheat people. To put them into eternal debt. But more than that, we know Dharmatma is a *killer*. We just have no proof! Whenever the police or the Organization think they have him, bribes and lawyers do the trick and he's walking the streets again. Besides, the fine for breaking the labour code is less than that for breaking a door on the Metro! We need the strongest evidence to see him in prison for good.

Meeta takes this all in, peering into an elaborately lit fountain near the hotel entrance.

Only two weeks of your life. One for training. One in the kiln. Whatever happens, the police will free the workers. The difference is whether Dharmatma ends up in prison, or walks free yet again.

Meeta inclines her head towards Pinku.

And the Organization can help you escape all this. Find you other opportunities. Just come and meet my people, Pinku says. First step. Trial offer. No obligation. They can explain much better.

She looks at him squarely and nods: once, twice, thrice.

XXIII

Take it all in, Pope. Farmland like this has sustained my civilization for 5,000 years. Look at the small brick homes, the fields of dusty green dotted by villagers at work. And then look there, in the middle of our pastoral scene: the Kiln, billowing black smoke.

Pan to the left and squint. In that field over there.

There he goes. And again. Look. No, no, no. Over *there*. There he is again: a head, popping up. And back down he goes.

Up. See his gaunt frame, his features contorted in fear.

Down. He waits for the better part of a minute.

Up. Note his clothes, dirt-stained and ragged.

Down. He stops; he hears it; then sees it: a pick-up.

The man lies low but the truck barrels towards him with such speed that the running man realizes he is spotted. The truck enters the field, unconcerned with what it rips up beneath its spinning wheels.

He rises again, fleeing for his life.

The truck stops and men, less exhausted, less spent, are out. They run with lathis and their steps kick up flurries of dust. The man is on his knees, panting, arms raised, begging for mercy his pursuers do not have.

He is beaten.

He is dragged.

He is taken.

Back towards the flaming belly of that Kiln where no one would go if they knew what awaited them there.

Where Meeta must go. Where we must go.

Meeta and Pinku stay at her apartment that night. He declares he will take up on her sofa. He turns the TV on immediately.

She prepares for bed, removing her make-up, applying Fair and Lovely skin cream, combing out her hair while sitting before her mirror, searching for something in her reflection. The same restless voice speaks to her from inside, urging her to slip into the night and re-emerge in another city where no one would know her. But lodged in her chest is a fully-blossomed conviction: all is not chance, that there was a reason Pinku found her, that she should give what he asked.

In those long months of solitude, she often reflected. Every relationship was transactional for her. She had never loved selflessly, never sacrificed. Even what she had experienced with Ram was tainted by supreme self-interest. Once, when flipping through channels, she stumbled upon a nature documentary about the ocean. She watched, horrified, as it explained whirl-pools, sucking everything towards a centre that crushes, and, in an atypical leap of analogical thinking, she compared the phenomenon to herself.

She puts down her hair brush and looks at herself, skipping past the surface beauty and plunging into the dilating pools of her eyes.

Come what may, she murmurs, as she puts out the lights and heads to bed.

The next several days pass quickly and with a grim inevitability, like the plod towards an execution date. Pinku and Meeta spend most of the hours at the offices of the Organization (whose name I purposefully withhold for reasons of confidentiality), located in the busy district of South Extension sandwiched between a Maruti dealership and a jewellery store. The offices are plain, appointed with linoleum and drab neutral colours while the place hums with the staff's determined activity. She had believed Pinku's fantastic story about the Organization and its work, but she is still surprised to see everything as he described it. Even more, Pinku is liked by the staff, both Indian and foreign! Valued for his work! Accepted by them!

Their main contact is a stodgy, older fellow named John Krista-dasa, quite serious and very passionate about the Organization's mission. At first Meeta is put off: he appears much like her clientele of recent months, though he treats Meeta with unfamiliar formality and respect, a paternal quality that unnerves Meeta because she has never experienced such a thing. She is unsure how to act around the busy staff as various members greet her, interview her, advise her, discuss compensation, and obtain her signature on lengthy consent forms which they explain because she cannot read. She ends up signing them with her thumbprint.

Orientation and training continue, and she passes through the swirl of it all with detachment. As they return for the second day, John lays out the plan over Café Coffee Day lattés and croissants. Pinku eats three. Meeta nibbles on one.

John's sharing goes something like this:

Meeta and Pinku will pose as a poor, young married couple

from Uttar Pradesh, living in a village just outside Lucknow. This was Meeta's home state, and Urdu was her first language, making it easy to assume her role. Pinku, a Delhi street child from the start, can only speak a smattering of Urdu that he used to deal with backwater types who visited G.B. He is cast as the silent type; the role will try him immensely.

John covers familiar ground. They will have one week to gather incontrovertible evidence to indict Dharmatma with concealed sound recorders and/or video cameras, the use of which she will be trained on. After that week, barring an emergency, the Organization will, in cooperation with the police, descend upon the Kiln. They already have enough evidence of abuse to justify the rescue and prosecute the low-level thugs who manage the site; the goal now is to finally bag the man on top.

Remember I've done this before, Pinku tells Meeta, not without some pride, and for at least the eleventh time since their reunion. All will be well, and such.

The gravity of what she and Pinku are to embark upon settles in. Her scepticism is not easily hidden.

She is warned by John that she may be placed in a complicated position. The Organization doesn't often send women in to pose and gather evidence. She shouldn't expect sexual abuse, John says, but it is a risk. One of the reasons they had Pinku reach out to her was to find an 'experienced' individual who knew how to 'de-escalate' situations. Meeta doesn't know that word, but once explained, grimaces. The middle-class women running around the office were too valuable to put in danger, she thinks, sighs, and shrugs.

We care about you, John adds in private after they break for a few minutes. He had intuited her thoughts. Your safety is more important than Dharmatma in handcuffs. You can decline to participate at any time, he says. His words carry no intimation that she would be weak or cruel or cowardly to do so. You are *valuable*, he says. Not here because we're trying to trick you to do our dirty work. Pinku spoke highly of you. Said you're smart and loyal. *That* is why you're here. We need good people to step into this together. We would understand if you want to decline.

We know we aren't paying much…

Meeta looks him in the eye. Inhales deeply. I'm not doing this for the money, she says.

Of course, he says. I didn't mean to suggest it. As she turns to visit the washroom, he adds, I have daughters your age.

She nods, only slightly reassured. *Come what may*, she tells herself, *come what may*.

'My name is Begum. My husband is Dhyan. I am from near Thavar. I am 20 years old, of low-caste birth, our land is poor, our cows have died, our family cannot keep us on. This new work is our life and hope'.

Meeta recites her assigned story like an incantation, especially at night as she tries to slip into sleep in a hotel close to the Organization's office, voicing the words until a peace covers her like a blanket. Meeta has already moved her few possessions from her keeper's nest.

The hotel room is cramped. She and Pinku are offered two separate rooms, but they choose to remain in one with two single beds; they are going to be 'married', after all. Pinku smokes bidis often, a compromise with his body's various urges as he undergoes withdrawals from other, more harmful habits. They watch TV together, or simply talk. They mostly avoid what lies ahead, though when the subject is broached, Meeta has a thousand questions about Pinku's prior work and the raids.

Though he has juvenile moments of show-offishness, shares off-colour jokes, and sometimes gives inane answers to questions, she still appreciates his familiar presence in the office among the well-off types – secretaries, lawyers, assistants, technicians, supervisors, advisers, police liaisons – buzzing around them all day. She takes reassurance from his confidence, even though it is often misplaced.

The training continues. There is a module on self-defence, and another with a young techy type with trendy glasses and a forced grin who is unnerved by her, clearly, and hurriedly talks her through using the recording equipment. It was all easy enough; just a matter of keeping things concealed. He also gives them a tiny mobile phone to keep hidden at all times, pre-programmed with a number to call should they need assistance. The Organization will set up in a small hotel for the week down the road, he explains. They promise that within an hour of a call or SMS, they should be able to arrive with the police in tow and cut the investigation off early. They teach her what the letters SOS mean.

As the final day winds down, they have the afternoon free. Meeta is struck by an idea. She asks for help making a call to *Shishu Bhavan*, the children's home where Sister had lived. She wishes to speak to someone who knew Sister Shanti. The Organization is willing to send her with a car and driver. She otherwise goes alone.

She is met at the gate first by the guard, and then by a Sister who Meeta recognizes as one who had pursued Sister Shanti in the Tibetan Colony. I'm sure you remember her too, Francis – the one we know as Sister Neepa.

I knew it was you on the phone, Sister Neepa says in greeting. She smiles and invites Meeta in, goes to fetch her a glass of cold water. Meeta is taken by the strangeness of the place with an old woman represented all over the place in murals, posters, and dioramas. Writing is on the walls, as you can see, Francis, a mix of scripture and Mother's sayings, but Meeta knows nothing of the woman nor can decipher the meaning of the words.

Sister Neepa returns and offers the water. Meeta thanks her and sips as she tries to decide where to start. I came today – wanting to tell you something. Sister Neepa nods with an open, serene face. Tell all of you MCs. You believe Sister Shanti has been lost. She has not. Not yet.

Sister Neepa shifts. May we walk? Her voice has a little tremor.

They begin to tour the facility and Meeta explains all as she takes in the various wards and disabled children, many who offer her unmerited smiles. In view of their easy play, Meeta weaves the sad story of Ram, Sister, and the mystery of his death since resolved. She tells Neepa, not without hesitation, of Sister's desire to leave the MCs, inwardly proud of the fact she has retained the word '*eks-claw-stray-shun*' after all these months. Sister Neepa is so troubled she can only look at the ground as they stroll. Meeta then shares what she is about to face in trying to rescue Sister, her signed confidentiality agreement with the Organization be buggered.

In all, her telling takes more than an hour. Though others have called for Sister Neepa during that time, Neepa will not pull herself away from Meeta, and yet she is reluctant to speak.

I don't know why I came today, Meeta says. I guess I thought Sister's sisters should know.

Sister Neepa touches Meeta's arm. Thank you. For coming. Thank you. For sharing. It is so hard to hear, so very hard. But I will tell the others. You say you leave tomorrow?

Meeta finds tears escape, and she forms a quivering smile as she rubs them away.

God goes with you, Sister Neepa says. Before you, with you, and after you. Meeta nods, just as a bell from a lower floor rings.

Sister Neepa says she ought to return to the children and prepare for the late afternoon schedule. She shepherds Meeta to the main gate and sends her away with an embrace that makes Meeta feel kilograms lighter.

Meeta rides back to the Organization in quiet thought, wondering whether it was appropriate to put this weight on the MCs.

She arrives back at the hotel. Pinku has ordered a feast of butter chicken. She declines to discuss the afternoon, but finds it impossible when their room telephone rings. Meeta answers. It is John. He explains that a Sister from the Missionaries of Charity called him about the upcoming operation, and before Meeta can mount a defence of her actions, he tells her to quiet down. There is no problem here, he says. The MCs have made an offer. They will send a pair of Sisters to stay in the hotel where we wait during the week. They will be praying for you and Pinku and Sister around the clock.

Meeta allows the thought to settle. The amount of stock she puts in prayers is near nil – for years they did nothing to deliver her from her circumstances – but the thought offers a surprising reassurance. She thanks John, they reconfirm details for the next day's early morning pick-up, and she hangs up.

Despite her better judgement they eat the heavy food and she and Pinku watch old Hindi movies on satellite until Pinku can't keep his eyes open. He rises, turns off the TV, bids her good night as he collapses onto his bed. Meeta, prepared and yet utterly unprepared for what the next day will bring, recites her incantation: 'I am Begum. My husband is Dhyan. I am from near Thavar...'

Pinku and Meeta must leave Delhi to return to it.

They travel the next morning by car, John at the driver's wheel. There are his expected admonitions, and his unease is obvious. Pinku acts nonchalantly and cracks jokes; the bad humour is a mercy. In quiet moments during the eight-hour drive, Meeta grasps the car upholstery, looks out the window at the enormous fields, the sagging power lines, the haze-filled sky and the near-empty Bihar Sampark Kranti Expressway, and ponders the immensity of everything.

They meet a man outside Lucknow who looks altogether average: his chin stubbly and moustache unkempt and unwrinkled dhoti. Yet he is a trafficker; a trafficker being paid by the Organization to slip them into the Kiln when a truck will come this afternoon looking for new workers. A complex soul he must be, yet one whose depths this story has no time to plumb. John gets out, waves his hand in confirmation of the deal. He signals to Pinku and Meeta. They take up their bags – filled with a few changes of clothing, their concealed equipment – and they stand waiting with the trafficker.

John mutters a few final warnings and encouragements. We are with you, he says as he embraces Pinku, then Meeta. Go with God. You have all our prayers.

The trafficker takes them under a thatched stall beside the road and keeps his words perfunctory: *quiet, sit, wait.* Meeta, feeling hunger stir in her belly, sighs. Just a week, just seven days – 168 hours – 10,080 minutes – no, now 10,079 – and change will have come and everything will be set right.

XXIV

Hold your head high, Francis. Straight ahead. That's right; the stakes have heightened; you are not above bodily harm here.

Where are we? you whisper out of the corner of your mouth.

The Kiln, of course.

When are we? you ask.

That very evening.

Quiet now. That short, grizzled man pacing before our line of 12 new workers demands obedience. He is Kasliwal, Dharmatma's lieutenant, and a brute. He speaks mostly in imperatives. His nostrils flare with every breath. His hands rest in fists. He wants all to believe he sprang into being this way, never having suckled at his mother's breast, nor had his bottom cleaned by another. Your eyes slide to his waistband. You're not mistaken; that is indeed a gun, an old *tamancha* country pistol. It distracts from the many English clichés he interjects into his speech: tight ship, tip-top, maximum penalty, hell to pay, *et cetera* and *et cetera*.

Quick, while his back is turned: afford yourself a glimpse of the compound in which we stand. There are three other guards there, perched on a trio of petrol barrels. They look tired. A pair of children watch from inside a block of a dormitory wing, backlit by a few dull electric lights. No one else chooses to watch this orientation.

Kasliwal drones on, inspecting us in turn. Pinku casts a deferential stare just under Kasliwal's eye line. Meeta can't help but meet his eyes, but only for a flickering moment. He glowers, but moves on down the row, stirring up dirt with each resounding step. Kasliwal pivots when he reaches us; he doesn't know what to make of the two of us, Pope. Best to stay on his good side, I should think.

A creaking metal door heralds a newcomer. He places himself under the sky-scraping pole from which a blinding floodlight shines. From his limned outline, Meeta recognizes he is none other than Dharmatma.

She sizes him up as she would a client entering her chamber. Within seconds she has a profile: a tentative pace – lack of confidence; hands held behind his back – prone to observation; shirt unbuttoned – a callow attempt at coolness.

Indeed, Meeta knows this one's type.

It's only towards the end of Kasliwal's speech punctuated with threatened violence does Dharmatma step forward and Meeta finally experience surprise. She has seen pictures of him, but they were grey, fuzzy things. His moustache is jet black, dyed; his hair similar. Up close, his wrinkles jump into sharp relief. He really is very old. He surveys the new arrivals, some of them, at least. His eyes skip from woman to woman, lingering upon the younger, the thinner, the prettier. Meeta looks away, playing her part well.

Dharmatma nods to Kasliwal and leaves. After a few final instructions about where we will sleep, and eat, and drink, and wash, and shit, we are dismissed and shown to our woven mats and straw pillows by one of the guards.

Tiredness dogs Meeta and Pinku as they stash their things and lay their bodies down. Kasliwal's final words are written indelibly on Meeta's mind: '*Work, for while you are here, you are ours*'.

The night passes without incident – and without rest.

For months Meeta has slept on a glorious mattress in her patron's apartment. A reed mat beside a stinky adolescent leaves much to be desired, and that small, selfish, clamouring voice inside belittles her for making this trade. She is inclined to agree.

She stirs in the early morning at the sound of others' rising, a nervous pit widening in her stomach. She changes her clothing when Pinku isn't looking, or doesn't seem to be, and she steps outside to watch as other women have congregated to wash. One woman, unable to pass a moment without a comment or lyric escaping her lips, greets Meeta. Meeta forces a smile and follows her example, waiting to fill up her pot at a shared tap. She cases the compound. It is different by day; less menacing, more banal. Roughly square, it has rusted barbed wire lining the perimeter wall and an imposing metal gate. No view of the outside world is offered except for what lies above: the sky coming alive with morning light, and the Kiln, already spewing black.

She stares too long at one of the thugs from the night before who watches from an observation tower. His gaze follows her as she returns to the happy woman's side.

Is there food? Meeta asks weakly.

Yes! It should come shortly.

It does. The gate opens with a tired moan and in rolls a pickup truck. The kids rush to line up first, taking proffered plates and accepting a scooped heap of mushy rice from two disinterested men.

After filing through the line, Meeta takes her plate and reaches for a second.

Oye!

One for me, one for my husband, she says.

Tell him to get in line himself, the man barks. Meeta glares at him, accepts her heaped portion, and uses her fingers to shovel the food into her mouth. She has not eaten for nearly a day.

Take your plate, Pope. I have mine here. I'm sorry there's nothing else to offer, not even a dash of curry or salt to enliven the dish. One mercy is that I've heard some diluted chai is coming. You slept poorly, you say? An aching back? Take care! If shooting pains keep you from work, you'll suffer the consequences. While you sit out the day in the infirmary (an unbearably stuffy room with a sagging cot) your debt will turn over. Dig itself deeper. Accumulate. If it can be avoided, never rest. Or else you won't be leaving this place.

Ugh. This rice. This *rice*. We eat unremarkable food in the MC home all the time in our dogged pursuit of poverty. But this, this, *gruel*, well, it's exceptionally bad. You can see Meeta gagging as she forces it down. Ah, there's Pinku, standing in the doorway, greeting the sun with arms stretched up. He rubs his hands together and seems in good spirits. He steps behind a wall where other men squat or stand and does his business. Inspecting the bottom of his sandal, he grates it on the dry earth until it's clean, runs his hands under the tap, and takes his own plate to join Meeta on the ground. He smiles, immune to Meeta's silent worry.

Suddenly, Meeta is up on her feet as her plate clatters to the ground like a fallen coin. She rubs her eyes. She had every reason to expect this moment's arrival but is still surprised at it. Only a few metres away, shouldering a pole with suspended buckets of water, is Ram.

He wears threadbare robes, walks with a limp, maybe from the old knife wound, maybe from Ravinder's blows. His cheeks are hollowed and his hair shaved to his scalp, making several new scars visible. Though his body is lean and sinewy, he is wasted.

Emotions conflict: too many, too quick to register. Meeta's mouth gapes, and his name sticks in her throat. Still, he turns towards her at the subtle needling her glare provides.

Pinku is up as well, and staring. But Ram turns away, taking his buckets to wherever they belong, as if he saw nothing, leaving Pinku and Meeta to wonder what has just happened.

Watch it, Francis! You almost dropped your bricks on my foot!

Sorry — this labour — is taking — it out — of me. *Whew!* We have to be careful not to show the watchers that we're spending so much time talking. They will not approve.

How does it feel? The pole across your shoulders, 24 suspended bricks at a time? I noticed you stumbling back there; I nearly called out, but at the last second you righted yourself. Your insides must be clamouring for food, your throat begging for water — I know mine are.

Ah! There it is! You're kneading your lower back! Remember what I told you? Rest, rest, just for a moment.

As I survey our co-labourers, fairly called the 'least of these', I see the emaciated men, sick from something terrible, out here at work, shedding life each day. Women carry stacked mountains on their heads. The small children tote a few bricks, or hunch over moulds with thick mud caking their hands. Think of it this way, if it helps: every brick you transport is a brick these others don't have to. Do it as if for our Lord himself, as Simon, temporarily bearing Our Lord's cross.

I've wandered. Let's take up our loads again.

You know already that the new workers, us included, were divided into separate teams. We have been tasked with taking bricks from where they dry in snaking rows in the field beside the compound to the base of the Kiln. Armed guards make sure we stay put. It is a cruel and effective engine we fuel: during the high season, over 30,000 four-pound bricks are finished here each day. All leavened with the secret ingredient of exploitation.

There she is. Out of the corner of your eye. Meeta struggles mightily. She, like us, is but four hours into a 16-hour work-day. What a wonder, these women who can balance 16 bricks on their heads! She is able to only do half, and the bricks have tumbled more than once. The jolly woman from this morning offers encouragement as she passes her by, but it doesn't help. Meeta is dehydrated; she is already exhausted. She regrets all the ice cream eaten during the past few months.

For every 16 bricks she carries she receives a token that represents a credit against her and Pinku's debt. She imagines how the debt accumulates like the bricks being transported: every minute some are taken away while new bricks are moulded and added into the vacant spot, without end.

She trips and the bricks fall to the ground. Each mistake of hers draws more attention, precisely what she doesn't want. Others don't help because it would mean wasting time or losing control of their own loads.

Except Ram does.

He lowers the load balanced from a pole across his shoulders, helps collect what Meeta has scattered. He does so wordlessly.

You recognize me? she asks through pained breathing, almost in a whisper.

He begins stacking the gathered bricks on her head. I thought you were a ghost, he says. Or a jinn. Meant to haunt me, he says.

She pauses, waits for him to meet her eyes. And Sister? She's here?

His look prompts a thousand questions. Meeta is horrified.

No, no, don't worry. She's not dead. He looks around, replacing the final brick on her head. I'll take you to her. Tonight. Only you; not Pinku.

Standing face-to-face, her momentary concern for him burns off. I'm here for her, Meeta says as she struggles under the weight restored to her head.

He nods, takes up his load, and continues towards the Kiln.

Despite her best efforts Meeta is on the cusp of sleep. Pinku already snores, but is surprisingly vocal. Being here has brought fearful utterances to the fore of his subconscious: separation, pain, beatings, and deprivation are all aired. One would never assume the things rattling around in his head just by looking at him.

When Pinku returned from his assigned work at the base of the Kiln he was drained of vitality. He tried to sleep immediately, but Meeta required him to tell more, if nothing else, to pass the slowly creeping time until Ram would arrive.

He was tasked with being a fuel man, one who has to feed the fire at the heart of the Kiln. To Meeta, this sounded a wonderful alternative to lugging bricks. John had explained how the Kiln worked during her training. She recalled that a circular trench surrounds the Kiln, and bricks are stacked so as to leave gaps. Air is allowed to enter and it passes through the spaces between older bricks to cool them while workers fuel the Kiln's fire via capped holes in the ground above the dirt-covered trench. The fuel men move clockwise around the Kiln tending to the fire, and as bricks are fired and cooled, they're removed and new bricks put in their place. It's a cycle: stacked, fired, cooled, removed, *repeat.*

So you were a fuel man, she said with some bitterness.

I was. But it is hard, a different kind of hardness than carrying bricks! When the caps come off and you have to drop the coal in, there's such heat! I worried for my hair! My eyebrows! The end of this week, I'll look like a spent match! Look, just look at my cracked lips!

Meeta suppressed a smile.

Naah, this is nothing to laugh about. Not with what happened next.

Meeta sat up. What?

See, I am having the equipment on me! Pinku leaned in close. *The camera!*

What? Why!

Never know when good footage is coming! But this was a mistake. I don't want the equipment damaged by the heat, so I'm worried, standing back, and this guy, Govind is his name, I don't know, maybe a few years older but looking like old stone because of the work, he sees me off to the side. I mean, I'm worried about the equipment, but I'm also worrying about *my* equipment, if you know what I mean. Who knows if those flames will render me inoperable?

Meeta sighs, making it clear she thinks Pinku's a fool.

Wait. So this old-young guy, he gets *angry*. Shouting at me to get to work. And just then Kasliwal is walking past. Out comes his gun.

What did you do?

I feared for my life! And turned on my camera! Well, Govind sees me tugging around in my lungi for the 'ON' button and Kasliwal barks at Govind. *This one is new! You're supposed to show him! No problems!* He's saying things like that. *An example I'm making of you!* And he does. Kasliwal threw Govind from where we stood and he rolled off and broke part of his hand while falling, I think. Not pretty. But, Meeta, oh, *great* footage, I'm getting. One day soon Govind will be proud of his contribution.

Today isn't that day, Meeta said.

No. Govind said all sorts of nasty things after that. Then Kasliwal said I was next, *et cetera, et cetera*, but I showed him I was afraid and trembled at his feet and was spared. Not sure what Govind will do next time he sees me.

Meeta and Pinku sat in the silence. Ram spoke to me, Meeta finally said. He recognized us right off. He's coming to take me to see Sister tonight. Says you can't come.

Pinku shrugged drowsily, curled up on his mat. Fine with me. I'm going to sleep now. Tell her I say namaskar.

The sounds all throughout the dormitory began dying down as workers and their families drifted off to sleep. Meeta sat, hugging her legs to her chest and rocking gently, listening as Ram's dreamy protestations echoed in their small, small room. This continued until the present moment, Pope, when Ram will finally approach and…

Psst!

The sound comes from behind the curtain, just outside their room, and makes Meeta jump.

Thank God, Meeta whispers to herself, rising from her mat to part the tattered sheets.

Ram signals with his head. They try to slip out, but a night guard posted at the sole entrance to the dormitory stops them.

It's just me, Ram tells him with a smile, like he's familiar with the man. I'm taking this new one to see Heeraji. Problems, she's having. *Feminine* problems.

The guard is unnerved, visibly so. Straight back after? he asks.

Ram gives an assuring nod, pats him on the shoulder. Meeta sees a flicker of the Ram she knew, all confidence and ease. The one she thought she knew. She darkens, letting herself fall a half-step behind him.

The pair walk in haste across the compound, under its single floodlight and the gaze of a pair of tired men sitting close to the main gate who sip tea. Ram goes rigid on recognizing them. They are Kasliwal and Dharmatma.

That you, Ram? Who have you got there? Kasliwal calls.

Feminine prob–. He cannot get the words out. His breathing quickens.

Meeta swallows, feeling her heartbeat rise to a clamour. Finally, Dharmatma leans creakily to whisper in Kasliwal's ear. The lieutenant nods, nods again.

One of the new ones?

Haan. Y-yes. She is, Ram hollers.

The young one? The pretty one?

Ram's eyes flick to Meeta. Yes.

Boss needs to see her afterwards. Inspection. Kasliwal gives a small chuckle, matched by Dharmatma. Ram offers a small bow. Meeta's mind races through a dozen imagined scenes, yet she pushes them aside as they continue on.

Ram can't help muttering: I shouldn't have…this is the worst… if I had waited till he was gone…

When they reach the other side, just out of Dharmatma's trailing eye, Meeta tugs at Ram's sleeve. What does this mean?

What you think. When he's here, the old man does what he pleases with the women. It may amount to nothing. He's fickle.

Meeta steels herself, feels for the audio recorder. It's tucked safely into the back of her dupatta. It was a matter of time, she says. Not unexpected. I'll figure something out. She touches his elbow and they lock eyes. For now, take me to her.

You need to be prepared. She's not—

Please. No more. Just take me.

He raps on an open metal door. The room inside is dark, though a flickering candle causes shadows on the wall to tremble and shake. Meeta's eyes adjust further. Dominating the room is a cot, and on the cot is a man, and seated beside the man is Sister Shanti. She looks up from her prayers, sans glasses.

Meeta takes a small step forward, gently pulling the sari back to reveal her face to Sister. Concerns about Dharmatma, the Kiln, her exhaustion, and the past fall away. She has imagined this moment since she last saw Sister, what she would say and how she would say it. But all the planned sentiments, arguments, accusations, and benedictions prove too heavy for her tongue. Speech fails her.

Ram, a bit bashful, wisely steps to the side.

Sister rises; looks Meeta up and down; goes to her; embraces her.

XXV

You didn't tell me, Sister says to Ram.

I thought you'd like a surprise, he says.

You didn't tell me, she repeats. She turns Meeta from side to side, putting her through an inspection. Meeta, you're beautiful. Really so. Something's changed.

Meeta inflates with pride.

Sister looks at Meeta's glinting jewellery catching the candle-light, her bright-coloured sari. You look like a…farmer's wife.

From the country. Dear Lord, are you...*married*? In, what, the last several months?

To Pinku, Meeta says.

Sister is horrified. *That* boy?

Meeta tries to contain her smile, but it explodes, the relief travelling from face to face about the room. Sister slides an admonishing finger across her cheek and laughs.

This woman, so collected, so at ease, is not who Meeta expected to find.

There is the obvious: Sister's head is uncovered and her hair, though short, has grown back, silvery and full; her absent glasses allow an unobstructed view of her dark eyes; though dressed in white, it is a sort of homespun fabric, without any blue trim. Beyond these things, she is agile, even spry. It's like viewing the Sister Meeta knew, but from a different angle. Somehow, the light strokes her features differently.

Ram floats over to a corner and watches while Meeta moves further into the room, looking for a place to sit but finding none.

Ah. Take my seat, sit down, will you. I'll look for another chair or something, Sister says. She steps out of the room and Meeta flashes Ram a look, lips pursed, eyebrows raised.

Meeta finally looks more closely at the man on the cot, a silent, unsettling witness to this odd reunion. His face is bruised, swollen beyond recognition. He breathes, but the air comes and goes in quiet puffs.

What happened to this one? Meeta asks.

Ram's solemnity returns. His name is Ajwa. He tried to get away. Went a little mad. His wife, she...died. And Sister – Heeraji, he says, catching himself – is nursing him. He's been asleep like that for a few days.

By the time Sister returns with a small stool, Meeta has forgotten where she is, her eyes tracing the broken body before her. Her hands clench her seat.

So, Sister says, sitting.

So.

They finally caught up with you too?

Meeta's gaze flicks to Ram and back.

The Goonda, Sister says. Ram, his name?

Ravinder.

Ravinder caught up with you and Pinku, saw fit to punish you the same way? Sent you here, did he?

Meeta suddenly wishes Ram had prepared Sister a bit more. She shakes her head. I've…not seen that horrible man in an age. Not since I was with you.

Sister looks at her intently. Then, how?

We – I – learned you were here. It was Pinku who discovered it. Meeta stops, struggling how to cut a long story to size. He approached me, told me we could help you.

How curious. The woman's affect dampens, as if the room's candle nearly flickered out.

Meeta starts. Sist—

Heera.

Heera. We're here for you. To rescue you. At the end of this week, an Organization will come and pull everyone out–

Sister looks away. Lists to the side. There is turmoil in her eyes that Meeta can't understand. Sister's right hand begins to tremble, and finally, she rises. She looks at Ram, then back to Meeta. Her face is troubled. Did you think of asking first?

Meeta is stunned.
Has no words.
Not a
one.

Finally: It's not – we're not here just for you. It's everyone caught here, under Dharmatma, it's—

Please. Go. Sister weaves her fingers together, closes her eyes. We can talk later. Her ease, her warmth, have vanished. I need time, yes, time, some time to be alone.

Meeta is already up, on her way out of the room, trying to stifle her desire to yell and shout and scream. *Rejection, rejection, rejection…gratitude impossible…beyond understanding…foolish, oh so foolish…*

Ram rushes after her, catching her sari and pulling it loose.

I don't understand her either, he hisses. They stand at the compound's edge, drawing eyes from all corners. She's herself, but different. Changed. I can't explain—

Meeta slaps him, hard, across the cheek. Her body is heaving. *All* your fault, she says. She curses him. Spits on the ground. There is a look in his eyes, a sagging hurt, dashed hopes. She realizes, finally, what any other would have been able to see. He was kindling feelings for her again, ready to revive the love or the facsimile of it that they shared.

Incredulous, she laughs. Not a mere chuckle, snort, or snigger. This is a full-bodied thing, travelling throughout the compound.

Ram's head is bowed, she thinks in shame, and it is several breaths before realizing the true reason.

Feminine problems, eh? Does she have them, or do you? says a low voice from behind Meeta. She becomes rigid, remembering that the world is bigger than her, Ram, and Sister.

Dharmatma. She needn't see him to know.

Come with me, he says to her. I have something to help even if the old didi didn't.

COME ON, Pope! We don't have all night. When those guards over there turn away, we'll dash to the side of that squat building where Dharmatma leads Meeta. It's a small suite, somewhat rustic considering his means. While Dharmatma is here, that's where he stays.

He has a number of kilns, but this one is his largest operation. Like many, he cordons off less scrupulous activities and maintains a respectable life on the side. He has a modest farmhouse (by the standards of the ridiculous wealth that permeate the highest echelons of Indian society), not so far from our esteemed Sharmila Gulzar's. There he has a wife (his third), three adult sons and one daughter (all but one from out of wedlock), a mother-in-law (his same age), a number of house servants (the most senior in his employ having stayed three months), and a Pomeranian he loves more than all the others combined.

He absolutely, positively hates his life.

He cares little for material comforts and would be an ascetic if he could. He only cares for the MORE of it all: wealth for wealth's sake. That's the itch he must scratch, the worship of which is his only religion. His family detests him except while in pursuit of some new, shiny bauble, in which instance they love him. This only increases his equal and opposite hatred of them. They are in his perpetual debt, sucking him dry, and they can't even fake gratitude. So he bumps from worksite to worksite, joking with his lieutenants like they're old school chums, sucking up fearful respect, plucking women in his debt and using that debt to his advantage. If he didn't poke these women – *his* women, he calls them – he'd have not done the deed in a decade.

This is the sick and sickening man Meeta finds herself with now.

Stand on that crate, Francis. You'll be able to see in the room, even though I'm sure you don't wish to.

The lair to which he brings her is as dark and grim as the worst *kotha* she's ever worked in. He switches on a lamp and two fans aimed at an unmade bed. She flips on the recorder when he's not looking. If she has to undress to ensure he doesn't find it, she will. If she has to let him in to keep her cover, she will. But oh, how she is exasperated.

She hates being traded by men, by men, by men! She thinks of John's patronizing words and feels a bitterness towards him and this whole operation, momentarily quelled by Dharmatma's hand stroking her shoulder. She snaps back to this moment, its musty smells, its immediate dangers.

I want you to understand you don't have to be here, Dharmatma says flatly.

I…don't understand, she whispers, exaggerating her timidity, inflecting it with innocence. She is unfolding a role, putting it on. I thought you said you had something to help me feel better.

Sit. No need to be so afraid. I understand, though. Me being the boss and all. But this is all up to you. If you and I have a little moment here, I make a note in my book here. Right next to your name.

But I can't read, she says.

Trust me.

What does a note mean?

It means more money for you at the end of the season.

She nods bashfully. She knows enough to see her fictitious name does not appear in the book.

But my husband—

Don't mention him, *betee*. Not around me. He'll approve. You're being paid, after all! I don't take what's not mine.

She nods again.

He puts one hand on her shoulder, than his second on her side.

A question, she whispers, just loud enough for the microphone to register. The man. The injured one with Heeraji. How did he become that way? Did he do something wrong?

His hands freeze. His breath is held. I have no idea.

And with that, his hands resume their creeping, he nuzzles her neck, and she curses, inwardly, knowing she needs more of a confession, and knowing what is coming next. She prepares her mind, as she always has, dimming it, deadening it. She makes herself pliant to record this man being vile, to one day parade it before the world.

His hands find purchase all over her, her belly, her thigh, grasping her breast. Her breathing is becoming shallow. She is hollowing out. From all the prior years, her body is prepared for undressing, opening, and letting in.

She is the same Meeta she's always been.

She is ready for this.

She can do the needful.

She cannot. She whirls around, spinning off the mattress, looking away. She doesn't understand the clawing sense at her throat, the sense of suffocation, a physical ache registering at points cast throughout her body.

Sorry, sir, she chokes out. My husband…I…no…me.

Dharmatma is wide-eyed, a monstrous vein throbbing at his temple. He rises up, lifts a hand to hit her, but simply spits upon her instead. You *tease!* You *whore!* You *bitch!*

She doesn't have a chance to regret it until it's already done, but she has done the unthinkable: she has smiled. It is big and powerful enough to taunt and shame, not just Dharmatma in the present, but every man, every single one, who has ever had the nerve to come to her and take what was not theirs.

Meeta, damning all consequence, basks in an uncontainable, effervescent pride unlike anything she has known before. That is, until Dharmatma throws a glass at her. In a near miss, it explodes against the wall and shatters with it any sense of invulnerability.

He is upon her now, hand at her throat, and she feels fear clamouring from within. She tries to scream but his hand claps her mouth. He is cursing her, and she is crying, gasping, fighting, begging.

He stops.

There is screaming, and Meeta has to close her mouth and listen to determine that it is not her own. Dharmatma fumbles to put his hanging beak back where it belongs, cinches his belt, and throws open the door. He steps out, and all Meeta can see is his form lit by flickering shades of orange.

She replaces her dupatta, ensures all is where it ought to be, and edges towards the door once he has stepped out.

A wagon is aflame. One of the wooden bullock carts for transporting bricks, right in the middle of the compound. Dharmatma is running around, demanding futilely that his men put it out. They scramble to fetch water as fast as the tap can dispense it. Chaos abounds, and Meeta slips out, across the square, back towards the dormitory where stirred workers rush to join in and extinguish the flames.

A million thoughts coming at a thousand kilometres a second register, chief among them whether she should dial John now and end this. It has been but a day, and look at the near disaster! She stumbles into her small room in search of the phone, fully expecting to find Pinku gone, pulled into the impromptu fire brigade.

He is there, docile, on his mat.

Meeta begins to cry, softly.

Are you alright? he asks, stirring.

Meeta wipes the tears away. She cannot stop her shaking.

While you've been sleeping, I've been in *hell*. God above, it's easy being a man.

But I've not been asleep.

Yeah? What have you been doing then?

Without rolling over, he lifts something, a small box. He gives it a shake.

In an instant she knows its contents: matches.

Wake up, Francis. What's that? I know, I know. Not enough sleep, body creaking, dysentery rattling your belly. You're not the only one feeling the effects of being here. I have little sympathy for——

Sorry. *Sorry!*

Being here, in this place, at this time – it's wearing upon me as well. I've been up for a few hours already, keeping an eye on Sister. I mean, Heera. I mean, Sister. There's still much to tell.

The bullock cart fire came and went, and, thankfully, there were no injuries for Sister to tend other than a sprained ankle. Many would have blanched and shrunk from the flames, but there were many here who spend their days exposed to bracing heat as fuel men. Even though the cart was a lost cause, Dharmatma made them fight the flames with vigour, as if he had something to prove.

After all died down, Sister was left alone, with the exception of the comatose Ajwa and a host of intrusive memories hastened by Meeta's appearance. Despite the fact she is no longer a nun, she still rises for prayer, still subsists on a deficit of sleep each night. In the solitude of her room, with little sound, she spent hours upon her knees, dozing here and there.

Meeta was quite right, Pope. Without putting too fine a point on it, Sister is much changed.

And much blinded to it.

There she is, coming out of her small door to greet the day in its haze of blue and yellow. Let's watch her on her way, Francis. Much can be learned.

Greetings abound. You see faces brighten as she visits with the women who queue for water, as she bends to accept children's hearty embraces. Men of all stripes offer her salutations and she bows in respect, a smile for all. Her right hand, ignorant of caste or faith, reaches out in warmth to the touchable and untouchable alike.

She continues her morning routine, visiting the guards next and ending with brutish Kasliwal. She is more veiled with them, but not much.

We're too far away to hear their words, but just watch their faces. She prompts smiles; I tell you, Pope, the light-hearted laughter of fearsome men is a strange sight, indeed. They are familiar with her, yet you see disbelief at this strange old woman, her open ways, her softness, her quick smile, despite, well, everything.

Dharmatma steps out of his lair, but first comes another woman, or, rather, a girl. She is the homely teenage daughter of one of the families here, the default victim of his advances. She bows her head and rushes to her family's quarters. Her tears are visible, even at a distance. Dharmatma is taciturn, starts barking orders before his grey cotton trousers are even zipped and his belt buckled. If this is any indication, today will be bad: for everyone, but especially for a few.

Sister approaches Dharmatma, greets him, commiserates with him over the burning cart. She says something provocative – he looks like he might hit her, but he suddenly bows his head, mutters a few words. What she does next is curious. She leans forward, takes his arm, in what I can only characterize as a stern maternal touch, and whispers in his ear. He laughs, uneasy, yet she holds on. She looks at him expectantly, her lips in a tight line, and he says something. I'm no lip reader, though I'm pretty sure it was 'never again'.

Before Sister is even a few steps away, her spell is broken and he is changed. The anger returns, and it is severe. He is off chasing Kasliwal while the morning gruel is dispensed, undoubtedly to work out how they will find the fool who burnt his cart so they can mete out punishment.

Sister's morning promenade finally ends as she stands with Ram, who looks out over the compound with his arms crossed.

You've seen how this place crumbles souls and tears bodies apart. But for Sister it seems the opposite. You have not spent much time with her here, but all it takes is a rambling circuit to see she is more…*happy*…than I have ever known her to be.

She and Ram talk quietly for a few moments, but then their gestures start to grow in size and urgency. They discuss something, surely the prior night's events, until they are bickering like mother and child. They pause when Ram notices Meeta step into the courtyard with Pinku trailing behind.

Look how Meeta has aged in just these two days! The girl looks positively haggard. Sister sees her too and looks away.

Pinku signals towards the mush line. Let's slot ourselves in line behind him and Meeta. I'm starved.

…all I'm saying is be absolutely careful, Pinku says. Don't go anywhere alone.

They'll do what they wish, Pink…I mean, Dhyan.

We could call John, Pinku whispers, looking over his shoulder. A few places behind him he sees Govind, the fuel man he got in trouble yesterday, and offers a conciliatory wave. Govind scowls.

No, Meeta says, missing this interaction. We can't call him. We've gathered almost nothing usable. I want Dharmatma to pay.

They quieten as they approach the vat of mush, taking tin plates in hand. It is then that Govind is pulled from the line by two guards. Kasliwal's voice booms from up in the lookout post.

You knew better, Govind.

Govind is petrified. He doesn't appear to have known better.

Better than to set fire to that cart! Kasliwal shouts.

Meeta and Pinku look at one another wide-eyed. How would Kasliwal have come to that conclusion?

Govind is shaking, looking all around for help, like a goat finally realizing why he's been fattened before Eid. He's brought to the middle of the compound, near the cindered wood, and made to kneel.

You were seen last night doing the act! Kasliwal bellows.

Govind pleads. He begs. He bleats.

Horrified, Pinku flicks on his hidden camera and positions

himself to capture it all.

Meeta notices that Sister is staring, not at the scene, but at her and Pinku. Her look is all accusation: see what you've brought us?

Meeta glares back defiantly, until Govind is struck with a bamboo stick.

Kasliwal relays the commands; Dharmatma stands beside him, whispering the orders.

Meeta's insides shout. Each blow makes her stomach churn, her legs falter, and she is very nearly reaching out for the man now, begging the sky and earth and gods to move and stop this suffering.

She steps out. Not Meeta, who, as you can see, Pope, is still as stone. It is Sister.

Her every step rattles the earth.

Get away, Heeraji! Dharmatma shouts.

She does not heed him.

Govind lies flat on the ground, emptied of breath, held tight by pain as more blows rain down

Sister places herself over him, directly on top of him, dirtying herself and choking on a flurry of dust. This stops now! she cries. By God, it ends this moment! She shouts it in English, which only a few understand, among them Dharmatma. She calls upon Ram and a few others to come and help her move him.

They stand back, unmoving.

Finally, they come.

Slowly at first, realizing by Kasliwal's grimace and Dharmatma's silence there will be no consequence to bear. The poor man is picked up, a worker for each of his four limbs, and carried to Sister's quarters. Sister rises, dirt streaking her face, her clothes dishevelled, laboured breath wracking her body. She glares at Dharmatma until he bristles, steps down, and leaves the compound by truck.

Meeta goes out to Sister and whispers, *Let's go.*

Sister obliges, reluctantly, willingly, painfully.

*

In 2008, in her 69th year, Sister was placed in captivity.

There was despair when she arrived at the Kiln. How could there not be? She feared she would be torn from Ram so soon after finding him. Malhotra and Sharmila Gulzar had just stared, stricken, as hired men with lathis swarmed into the compound like rioters in a film scene. They pulled Ram up as he screamed, owing to his infected leg and his fear, and Sister shouted all manner of harsh words. Ravinder revealed himself, demanded the money, tortured poor Ram by twisting his leg. Sister denied having a paisa on her, and only then, amid Ram's screams, she told a desperate half-truth: the money was given away to the poor. Ravinder was not pleased. The thugs beat Ram thoroughly, but, as is obvious, did not kill him.

After Sharmila's, the drive to the Kiln took but an hour, but felt much longer for Sister and Ram. The back of the truck was suffocating, and Ram's blood-spattered condition was dire as he floated in and out of semi-consciousness. Sister rested the boy's head on her lap and her tears mingled with his matted hair. The one-of-a-kind sickly-sweet smell of his blood permeated everything, and she prayed and wept, mostly out of fear, but also gratitude that Ram was still, despite all expectations, alive.

Kasliwal met their truck and Ravinder spoke with him briefly. It was a few hours into the morning, and the arrival was a distraction from the work at hand. Bringing these two here had already been cleared with Dharmatma, Ravinder told him. Kasliwal nodded, and his men dragged Ram out of the truck and cast him into an oven of a room. Sister, covered in DirtSweatBlood, went straight up to Kasliwal. There was an unprecedented fury in her eyes that her glasses amplified; Kasliwal shrank. Even before Ravinder had left, she told the overseer how it would be. Yes, we are your slaves, she said. Accepted. No argument. But that boy is near death. I will do whatever you wish, but you *will* let me tend his wounds.

Not a QuestionRequestSuggestion. A Command.

Kasliwal, slow to betray it, respected this.

For two days, Sister prayed over Ram, forsaking food as she cleaned his wounds, begged for medicines. Her blue-striped sari, the blood and sweat-stained clothing that had carried her into her search for Ram and represented the final vestige of her religious life, was burnt. Her crucifix and rosary were confiscated. She was given ragged robes instead, made to look like a grieving widow, like a Delhi street sweeper, like a beggar. She didn't care. All was Ram. Miracle of miracles, he recovered, but only to find himself in a lower level of hell.

She observed the Kiln's squalid living conditions, the workers' malnutrition, the callous and sometimes brutal enforcement of rules on innocents' wasting bodies. She knew that the work these people did was a futility, that theirs was an unbeatable, ever-inflating debt. A rage could swell in her in an instant, arriving in waves like a malarial fever, only to abate in Ram's presence.

One night, after a few trying weeks adjusting to the rhythms of the place, she had a stunningly obvious thought: she was here. She was *here*. Yes, it was a group of thugs who caused her to be here, but maybe, just maybe, she was led here. That to move from point A to point B to point C in her life was remarkable, and that instead of being a curse, maybe this was where God, in his awesome and inscrutable manner, saw fit to bring her. She spoke words that felt gifted to her by the Spirit:

I will observe the goodness of those here.

I can minister to them.

And them to me.

So simple, yet it felt like a breach in the brick prison in which she found herself, and the world opened up anew.

*

Sister spends the rest of the day quietly as she tends to Govind's split-open back and to Ajwa in his coma. Govind is conscious and spits curses between moans. They are aimed at the one who burned the cart and cost him these wounds. She uses old rags and finally exhausts her supply of iodine that she had begged from Dharmatma some months back. Govind mutters a name,

216

'Dhyan', over and over. Sister doesn't recognize it. Finally, he rests.

After fruitlessly trying to wash the brown from her hands, she lifts them up to the light. All crinkled and gnarled, she takes in their iodine-darkened hue. It reminds her of the hennaed hands of a bride, sends her back through time, thinking of lovely designs made memorable in part because of their impermanence. A lesson in beauty, the tattoos would fade, like a child's youth, like good looks, like health, and could be savoured more in the present owing to that foreknowledge.

Meeta comes to her mind: Meeta, Meeta, *Meeta*. She's nearly all Sister can think about since she turned up. Her presence was remarkable – incredible! She wondered at it, as she did a great many things these days.

She can understand Meeta's hot anger. Sister's ingratitude would seem stunning on hearing that a rescue was at hand, that such risk was taken for her. In Sister's months of looking back at the few days spent with Meeta, there was so much she'd got wrong with the girl. She assumed that no chance to rectify her mistakes would appear. And yet! Meeta, here, in the flesh, standing before her!

She wished she had explained herself when Meeta presented the possibility of freedom, but with Ram there, her tongue seized. If Meeta hadn't been such a surprise, she would have had time to prepare an answer. Instead, she succumbed to her stupid base instincts and sent Meeta away, reeling.

Francis, you may be straining to see how Sister could thrive here, let alone tolerate this place. You may wonder if her sanity is intact. I would counter it is not so difficult to imagine:

1. Her age keeps her from the most truly difficult labour.

2. Austerity and discomfort are not foreign experiences.

3. Ram is – on the surface of things – safe here, and, in a way, being made to pay the consequences of his actions. What would become of him outside, once brought under the law's harsh scrutiny?

4. Being here with Ram is a God-ordained gift. She is called to lighten his load, to help him in the difficult process of living

after committing great harm.

5. Finally, after a short while here, she has come to understand a powerful other calling: it is not just Ram she was brought here for. Her circumscribed choices had brought a welcome clarity after years of struggling with doubt and guilt under and against the MC Rule. Her world had finally constricted to a size and mission she could manage: the care of each body and soul caught in this place. Not just those bonded in debt, but those who exploited them. Each was hers to minister to, vicious and venal and victimized alike. Every…Single…*One*.

And then the appearance of Meeta and Pinku threatened to upend a life she had come to accept and made the future as unpredictable as ever.

Ajwa sucks in his breath and moans, the first sound he has made in days. Sister jumps. She examines his worst wounds, sees them festering despite her efforts at bandaging them. His eyes remain shut tight and his chapped mouth open. His body, without food, is consuming itself.

Sister knows Ajwa. She knew his wife.

Ajwa is gentle, diligent, and kind, despite all. The pair were low-caste, married for somewhere around a decade. Both looked older than their 30 years owing to malnourishment and toil. His wife, Aania, was pretty, despite all she suffered in life, a really lovely woman. And a week ago, she was found dead.

Whether she had chosen or been forced, she drank as much engine coolant as she could stomach, stolen from the compound's supply depot. Two guards brought the corpse to Sister, almost like they hoped the Christian power of resurrection lurked somewhere inside Sister's fingertips. All she could do was weep and curse and pray, all while under the watchful gaze of the men who carried the body in. One eventually stirred, whispering that no one had yet told Ajwa.

The suggestion was clear. Would Sister be the one?

At first she told them no, to do their own sorry business. She relented as they quietly filed out of the door. Just stay the hell away as I do it, she said.

She found Ajwa at the base of the Kiln. He was piling baked

bricks on a cart. He gave Sister a wide smile, which she did not return. The work paused. His co-labourers stood watching with dim curiosity as Ajwa fell to his knees and his world collapsed.

Asked later, she could not remember her precise words, for what followed shocked her beyond measure. He rose and pushed her, unexpectedly, as a reflex, as if she was the embodiment of the news she carried. She fell to the ground, and the other men jumped to assist her, calling out to him. But there was no response from Ajwa. He followed his most fundamental instinct: to run, fast, far, and away.

You and I have already seen the outcome, Pope. Surely you remember: *Up, Down, Up, Down.* Men hurrying from the truck, soon to break Ajwa's body. You can play back the scene, seeing new layers of context. Who knows what went on in Ajwa's mind? Surely some semblance of thought must have returned, some notion that a plan was needed for escape. But maybe not. It's possible all he could do was distance himself from that bilious apparatus and its masters and the misfortune they cause.

All of this Sister recalls, literally re-views, as her fingers run over the beads of a rosary that isn't there, as she reaches to adjust glasses long since disappeared. She lays a hand on Ajwa, before realizing that his prone body no longer rises and falls.

Ajwa Ezzah, husband to the departed Aania Ezzah, has joined his wife in death.

Pinku holds the mobile in his hand, flipping it open and closed, open and closed. Meeta paces.

Knock that off, won't you? she says.

Quit your walking to-and-fro, he says.

I don't want someone seeing you with that!

We need to call, Meeta. This has become utmost dangerous, and we've already got some good material. The boss trying to poke you, then beating up innocent, poor so-and-so for burning…well – you know. It could all be over in just a matter of hours. Think of it! All these people saved! Us too!

Meeta clenches her eyes. The anxiety she's been carrying feels like it's gnawing a hole through her gut. It could be so easy, just a single SMS...

But think of the next batch, Meeta says. And the next. They'll close for a month, recruit, and all will be back to normal – no change! And Dharmatma will have his next victims! What then?

We only can do what we can do.

Just a little more time!

But Dharmatma could come for you again. I can't let that happen!

Meeta can't help but smile at Pinku's protectiveness. The thought of Dharmatma's hands on her makes her tense. She forces herself to breathe deeply. Finally, she shakes her head.

You recruited me for this. There was always the chance that someone would make a grab for me, and we need to end this—

Well, I was an idiot then! This is a big mistake! I shouldn't have! I'm messaging John.

Don't do that.

The new voice, coming from behind their curtain, makes them jump. The sheet parts and Sister Shanti steps inside their room. All fall silent. Pinku sits slack-jawed while Meeta makes her derision known.

Sister speaks again. What help would you need to bring this to an end?

XXVI

Their plan, dear Francis, resembles the story of Daniel cast into the lions' den, but in this version, Daniel dives in, shouting MUNTER JUNTER! and magically expects the lions to clamp their toothy jaws shut except for when he commands them to speak and confess all of the people they've ever eaten.

It is, in a word, folly.

Sister has the microphone hidden – Meeta helps affix it after Pinku checks its batteries – and will go to Dharmatma's quarters. She has told them that Dharmatma's visit to the Kiln is likely coming to an end. Word of Ajwa's death has apparently rattled him. It is not so often victims of his violence die on site

– they are often courteous enough to do so off premises, where disposal is tidier and a few lies can cover up that a labourer's sudden departure is owing to death.

Sister remains stoic through the preparations. She had explained very little of her change of heart; simply that Ajwa was dead and that she would share more later. Meeta and Pinku, unsure of what to say, offer Sister inane advice about what lay ahead – *don't turn your back,* naa, *face him for the microphone to catch what he says* – but she doesn't hold it against them.

Finally, Meeta asks the question. Are you sure about this?

Sister looks at her squarely and nods.

I'll pray for you, Meeta whispers as Sister heads for the courtyard door.

Me too, Pinku says.

Sister nods again, and departs.

Come close, Pope. We can only watch this from a distance.

Look at Sister's fortitude. Each step is measured, determined. Kasliwal, still loading the body along with some of his men, orders her to go back inside, but she silences him with.

I will speak with Dharmatma, she tells them.

He wants no distraction, Kasliwal says.

Let me pass, she commands.

He lets her, and Sister steps into the lair, disappearing into the dark.

It is close to an hour before Sister returns. A *psst* at their hallway curtain makes Meeta, makes all of us, jump.

She enters, and Pinku opens his cell phone to illuminate the room. The contours of Sister's face glow with the soft blue light. Her countenance gives way to a smile.

Excuse me, she says, passing the audio recorder to Pinku. I must check on Govind.

But what happened? Meeta asks, stunned.

Listen, Sister says. And she departs.

Pinku is quick to change the microphone for earphones, and he and Meeta each hold one to their ears to listen.

Sister Shanti: Good evening, Dharmatmaji.

Dharmatma: What are you doing here?

SS: Here for a talk. About what happened with Ajwa.

D: Get out.

SS: You need to tell me.

D: Are you out of your fucking mind? You old hag. Who do you think you are?

[Silence.]

SS: That is a complicated question. For years, I was a nun. You know this, no? I would go to confession with the priest every week. I kept a journal of my sacrificial acts. I catalogued everything. I tried to purify my soul.

D: I have no time for this. Get out.

SS: Dharmatma, you are keeping so much bottled up. I see it. All the hatred, for others, for yourself.

D: Get out!

SS: I will not. You will hear me.

[Indistinct; scuffling sounds]

SS: I am giving you a chance! A fleeting chance. Because there can be no change without telling the truth.

D: I have no reason to tell you a thing.

SS: Yes, you do. I tell you, you can feel such freedom if you simply tell. I am giving you that chance. Make known what you've done.

[Silence.]

SS: What do you think I come here for? How do I benefit? I am trapped in this place. Get nothing from this. I do this for your own good. I imagine you've tried every form of escape, but none has done you any service. Your shame, it stretches over everything.

D: That's cow shit.

SS: Cow shit, indeed! No matter how hardened you've become, you will only hate yourself more. So simply confess.

D: What if I do?

SS: You have a chance to see past your shame.

[Silence.]

SS: I want to tell you something else. Even in your shame – and you and I both know you have a great deal to be ashamed of – the God of the universe smiles at you.

[A man's laughter.]

SS: It's true. You are His son – His creation, and He takes pleasure in you, simply for *being*, despite all you've done. He saw you in innocence and in each wrong-headed, evil choice you've made. He hopes like a loving parent for a reconciliation that may never come.

[More laughter.]

SS: I do not joke. This is what I believe. Dharmatmaji, your soul is dying to know its worth, and it can. Here. I will confess first. I will tell you what I have never told another soul.

[Silence; an engine starts in the background.]

D: Go on.

SS: I hate you.

D: You are not the first.

SS: Ah. Sorry. That's not what I'm confessing. No. I have hated so many in my life. When I became a nun, I volunteered to face the misery of the world daily and do what I could to reduce it. I didn't know what this would do to me. I thought the bargain meant all costs were paid with the leaving of things.

[Silence.]

SS: I was so young. But the years meant confronting devils and demons, within myself and without. Examination that I thought would lead me to holiness, but only meant sadness. Bitterness. I was not who I intended to be. The benefit of my bargain went unrealized. No, my confession is this: despite my hatred for what you've done, my confession is that I have love for you, even as I hate you.

[Silence.]

SS: I mean what I say. I see the evil of men and I want it stopped. I want justice. Revenge. I always thought it an impossibile command to obey, but here, you have finally taught me to love my enemies. To everyone else you've hurt, they would see this as a sin, maybe greater than any of your own. To love the author of our misery! But I can see you with eyes of faith, see you as a child of God. And so I am here, urging: confess, turn from your wrong, do all you can to make it right.

[A snorting sound.]

D: God and gods hate me. Despise me.

SS: All I know is that as soon as I have measured my God, taken stock of him, he does something that upends everything I thought I knew. He is wild. Simply wild. Beyond expectation.

D: Where would I even begin?

SS: Start from this moment and work backwards. Try it. Perhaps with cold Ajwa out there and his poor wife, Aania.

[The sound of a cork removed from a bottle, then drinking. Slurping. A long period of silence.]

D: I…took Aania. For my own. Had her stay the night with me. She…conceived. It was months later that I found out. Ajwa, he could not have been the father, she said to me, because of some…bodily malfunction. I…told her…to get out. Not my concern. To go do something about it if she didn't want the child.

SS: So she killed herself.

[More slurping.]

SS: And Ajwa, what did he do?

D: Ran. Away.

SS: And what did you do?

D: Caught him. Had him beaten. The poor fool. Don't look at me that way.

SS: Have there been others killed on your orders?

D: Yes.

SS: How many?

D: I don't…I don't know.

[Long exhalation.]

SS: How many?

D: At least 12.

SS: And how many beatings?

[Silence.]

SS: Too many to count?

D: Too many.

SS: I see.

[A long silence; up to a minute.]

SS: What can you give up to right these wrongs and free your-self?

D: I have no idea. I thought you would tell me.

SS: Oh. Oh no. I am only a messenger. Pray to God, or your gods, and seek truth. And live. I am no priest. I can't absolve you of what you've done. You have revealed much already, enough for you to think on for a long time. But I will come tomorrow night, if you wish, and we can talk further. Turning from evil and reconciliation are process-es. This has been a first step, Dharmatma. Everything will depend on what you do next.

[Dharmatma does not speak again. There are more indistinct sounds; a door opening and closing; Sister's footsteps. The audio recorder is eventually turned off.]

When it ends, the hour is exceedingly late. Meeta clasps Pinku's hand and squeezes it. In such a short time they travelled from anticipation to fear, dread to astonishment. Tears well in her eyes; wonder has taken hold. Sister has done it, Meeta whis-pers. She has actually done it.

They tuck the device away like a great treasure and go to their respective mats, dreaming of what the next day would hold, what Sister might further uncover, and how this whole life-steal-ing operation was soon to come toppling down, brick by brick by brick.

The poor, poor fools.

The bell clangs.

It can't be – it's surely not time to rise and start work. A quick glance outside: the moon is full and bright.

Line up! shouts one of the guards, poking his head into the dormitory. Everyone! Outside!

Unfortunately, Pope, we are not exempted. Up, up, up. Give

a good stretch.

What's going on? Meeta asks, poking her head into the main corridor. One of the other workers shambling towards the compound's centre forces the words out through a yawn: No ideee*aaa*. Maybe someone is in trouble.

Meeta shoots Pinku a worried look. The pair follow the others, and the two of us follow them.

The assembly swells over 10 minutes. The guards, equally annoyed at their disturbed rest, are harsh with stragglers. Anxiousness makes Meeta alert. Whispered words float around. She tries to keep her head down, but can't help casting furtive glances around those assembled. Kasliwal perches himself on a crate, making his shortness all the more apparent. Sister is there, and Govind, the injured one, has been made to rise too. He does not look at Kasliwal, but glares unflinchingly at Pinku with his unswollen eye.

Please stop fidgeting, Francis. It's not helping matters any.

Meeta tries to draw Sister's attention but she is distant, nearly sleeping where she stands. Meeta looks for Ram, and he's there, staring into space. He suddenly turns to look at her. She screws up her eyebrows questioningly. He shrugs; no clue what's happening, either.

Still, Kasliwal doesn't speak. The guards are in the dormitory now, and Meeta feels beads of sweat – one, then a second – slip down her face. A child cries out, quickly hushed by her mother. Meeta thinks through possibilities. What will she do if discovered, which way will she run, will she scream, will she kneel, will her heart explode?

Dharmatma finally shows himself. He snaps, and a guard brings another crate, sets it next to Kasliwal's. Dharmatma steps up and surveys those gathered with a bleak look of disdain.

A moment later, a guard bursts from the dormitory, his hands filled with small devices. As he reaches Kasliwal, he lifts them into the air, and you see a number of things transpire simultaneously:

Kasliwal looks at Sister and shakes his head.

Dharmatma's face clouds, his jaw clenches.

Govind smiles broadly.

Pinku sprints for the open gate.

Meeta shrinks to the ground.

Her mind goes blank. She has not recovered her faculties when guards descend upon her – and us! – and cast us all into a darkened room, darker than any she or we will ever chance to enter again.

Brace yourself, Pope! Brace yourself!

XXVII

I hope they weren't too rough on you, Francis. My wrist has never been so strained, but I imagine I'll complain of much worse before long.

Yes, Meeta is here in the dark – that sound is her weeping – but Sister also has been caught in their net. God knows where Pinku is and whether he made it out. I have my fears.

It's a surprise they would consider the pair of us in on this little conspiracy. I'll point out that if the danger grows too severe you can always put these pages down. I know you didn't sign up for potential InjuryTortureDeath when we started. But remember that Sister and Meeta don't have this option.

As usual, the Likely Pair could not care less that we're here with them. They are caught up in their own swirling fears. Sister is quiet, spent, and silent. Her thoughts trip between the corporeal and the disembodied, the here and hereafter. Meeta is consumed with three things: the pitch black, Pinku's assured death, and what will come next. The only flickering light in this mess is that Ram, while despised, was spared.

Don't go over and comfort her, Francis. We're here to observe, not to minister. Besides, it's Sister who rises up, stumbles through the dark, and reaches for Meeta.

The girl's sobs quieten and Sister whispers:

You are brave…
…you are strong…

...you are lovely...
...you are worthy of love...
...I love you...
...I find my Lord in you...

She hands profound truth to Meeta, and the words bring Meeta new tears, even as Sister wraps her arms around her, holding her tighter than she's ever been embraced before. Meeta's fear abates, relents, releases its hold, then grips her again. Sister places a gentle hand on Meeta's head.

Sister's breathing slows, comes and goes in uneven huffs. Her body tenses, enough to cause Meeta to stop crying and wonder what has stricken Sister.

Sister? Sister! What's happened?

Nothing, Sister says, skipping a breath, and then floats back to her corner and sits cross-legged. Sister puts her hands before her and shuts her eyes.

Meeta cannot see any of this, not at first.

Sister's fingers begin to dance over invisible keys. She is summoning new music, can hear it in her mind, an improvized song.

But Pope: listen. We can actually hear the invisible keys resound.

As Sister's playing picks up, it becomes virtuosic, painfully beautiful. Meeta sits up, confused where the music comes from. She's heard piano before, but couldn't even identify the instrument if asked. Bewildered by what she hears, she is even more amazed by what she sees.

Sister emanates light, almost glowing, subtly but definitely enough to see, and the light pulses with changes in her playing. She appears priestly, as if presiding over the Blessed Sacrament, the altar and monstrance.

This song, Pope, is a haunting thing, its emotions expressed so very clearly. Love and regret, joy and anger, a whole life summed up in its bars and measures, all of it melding into something so astoundingly beautiful that Meeta does not even think of their circumstances.

It is over too soon. The light fades. Things settle down to silence after a time, just our breathing, as we contemplate life, death, and the strange lightness we feel while cloaked in dark.

It is then that the door opens.

Daylight stretches around corners and pours in. Ram enters. A guard joins him. The world is recalled.

Ram sees us all stricken and goes to check on Sister, and then, unsure how to approach Meeta, claps his hand on her shoulder. He searches her wide-open eyes.

I brought you water. They wouldn't give me any food but—

Do you...know...what they plan? Sister rasps, not acknowledging the miracle in what just occurred.

Ram glances up at the guard, then shakes his head. I keep thinking over how this has happened, he says. Kasliwal won't tell me. He doesn't even want to look at me. They never search the dormitories, at least they haven't before; what would they find? The only thing I can think is that they were told; someone, somehow, knew. Govind probably, trying to get back at Pinku for the beating.

Seems a...reasonable thought, Sister says.

I'm so sorry, Ram says, through new tears.

Sister forces herself to sit up, and nearly slumps back to the ground. She pulls Ram close and searches his eyes even as he tries to look away. She gives him a tired embrace sealed with finality, and tells him she loves him more than all the world. And then: Don't lie to us, Ram, she says. There's no need.

Ram's body convulses, almost as if thrown backwards by an invisible force.

It was not Govind, she says. You and I know it.

Someone else then...

You knew what we were attempting, what we hoped to accomplish. You knew. And you have reason to see us fail.

Not true. Not true!

Meeta is still stricken, still uncomprehending.

I know, Sister says, because it was my same fear. The fear that when all was said and done, you'll be removed from one purgatory and put in another for what you've done – prison, most likely. Not for Manoj, but for the 18 others you cast to the side.

Stop...stop saying this. How could you...think that I...risk your lives—

Sister smiles, a small smile, pushing through tears. She reaches to hug him again, but he pushes himself away, until he collapses on his knees.

Turn away from all this wrong, whatever you do, Ram. And when your guilt feels beyond bearing, remember I am willing to forgive. Always willing.

Meeta is too frightened to speak. The guard, visibly unsettled, comes in and pulls Ram up. Come on, come on. Be a man, eh? he says as they leave.

And in an instant we are plunged back into the dark.

When the door opens again and our eyes adjust to the light, the visitor is not who we would expect.

It is not Dharmatma coming to gloat.

Nor Kasliwal expressing regret.

Nor Ram with an apology.

It is a little toad of a man, none other than the original orchestrator of this mess: Ravinder.

Hello. He brandishes a gun, visible even in the dim light.

Sister makes a point to stand and face him, even though she is exhausted, shattered. Meeta is still too astounded to speak, unsure of what Sister is up to.

Come on, he says.

Sister follows. Take my hand and rise, Francis. We shouldn't dilly-dally.

Ravinder sees Meeta isn't moving. Guard! Get this girl!

Sister suddenly snaps, Do not even *think* of touching her. She goes to Meeta, feeble as she is, and bends down. She is whispering, and at first you think it is soft encouragements. But I can tell you Sister utters a prayer, for her own strength. *Help me... face this Calvary...this is my passion...you are my passion...give me love...strength to face...hope for...nothing can separate us from your love...*

Meeta does rise, and leans onto Sister. Her steps falter, but the pair walk together. *God is here*, Sister says to Meeta, *with us, with us…can you feel him?*

The words echo and bounce around Meeta's mind unregistered.

Ravinder grunts. Sister pauses before him. I feel sympathy for you, Ravinder. Your wife knows what you do? Would your children be proud of their father?

How did you…

Wedding ring. An assumption about the children. She looks so tired but continues. Whenever I meet monsters like you, I remind myself that you came from a mother, innocent, and that you've erred, and been wronged. I tell myself monsters don't just spring up from the mud. We make them. Let them be made. Like bricks. Formed and fired and sent out into the world. Products of all our hands.

Ravinder produces blindfolds.

Sorry, Heeraji, the guard says, taking them from Ravinder's hand. He first tightens one around her eyes.

The guard goes next to Meeta and the pair of us to do the same. Meeta lets out a cry as the dark becomes permanent, but Sister speaks benedictions in her ear.

By now, we are in the courtyard, being ushered into the back of a truck.

I'm sorry for whatever hurts you carry, Sister says, her words aimed at Ravinder, though she doesn't know where he stands. I know you intend to hurt us. I just ask you do what you must, but make it without pain. Without all this torture and misery. Don't play the part you've been cast, eh? You hearing me?

Ravinder has been distant ever since mention of childhood, children, his son. He nods, though Sister cannot see, and closes the truck's tailboard and locks it.

A silence descends. I can feel the fear rising in you, Francis, the fate ahead sinking in, just as it has for Meeta, and for Sister. How does it feel, being a lamb led to the slaughter? Does your life unspool before you? All RegretsJoysFears ramming together? Or do you too feel a transfiguration at hand, like Sister? The end of something difficult running its course? The arrival of a new day, heralded by a pink and orange polluted sky, or maybe a cleansing, life-giving monsoon, or maybe the retreat of turbid air and the relief of cool spring?

Right. Maybe I ought to be quiet, too.

The ride is not long.

I've managed to pry my blindfold off. Let me help you with yours.

Yes, it's true. There's not much light, but at least there's a little.

I can see you doing the grim maths. Going all the way back to the beginning. How many were to die in this little story of mine? Yes, count them off on your tied up fingers. You don't seem to be thinking clearly, so let me help you. The answer is that Adiba, Singh, Latika, and Ajwa have departed. Leaving just one more. And I shared from the start that Sister dies. I see gears of wonder churning behind your eyes.

Meeta and Sister are in the corner of the truck's body opposite us. The Likely Pair make for quite a vision. Sister, for some reason her hands left unbound, has a hand on Meeta's forehead while her other arm enfolds her. Meeta is sobbing, voicing her fear again and again, and Sister speaks words to her, tender words. She tells her of a place beyond all suffering, a place she believes is very real, and the knowledge of it is the antidote to all her fears.

There are other words exchanged, but they are not for me to disclose. They are a gift, from Sister to Meeta, and Sister would not appreciate knowing I was the one who shared them.

The back of the truck swings open. Ravinder sees us, couldn't care less that our blindfolds are removed. He moves like an automaton, preparing to do what he is about to do.

He grabs Meeta, and Meeta, she thrashes around and hurls insults and sobs until she hits the ground and the air is knocked from her.

Cry out, Pope! Cry out with me! Don't let this evil go unprotested!

Take me, you *beast!* Sister shouts. She manoeuvres to the edge of the truck's body, nearly falling. Me, me, me first! I can't watch my daughter here leave this world. Grant me this!

He pulls her out and…calm yourself, Pope. Just…just for a

moment, and witness.

Sister looks terrorized as she kneels in the loamy soil. Our eyes deceive us.

Fear is suppressed to the tiniest corner of her soul *5* each breath billows love, a supernatural love, from her top to toes and back *4* Meeta looks up from the ground, *3* stunned by Sister's countenance *2* that catches the sun and *1* reflects its glory.

Ravinder raises his gun.

In 1970, in her 31st year, Sister Shanti was ready.

After months of study, she awaited a letter eagerly with the other Sisters while completing their tertianship in Rome. The years with the MCs had passed, nine to be precise, and though there was much pain, she felt she was part of something that could change the world, or, at least, herself.

The letter Sister Shanti posted was like those of the other Sisters, asking Mother whether they would be permitted to take final vows. The period of waiting was agony; the response was no mere formality. There were other Sisters who had received deferrals and they took it as a great shame. After so much preparation, would Sister be told 'no', be made to wait six months, a year, or told she would never be accepted as an MC? She had felt a half-step out of touch with the other Sisters, always a little out of place. She took to longer prayer and increasing corporeal penance to purify herself, ready to accept Mother's determination as God's will.

The letters finally arrived. Sister Shanti's said 'yes'.

During the eight-day silent retreat that would precede the profession ceremony, Sister revisited her past. She was frightened to do so at first, stumbling back into all that had been lost and traded for this life, and the years she had accumulated since making the trade. She had already lost the shine of youth and needed glasses for reading. She could glimpse her reflection and easily imagine what her wrinkled older self would look like. She sometimes pictured Walter beside her, or a nondescript, moustachioed husband and three babies in her arms. She saw small visions and the yearnings that accompanied them as chaff to be burned off in the purification process. She hoped final profession – symbolic of marriage to Christ himself – would kill certain desires and dreams, lay certain doubts and accusations to rest. All the while she wondered whether she was worthy of this calling, whether she was still pretending at something, attaining to the impossible.

Superiors told them such concerns were common, the devil's deceptions. Always one to struggle against such sure declarations, Sister Shanti continued wondering.

The day of the ceremony arrived. They put on their new saris, trading in plain white robes for those appointed with blue stripes. It began with a procession to a glorious old church as Catholic townspeople gathered on the road to celebrate them. Feeling like her doubts trailed behind her like a ball and chain, she prayed every step of the way: *'Nothing can separate me from the love of Christ. Nothing can separate me from the love of Christ.'*

Mother Teresa was there waiting for them in the church, and her face radiated joy. Sister felt time slow, the organ music and cheer falling away as she scanned the assembly for her family's brown faces that she knew would not be there, for Walter's smiling face, but felt tears well up all the same at their unremarkable absence.

She and the new Sisters took up their positions, forming a half-circle around the altar. After the homily, which felt interminable considering the circumstances, the Archbishop read each Sister's name and they responded in turn by reading their vows and receiving a crucifix that Mother had raised to her lips and blessed with a kiss.

Sister Shanti, on her knees, was all but enraptured by the moment, taken to a place where the present and past blended together. She focused upon the words she prayed as an anchor tying her to the here and now, *'Nothing can...separate me...from the...love of Christ.'*

Finally, her name was called: Sister Shanti!

She rose, bolt-upright, and spoke with a plain serenity delivered from above:

Lord, you have called me!

THE END

In but a few moments, Francis, we've travelled across time and space. The sun is setting and the Delhi sky is aflame. Children are caught up in flying their kites and their laughter, it floats on the air just like their *patangs*. Just lovely, it is. Absolutely so.

Years have passed since that terrible moment with Ravinder and the gun. Nine to be precise, and it is only a few weeks after I made the decision to sit down and write you this rambling letter.

I should be back at the MC home at this hour, winding down the day, but I'm here instead, with you.

What's this?

What became of Meeta, you ask? And Sister? And of all the others? You're right. At this point I'm simply playing coy.

Sister did die. But just not then.

The moment was incredible. Though present in body, Sister was spirited away, just – taken – even as the gun was raised to her head, the bullet chambered, its pointed tip ready to channel its way through her life.

Ravinder pulled the trigger and...

Nothing.

The gun did not fire.

Ravinder worked with the parts of the gun, trying again and again, but something caught, something was stuck.

It would not fire.

Sister kneeled there. I don't wish to offer an image of the Saint, distant in prayer, ecstatic in communion with the Father above. She looked exhausted but at ease. Her body struggled to stay erect. She was still very much in the world, but the world had fallen away.

Ravinder loosed vitriol. That gun wasn't the only weapon he carried, he muttered under his breath. Tucked away, back in the glove box, was a knife, one you'll remember well.

As he went for it, Meeta called to Sister, encouraged her, blessed her. If you asked her later where the words came from, she'd tell you she did not have a clue.

Ravinder returned, clearly reluctant to do what the knife in his hand portended. He waited, and stepped towards her.

Meeta screamed till she could no more. Her cry blended with a car's klaxon horn that grew and grew in strength.

Ravinder couldn't help but follow the approaching car with his eyes. After all, it barrelled towards them. He took flight even before Meeta and Sister and you and I could figure what was coming.

They tore out of the car in a blur. First was a figure bedecked in white, appearing like an angel before them: it was a Sister, Neepa, with her hand stretching forward as if to still Ravinder; then fatherly John Kristadasa; then two policemen; and then, counter to all explanation and expectation, was Pinku, complete with a lopsided grin.

Salvation, in a form, had come.

The police tackled Ravinder and Sister Neepa nearly tackled Sister Shanti and wept over the woman, so distant, she bordered on the catatonic. John and Pinku untied Meeta's hands, and all she could say through her trembling and tears was thank you, thank you, *thank you.*

They brought a doctor to tend to Sister and Meeta. He met them in a hotel where the pair were put up, on Meeta's request. As soon as he pronounced them well, Pinku and John joined the efforts of the small army of police and Organization staff who were busy processing and sorting out arrests and evidence and what to do with the Kiln's workers. When they finally reached the bottom of their to-do list, they remembered the unlikely Likely Pair, tucked away for several days to relive their traumas and succour one another. They provided Meeta support for what came next, paid extra for her services, relocated her to a donated flat for a few months to get sorted out, everything above board. Sister was given the same, and she accepted the resources. The Missionaries of Charity were willing to accept her back with open arms, and despite Sister Neepa's kind and persistent invitations, Sister would not return, though she thanked them for all they had given her, every moment, and she meant this. When it was finally vacated, she returned to her childhood home to pass into her twilight years and finally explore the Great Unknown.

And now, with the immediate fear for Sister and Meeta put to the side, you've still got a handful of questions tucked away in that robe of yours.

What of the others whose lives we touched?

Where I have knowledge, I will share it.

Ginna: old, terrible, dear Ginna. She was emptied after Adiba's passing; who would have thought she'd feel it so deeply? Like Zaccheus, her first step was divesting her mountain of ill-gotten gains. She sold her *kotha* and gave the money to the girls and to her dismissed prostitutes who still worked up and down G.B. Road. A priest at old St Mary's took pity upon her after hearing her story and unlikely reconversion. She is still widowing and winnowing her days away, sweeping dust and the memories of how she spent so very many years so very poorly as she tends to that church and gets by on its charity. I sit with her every once in a while, when I pass by there. She's reluctant to talk about the past, and I can understand why.

Pinku, that urchin, found himself in circumstances I still struggle to believe. He has two young sons, and his wife is a plump, whip-smart university graduate. Can you believe it! He, not a day of school in his life; she, somewhere near the top of her class! They met at the Organization. That's right – all of the sordid details of what just transpired weren't enough to keep him from plunging right back in and continuing to work with John on further investigations. His wife-to-be was none other than John's assistant. A love marriage if there ever was one! Can you imagine what the meeting of the parents would be like to arrange that marriage, if Pinku's could even be found? With the arrival of his twins, Pinku is finally winding down his career infiltrating dark places. God knows what other trade he'll find to ply. I can imagine the stupid, good-natured comments his dear wife has to put up with.

Sister Neepa became Superior herself of the *Shishu Bhavan* children's home after four years spent in an MC home in Port-au-Prince, and is as kind and gentle as ever. I consider her a dear, wise friend. Mohsin, at Meeta's insistence, was rescued by the Organization, and the small, brave boy guided John and Pinku to the sweatshop and its moving shadows just as he had led the Likely Pair. Mr Shah Jee and I share a chai every once in a while. He still peddles drugs in his pewter pots, but promises me he'll stop someday soon.

Other endings are not so cheerful. After all, this is real life.

Ravinder, as you know, was apprehended despite a half-hearted effort to run. You saw him shuffle in the Tibetan Colony – though surprisingly nimble for his girth, it wasn't enough to get away. He went to prison. There was no rabid pack of lawyers to get him out of a sentence. I checked in on his wife and son just the other week: the son placed highly on his entrance exams and is readying for university. Between you and me, they are better without him.

Dharmatma did what he does. Lied, obfuscated, evaded – all through his lawyers, of course. Despite all the evidence recovered, he continues doing what he does. He's upped his security. Entrenched in his ways. Buried in his shame. He makes his bricks, makes his bricks, makes his bricks, and suffers for it.

Then there's Ram. The one whose crimes and lies were the pulsing heartbeat of this entire narrative. He went to prison, too, a severe pain for Sister to bear. There was legal help for him, secured by Sister through her web of relationships spread throughout Delhi. After all was said and done, he was made to pay with only eight years of his life for his crimes. Many were outraged in the press. Eight years for 18 lives! It was not enough for all the pain he'd caused. I felt a good deal of conflict over how those legal proceedings transpired, as I knew Sister did. He was like her son, after all. It was only a few weeks ago that he was released back into her care after years of regular visits to him where she supplied him with medicines and extra food, with care for his injured soul.

Speak of the devil. Here Ram is.

Ram has just ascended the stairs, joining the two of us on the roof. Even after all of this, he is under 30 and still looks handsome; beautiful even. That new heaviness you feel is not from a cloud blocking the sun. There's a good deal of tension that lingers between the two of us.

You'd better come, he says, mainly to me.

Let's go in and see her, Pope. Please, take my hand. The descent to her flat is as difficult for me as scaling a mountain.

No. 4. We've arrived. I feel some anxiety and much sadness, even though I've been here many times, especially as the decision to write to you took shape.

We enter.

Sister Shanti is here, ah – I mean Heera – laid out on a small bed with a window view. She is shrivelled and wrinkly and serene; though she does not look well, she still smiles faintly on seeing me, wheezes my name.

Your eyebrows leap. Just so; the final piece of the puzzle slots into place.

As I've proven unable to call her by another name than Sister Shanti, she's always been unable to call me anything but Meeta.

I am Meeta. Meeta is me.

I see your mind at work, the steam spewing from your ears… but wait – she said – this happened – it can't be——

No. Quiet yourself. Worry not. We needn't delve into the details just now. Besides, we…we must tell Sister goodbye.

Ram has her one hand and tears stream down his face, and I bow by her side, and I thank her for the gifts she has given me. She is so weak, she can hardly speak, and I linger with her, close at hand. I have seen much death up close in my time as Sister Immaculata and know that this is the end, that though her heart is strong, it is weak, and weakening, that this is the end, that she is slipping, slipping away, and this is the end, and now she is gone, departed, and my sadness and happiness, they embrace, because I know: this is not the end.

This has been a mystery story, Francis. Who killed who, stole what, died when, lurked where, and why. I've worked hard to tie all of these events up nicely for you as a gift of sorts. But it's not merely that kind of mystery. This story speaks to the MYSTERIUM TREMENDUM: the ultimate mystery that repels and attracts, fascinates and makes us tremble.

The revelation of my identity is nothing so dramatic as split personalities. There was nothing malicious in my little deception. We Christians speak of being born again and the popular notion is that who we were dies. Not true! Meeta is my old self, living inside this same sari-bedecked skin. I am the girl of 9 being raped and the Sister rising to take final vows at the same moment. I am every age I have ever been, all at once. All Meeta's pain is mine, and her sin, but so is her beauty. And, fortunately, none of the glamour.

You know the parable of the sower? Various seeds are strewn about a field, but not all rise and thrive. Some are choked by weeds; others eaten by animals; others fall on bad soil; some grow quickly and then wilt under the harsh sun. Others planted in good earth flourish. It is a metaphor for life in faith.

The larger mystery, to me at least, comes from an image granted by St Thérèse of Liseaux: how does a sprout grow tall in the most terrible of soil, bearing the harshest sunlight and most unbecoming weather, to somehow thrive and live and grow into a little flower God can pluck and take supreme pleasure in?

Ask me why I am here. Go ahead. Why kind Rifat is dead, and why Anu is pimping other girls, and why no one knows into what pit Deepti has fallen. Why those factories of misery – the Kilns and Sweatshops and Streets and Childhood Homes of this world – continue churning out generations of broken people? I don't have the precise answer, even though this is my story. I suppose I will live the rest of my days to ponder the question, and take solace in the fact I need not know; only live in the mystery.

At long last I return to my earliest point and purpose: Sister's canonization. I told you that Sister was responsible for a staggering 142 miracles during her life, far more than most saints could claim. All counted, 139 people were rescued from the Kiln. I count her playing and illumination in the dark as 140. The gun's failure to fire as 141. And, at 142, I am her final miracle.

I am certain posthumous ones will follow.

We could argue about what a saint is or is not, but I am beyond convincing otherwise: a saint is a person who touches you and you become alive in a new way; one who suffers from all the same doubts and fears and failures as the rest; who knows perfection is unattainable and rejoices that it is so. Give me the Shantis of this world, who are free to love because they know they are loved. Who are utterly human, and who shine with holiness nevertheless.

Sister Shanti of Delhi – no, forgive me: Heera Chayn – should be recognized as the saint she was, the saint she is.

See to it, dear Francis. See to it.

ACKNOWLEDGMENTS

My research in Delhi was immensely special in part because my parents lived there at the time. The network of relationships they cultivated helped inspire characters and many of *Little Flower*'s twists and turns, and it's a joy to retread the book and see myriad details plucked from the opportunities they provided. Without my parents, there would have been no book, and as always, I owe them an enormous debt.

From that trip, I'm grateful for the hospitality of two Missionary of Charity homes that permitted visits. Also, a number of people I encountered were involved in advocacy and action for the protection of vulnerable children, and I offer up my admiration for the staffs at Kat-Katha, Bachpan Bachao Andolan, and International Justice Mission. I look back on other particular conversations, and I'm grateful to Sister Nirmalini, Eirliani Abdul Rahman, Tarquin Hall, Y.K. Sikri, and Pradeep and Jyoti Aggarwal of the organization Light Life Freedom.

Though my time was short with them, the Delmas 75 Writers' Group in Haiti left an impact, offering me a place to share my words and foster a blooming appreciation of poetry. Thanks to Ruth Hersey, Jennifer Stuck, Timothy Plumberg, and Magalie Boyer.

I had a lot of help bringing this book into your hands, and special thanks need to go to Mark Ecob, Zehra Jane Naqvi, Michael Benson, Justin Wright, and Dhiren Bhal of Wordsway Copyediting. Melissa Desai's insight into an earlier draft of the book was tremendously appreciated.

This book was the result of a crowdfunding campaign and I'm deeply grateful to the friends, family, and readers who made its publishing possible through their generous support:

Judy Mikalonis | Shelley Hom and family
Chuck and Nina Clark | Kelli Singltone-McMullen
Chuck and Maribeth Highfill | Mark and Patty Wright
Greg and Carol Reller | Peter and Wendy Hileman
Jef Williams | Mikie Spencer | Kristen and Darren Lowe

Sherry Sara Thomas | Kevin and Jen Deane
Melissa and Hannah Harris | Yuan Tang | The Cale Family
Beaver and Kathy Brooks } Lisa and Bella Parrott
Suzanne Stanfield Lynskey
P.J., Erica, Kali, Liam, and Ashton Oswald
Rhondi, Darci and Sarah | Janice and Steve Daulton
Renee Stein | Dr. Stephen and Mrs. Stephanie Perry
Linda Daulton | Mark and Cyndi Nine
Phil and LeeAnn Oswald | And to a handful of other
contributors who wished to remain anonymous.

Although I consumed far more books than these in researching and writing *Little Flower*, the following selections were foundational and require mention:

An Unquenchable Thirst, Mary Johnson
Capital: A Portrait of Twenty-First Century Delhi, Rana
    Dasgupta
Mother Teresa: Come Be My Light, Edited by Brian
    Kolodiejchuk
No One Can Love You More: Life in Delhi's Redlight District,
    Mayank Austen Soofi
The God of Small Things, Arundhati Roy
The Vish Puri Mystery Series, Tarquin Hall
The White Tiger, Aravind Adiga

Finally, to Katharine and James, you bless me tremendously each and every day.

Made in the USA
San Bernardino, CA
05 June 2018